SOUL WEAVER

SOUL WEAVER

―――∞∞∞――

HAILEY EDWARDS

New York   Boston

Forever Yours
Hachette Book Group
237 Park Avenue, New York, NY 10017
www.hachettebookgroup.com
www.twitter.com/foreverromance

Originally published as an e-book by Forever Yours

First print on demand edition: October 2012

Forever Yours is an imprint of Grand Central Publishing.
The Forever Yours name and logo are trademarks of Hachette Book Group, Inc.

The publisher is not responsible for websites (or their content) that are not owned by the publisher.

The Hachette Speakers Bureau provides a wide range of authors for speaking events. To find out more, go to www.hachettespeakersbureau.com or call (866) 376-6591.

ISBN 978-1-4555-7391-2

SOUL WEAVER

Chapter 1

SOFT SNORES CARRIED from the darkness on Nathaniel's right. Weak sunlight slanted over his shoulder, cut through the gloom, and illuminated the weathered face of his mark. The mattress squeaked as the man rolled onto his back. His tangled limbs twitched in peaceful sleep.

Nathaniel traced the cool metal handle of his shears, sheathed in their fitted holster.

The black marker on the man's soul pulsated, calling to Nathaniel. The only sounds came from a pay-per-view skin flick he'd already seen playing in other seedy motel rooms just like this one.

He crossed the room and glanced at the nightstand.

Pictures lay spread like glossy fans across the chipped laminate surface. He glanced away. Soon he'd know the story behind those photos as well as he knew the man who had taken them.

Knocking a fly from his ear, Nathaniel sent the pest zooming around the room in circles.

He lifted his pendant over his head and tucked it into his

pocket. His skin rippled and faded to the golden outline of his spiritual form. He winced as the psychic bond between a soul harvester and his prey snapped into place. A deluge of sickened thoughts branded their knowledge inside Nathaniel's skull as he slid his fingers into the handle of his shears.

"She wanted it. Begged for it. Should've made it last. Damn camera. Ran out of batteries. Now I won't remember it all."

Nathaniel's gut clenched. It never got easier. Each time his stomach roiled as bad as the last, maybe worse. His mark's twisted pleasure trickled through their connection. He shivered with loathing and tightened his grip.

"They'll never know. No one ever knows. I liked the look of that blonde. Could've had them both. Be ready next time. She'll still be there. Waiting for me."

"Enough." Snarling through gritted teeth, Nathaniel made his accounting. "You've taken innocence not yours to have, and you will be held responsible for that loss."

He braced his hand over the man's heart. Steady thumps pulsed beneath his palm as he sank intangible fingers into the man's chest. There, on his left. He'd found it. Miniscule thing it was.

Cradled inside the man's rib cage, Nathaniel's quarry clung to its host.

The marked soul slithered right outside Nathaniel's grasp. Sinking his wrist inside the man's body, he growled his frustration. Disgusted, he plunged deeper, opened his fingers wider, and sifted through organs and tissue until his fist closed over his prey.

The man's eyes popped open wide, his gaze searching the room. "W-who's there?"

His feeble swipes through the air might as well have swatted flies. The urge to take a pound of flesh from the man's wrinkled hide tempted Nathaniel, but he could only touch fellow spirits without his pendant to ground him, to wrap him in flesh like the odd gift to the world that he was.

On a choked sob, the man began begging for pity, for leniency, for *mercy*.

The words should have burned his forked tongue as he spoke them. Instead, he blathered on about things he'd left undone, words he'd left unsaid. As if he hadn't ended lives while indulging his sick tastes. Without a thought about who his victims left behind as he silenced their voices.

A tic worked in Nathaniel's cheek. He would not snap. This death would not be the one to break him, though if it did, he could hardly be blamed. Teach a man to kill, and he lusted for blood. Show him how scales are balanced, and he will discover how they can be tipped.

He chuckled darkly as hatred unfurled in his chest. Pity had no place here. In any case, he'd run dry of that emotion long ago.

A twist of Nathaniel's wrist pulled taut the length of soul writhing in his fist. His mark's body strained and bowed off the bed in an effort to remain connected.

He snipped the man's soul free with a quick clip of his shears, and the body fell in a limp heap against the mattress. His mark's sightless eyes stared into nothing. His parted lips dry.

Holding the swath of soul at arm's length, Nathaniel retrieved his pendant and threw the chain over his head. His skin prickled as he became corporeal. Once he shook off the sting, he reached for the short velvet pouch hanging from his belt. He freed it, forced the mouth open, and shoved the hand holding the blackened soul down the gullet of the bag. Familiar suction nursed his fingers as a vortex swirled around his hand and a portal swallowed his arm up to his elbow.

Heat singed his fingertips as his hand burst through the bottomless bag and into a soul pit.

He smelled flesh cooking and knew it was his. Of course, if he hadn't worn his pendant, his soul would have been sucked into the bag—into Hell—too. Any spirit not tethered by a body would.

Considering a soul lost to the pits was a spirit lost for eternity, he'd suffer the burns any day.

Wrenching his arm free of the bag, he wiped the residue from his fingers on the bed's soiled sheets. He cinched the ties, closed the bag, and reaffixed the pouch to his belt.

His shears still vibrated from the power that had radiated from his spiritual form. Holding their jaws open, he sliced through the air and opened a rift. He was intent on returning to his home, but his blood hummed from the kill and his mind itched for distraction. He took a step, and that same pale sliver of sunlight glinted off the toes of his boot.

His head was heavy, and lifting it was difficult. Through the crack in the curtains, the mortal world beckoned. He craved fresh air to clear his lungs, needed the feel of sunlight warm against his skin. He longed to walk among the living and leave the taint of death behind him for a while.

After exiting the motel, Nathaniel ambled through the parking lot and onto the crumbling sidewalk. Cold wind slashed his cheeks, numbed his face. Slush froze in the cracks and pried the concrete apart.

A rumbling growl overhead diverted his thoughts from

the urban decay of the block where his latest mark had resided. Above him, a roiling blanket of clouds stretched across the horizon. He stumbled as he experienced the same instant of vertigo he always did when faced with the clouds' darkened underbellies rather than their luminous crowns.

His steps slowed, giving him time to regain his balance. He touched his hip, feeling the reassuring presence of his shears and soul bag. Rubbing his palm across his pants, he knew there was no blood to wipe from his fingers. The stain ran deeper, having seeped into his soul and corroded it.

A truck sped past, spraying his pants with icy slush from the roadway. Nathaniel paused for a heartbeat before shaking the sludge off. His soaked pants slicked to his leg, and his boots sloshed on his next step.

He glared at the driver, but his lips parted when the truck's front wheels locked, sending it skating across a patch of ice. He watched with morbid fascination as momentum carried the truck through the intersection and into oncoming traffic.

His shoulders tensing in anticipation, he cringed as the truck plowed into the side of a sleek van with a sickening crunch of steel on steel. Metallic screams filled his ears as both vehicles exploded through the guardrail and vanished from sight.

Silence engulfed the strip of asphalt where Nathaniel stood.

He wasn't human. He had no duty to those people. He had done his job, collected his mark.

He swallowed hard. Help would come. Someone must have heard the cry of metal grinding over pavement. His fingers twitched with the urge to slice a rift. He should take his shears and leave.

The harvest was messing with his head, making him feel kinship with these mortals whose lives had spun from their control. *Madness.* This was insanity. He took a step and glanced around to prove he was alone. He was. He took another step, and another, until the pounding of his feet became a full-out run. He slid to a halt at the gap where twisted railing curled as if pointing a sharp finger down the slope and into a ravine.

He tore his gaze from the violence below to scan the turbulent skies, expecting the gloom to part and his angelic kin to descend. No light pierced the thunderheads. No peace settled into his bones at that stolen glimpse of home. Nothing happened. That delay meant one thing—there were survivors.

For now, the mortals would be left alone to live or die. Only then would angels intervene.

At the bottom of the ravine, the black truck flashed its silver underbelly. Its cab was crushed, the driver's side door collapsed. Glass was strewn like glitter across the ground. The van slumped on its side, its front end an accordion of crumpled metal. Exhaust hissed from its bowels.

There were survivors? If not for the absence of his kin, Nathaniel wouldn't have believed it. He shifted his weight and tested the incline. Brittle kudzu vines tangled around his boot on the first step.

His every step tampered with the natural balance of things. Death was inevitable.

Rolling his shoulder, he shook off the imagined burn of the implant heating beneath his skin. The sterling triquetra embedded to the left of his spine marked him as property of Delphi, the reigning governor of Hell. Part of Nathaniel's initiation into soul harvesting had been a vow of service to Delphi. Dark vows stamped into his memory.

Forget all you know of Heaven, for you have forsaken it. Hell is your home now, and I am your new master. Mortals are ours to patrol and ours to punish. Form no attachments. Their lives are fleeting and intervention in their deaths is forbidden.

Nathaniel's vows were sealed with blood—both his and Delphi's. As the first fallen angel recruited for Delphi's campaign against mortal corruption, Nathaniel wielded power second only to the master seraph. Unique even among his fallen brethren, Nathaniel was the Weaver of Souls.

A duty he would have never asked for and a title he would have never wanted.

But who among his brethren would he burden with his tasks? None deserved to know how mortal souls felt once they had been stripped bare, shredded, and repurposed. Harvesters wore their wings with gratitude. Wings he had woven, wings fashioned from the souls of the damned.

Yet if Nathaniel did more than watch this tragedy unfold from the sidelines, Delphi would retrieve the shears and toss him in one of the soul pits burning on Hell's borderlands for eternity.

Mercy was not in Delphi's—or his—vocabulary. *Justice, vengeance*…those were words they knew. Why should they care if a few mortals faded from existence? After all, the human body served only as temporary housing for the soul. Their forms weren't meant to weather eternity.

He should leave, not continue his downward slide into the ravine, toward the wounded mortals, but he wanted…what? A bird's-eye view of a different kind of death than the sort he dealt in? He had been the cause of it often enough to know with unfailing accuracy how those final living moments would play out.

He leaped the last several feet to the bottom and sucked in a reverent breath at the sight before him. A wavering aura bathed his bleak surroundings in sunset colors.

Homesickness speared through his chest. *Aeristitia*.

Except that in Heaven's first city, this sight would go unnoticed. When standing on streets constructed from flawless clouds set in gilded skies, even the shimmer of rainbow souls paled in comparison to their surroundings. Streets cobbled with golden pavers, houses erected of snowy marble, even the trees were frozen in eternal bloom. Aeristitia was called Paradise for a reason.

Nathaniel's new existence was monochromatic by comparison. Here on Earth, everything seemed muted, darker, and hungrier. He'd grown used to it, though, and learned to thrive amid the mortal chaos. What that said about him, he didn't want to know. What he did know was that he hadn't seen anything so beautiful in an achingly long time.

Circling the van, he found the aura's source lying in an ever-widening puddle of her own blood. The nape of his neck prickled and he returned his gaze skyward. He couldn't be caught here. The loss of his shears would cripple him. Assuming his shears were all Delphi took from him. His life, well…he wasn't worth much without those shears.

As he turned on his heel to go, the woman's pained whimper froze him in place.

"Please…help." Her chest rattled when she spoke.

Those two words shattered something in his chest. How easily he'd dismissed his mark's pleas, but hers sank hooks into his heart and tugged. He glanced over his shoulder and found he couldn't look away a second time. Approaching her with caution, Nathaniel gave himself time to reconsider. Dropping to his haunches, he stared at her aura's unfamiliar spectrum. His job meant dealing with only the foulest offerings of mankind. Her purity of spirit humbled him.

The woman's eyes blinked open. Her irises were the color of dark chocolate. "You're…an angel?"

"Afraid not." He hadn't been one in too many of man's ages to count.

She stared at him while disbelief furrowed her brow. His aura held golden traces of his prior calling, invisible to all but his kin and the dying.

He grimaced while she continued to appraise him with a mixture of hope and doubt.

The sharp burn of old shame made him reluctant to admit he'd once been the very being she called him, even if it might have comforted her. Better for them both if she spared her strength and her questions.

She reached for his knee. "Stay." Her lips moved without making a sound before slacking as her eyes rolled back in her head.

He cupped her mouth with his palm, but no air stirred. As he searched for a pulse, her heartbeat vanished beneath his fingertips. A hard shudder racked her body, lolling her head and turning her face into his palm.

He caressed the frigid softness of her cheek, then removed the silver pendant from around his neck and deposited it into his pocket. His flesh dissolved into the fractured light of his spiritual form.

Reaching out a tentative hand, he caressed her soul, and its silken texture glided through his fingers. At his touch, her aura flickered, struggling in his grasp, trying to escape him. His fingers tightened and her light dimmed.

Intrigued by the odd behavior, he released his hold and its brilliance flared. He closed his hand around the column of spectral radiance and once again it dulled, writhing to be freed.

How could she have gone through life with such a vibrant soul and yet meet her end without a loving tie to another living person? He dealt with a lot of untethered souls, and hers was undeniably one of them. Even as feisty as her spirit seemed, the journey to Aeristitia was a long and merciless trek if made without a guide, and none seemed forthcoming.

His thumb stroked her soul until it grew complacent.

The bond of affection so many took for granted suffused their souls with a lustrous shine, and that light acted as a beacon to capture the attention of Heaven. Hers was resplendent, and it pained him to know there would be no warm welcome for her. No glowing acceptance or reunions with loved ones already passed. The best she could hope for was belated acceptance before the fabric of her being dissolved into the atmosphere of the holy city, or she was left alone to wander the Earth until it too ceased to exist.

Her soul—a vibrant and tangible reminder of her death—wilted in his hand. He searched the skies again and found them clear.

Panic stripped him of all logical thoughts. Urgency pounded in his heart as adrenaline spiked in his veins. If he didn't act now, her soul would be lost. His angelic kin wouldn't *dream* of overstepping their bounds. No, this line was his to cross.

He clenched his jaw. "Damn me for a fool," he muttered. It wouldn't be the first time.

Gently, he coaxed her soul back down into the pain of her twisted shell and whispered promises of atonement. Crimson flecks speckled her cheeks while everything below her neck was saturated with blood. He peeled aside her sweater's collar, exposing her left breast. A cylindrical pipe, no thicker than his thumb, speared through her chest.

A twist of his wrist freed the metal with a suctioned pop. He tossed it among the wreckage of fiberglass and steel littering this winter wasteland.

He could use his talent to spare her. He was the Weaver of Souls. He could be this woman's savior. One time he could thwart his own nature and grant this single exception to Delphi's rules.

While he lacked the innate healing ability of his angelic kin, he could manipulate her soul. It could be bound within her body, for a short while, and her healing could be left to other mortals.

His nose burned with the pungent stink of Dis, a sulfuric reminder of what eternity held for him if he got caught. Well, he reasoned, better damnation for a selfless act than his current state of purgatory for a lapse in judgment.

Nathaniel gritted his teeth and sank his fingers to the knuckle inside his insubstantial chest with agonizing precision. He gasped through the startling pain of it.

When his victims begged for mercy, he ignored them, always. Now the horrible pain shredding his soul had a plea perched on the tip of his tongue.

He swallowed the words, knowing anyone who answered his cry would drag him before Delphi for sentencing. He couldn't let that happen.

Souls don't rend, as a rule, and his was no exception. If he'd thought his shriveled soul would abandon him on principle, he'd been wrong. Damaged as his spirit was, it strived to remain whole. He resorted to freeing the shears at his hip and snipping a section free.

His frantic heart pounded as his vision wavered and his sight dimmed. Unimaginable pain ripped a stark growl from his throat. While panting through a moment's break, he was struck by how much more like burlap his own essence seemed. How coarse and threadbare it shined in his hand.

Nathaniel laid the burned golden patch of his soul against the hole left from her impalement, then withdrew a hooked needle and threaded it from the copper spool in his pocket.

A few precious minutes were all she needed. If he trapped her soul in her body, mortals would come and resuscitation could begin.

His quick stitches secured her buoyant spirit. Even if it wanted to, it couldn't wander away now.

Searching the clouds one last time, he noted her escorts still hadn't arrived and their absence was telling. It proved she would have died alone and been lost. Now he hoped she would remedy her situation, reach out and forge ties of friendship…bonds of love.

Cries from a pair of motorists overhead drew his attention toward the forgotten guardrail and roadway beyond. In the distance, sirens wailed and horns blared.

His fingertips brushed the woman's pale lips and they parted, exhaling warm breath across his palm. "Make better use of your time, *meira*. No one can know when it will end."

His skin prickled with awareness as he sensed the belated approach of his angelic kin. He spared a glance at the forgotten truck. Waves of blue-green rippled around the cab. Despite the truck driver's hand in this tragedy, his soul held a brilliant gleam. It was his light calling attention to their location, which meant Nathaniel's time had run out.

They would overlook her soul in its untethered state and therefore his handiwork as well.

After all, choosing to spare a soul required independent thought. Not an angel's strong suit.

He stood drunkenly and gasped through sharp pangs in his chest as his wound cauterized. Palming the shears, he slid his fingers into the familiar handles.

He lowered his gaze to the woman and felt a sharp stab of regret that he couldn't lift her up and carry her with him, to heal her fully and make her realize her mistake. Laughter bubbled in his chest, a rough and bitter sound.

Humans weren't meant for keeping. For culling and cultivating, yes. But to covet or care for one particular person…no reward could be worth that risk.

His shears opened wide, sinking their razor teeth into the air and biting down to slice open a rift. He stepped through the portal and straight into the void.

Chapter 2

GLITTERY DUST MOTES coalesced above Chloe in a darting swarm of fractured light. Gold spots swarmed her vision. Pain seared her chest as the dots gathered and crushed downward with brutal force.

She lashed out, stirring the air with flailing hands and displacing the solidifying mass. Faster and faster the glitter swirled, taking on a masculine form.

His hard eyes bored into hers. His full lips curled with disgust.

Her reality slipped as she found herself drawn into the hateful gaze of the insubstantial man looming over her. She reached out to touch him, and his cold eyes narrowed to thin slits. Glaring at her outstretched hand, the terrible pressure he exuded lessened.

Her skin met his…and passed through. He chuckled darkly and reapplied his bruising strength to the valley between her breasts. He was killing her, and she would die staring at the twisted smile on his face.

His deep voice rolled through her head. *"You've taken an innocent life."*

"No." She planted her palms where his chest should be, but they met with open air. "Please don't do this."

She begged for mercy he never granted. Her pulse roared in her ears. Her limbs grew too heavy to lift. His hand plunged inside her chest and she screamed....

Chloe jackknifed off the couch and hit the floor. The book she'd fallen asleep reading thumped onto the carpet beside her. She lifted a hand to her burning throat and licked her cracked lips.

A dream. He was only a dream. One that ten months of therapy hadn't been able to erase. No matter what she tried, he kept coming back.

She trailed her fingers down her neck, past her collarbone, and into the loose top of her nightgown. Tracing the circular scar over her heart, she smoothed the puckered outline from where the pipe had punctured her.

I'm lucky to be alive, she reminded herself. The other driver hadn't been so fortunate.

She glanced around. Everything was as it should be.

Her book lay open-faced on the carpet. She picked up the paperback and lovingly smoothed the pages before placing it on her coffee table. Her night-light flickered and died as the rising sun bathed the room in a golden glow. The television blared infomercials, but she had no neighbors to care. She had no one at all really.

Chloe hadn't always been so alone. The nightmares just made it seem that way. She remembered a time when this apartment had hosted family dinners. When Dad could always be found reading by the fireplace before bed while Mom worked on her latest quilting project in her craft room. They had both passed on now, and their absence left her locked in familiar patterns and surroundings.

When her breaths came easier and her pulse became less frantic, she rose from the floor and headed for the bathroom.

She curled her toes as her bare feet crossed from the plush carpet to chill tile. Gooseflesh dotted her arms, but she couldn't blame the cold for those.

Her medicine cabinet held a cheery assortment of prescription drug bottles. Her fingertip skipped along the white caps until she found the one she needed and dumped a half dose into her palm.

Her eyes closed as she swallowed the pill dry, her nose wrinkling at the bitter taste, but already she imagined her hands steadier.

She would get used to the lower dosage. The key was consistency. Weaning herself from the pharmaceutical crutch wouldn't be easy, she knew, but she refused to be medicated for the rest of her life. She'd witnessed Mom's decline after Dad's death and had no desire to follow in her footsteps.

With some fortification from her pills, Chloe shrugged off the past eight hours. Once she was dressed in a crisp button-down shirt and khakis, she headed downstairs to open her store.

Bookcases loomed in shadow as soft morning light crept through the windows. She inhaled the welcome scent of old books on her way to the front door and frowned as a long silhouette slanted across the small outside porch.

Early-bird customers were a rarity she didn't mind. Hers must be the only bookstore left that sold more books than coffee, and she planned to keep it that way. She flipped the sign and the lock. An expectant face stared back at her through the glass panel.

Oh, snap. She'd forgotten she had an interview scheduled for today. Chloe's hand froze on the doorknob as she made eye contact with the woman. Her interviewee was here. She couldn't turn back now.

When her parents had been alive, the three of them ran McCrea Books together. Now Chloe was the lone employee, and it was past time to lighten her burden.

The store could support another worker comfortably, but the idea of replacing her parents hadn't appealed to her. It still didn't, actually. For three generations, McCrea Books had employed only McCreas. Now the paycheck she endorsed would go to someone who wasn't a blood relative.

It's not as if I have a choice. The bills had to get paid around here, and she was falling down on the job. Sleepless nights bled into listless days. Even though her medications helped tame her social anxiety enough so customer interaction was possible, sometimes even enjoyable, they couldn't fix everything.

Her nightmares and borderline agoraphobia had spiraled out of control after the accident. Now these four walls acted as her security blanket. They bundled her up and away from the outside world and the bad things that happened there. Opening her door to that world took as much courage as her doctor-recommended doses could muster.

"Hello? Ms. McCrea?" A hesitant voice pulled Chloe from her thoughts.

Her cheeks burned. Clueless about how long she'd stood talking to herself before the woman broke the awkward silence.

Pulling open the door with what she hoped passed for a smile, she said, "I'm Chloe McCrea." Her palms were sweating, so she shoved her hands into her pants pockets.

The woman smiled. "I'm Neve Byrne." She glanced over Chloe's shoulder. "Mind if I come in?"

Chloe stepped aside and Neve entered with a wide grin plastered on her face.

"Wow. This place is gorgeous." Neve turned a slow circle. She walked to the register and ran her hand across the aged countertop. Her purse snagged on a cup full of pens and sent them skittering across the floor.

She scooped them up with a laugh. "Sorry about that. I guess I'm kind of nervous."

"It's fine." Bending down, Chloe lifted a pen stuck beneath a magazine rack by her foot. "Don't worry about it."

When her gaze slid across the floor, she noticed a hint of white sock peeked through the toes of Neve's canvas tennis shoes. Even the knees of her jeans gaped as her weight shifted. When she leaned over the counter, replacing the cup, her shirt rode up and exposed a ribbon of skin across her midriff. An angry scar ran a jagged, purple line from her navel across the top of her hip bone.

She tugged on the faded hem and shifted uncomfortably under Chloe's blatant stare.

"Sorry." Chloe cleared her throat, tucking the pen into her pocket while wishing her dad's attempts at teaching her manners had stuck. "So, are you local? I don't think I've seen you around town."

Not that she saw anyone outside of her store these days.

"No, I moved here last week. Piedmont seems like a friendly place." She paused. "Have you lived here long?"

"My whole life," Chloe said with a trace of pride. "This is home. I wouldn't want to be anywhere else."

"That must be nice." Neve's knuckles whitened where she held on to her purse strap for dear life. "To belong somewhere, I mean." She fidgeted some more before exhaling on a rush of words. "I know I don't look like much, but I'm a hard worker, and I really need this job. I promise I'll buy a better outfit out of my first paycheck, and the place where I stay has showers…." She paused long enough to gulp down a breath and thrust out an application Chloe hadn't noticed clutched by her side. "I hit a rough patch back home, so I thought a clean start in a new town—"

Chloe held up a hand as much to silence Neve as accept the piece of paper. She knew all about rough patches. Even ten months after her car accident, her nights careened out of control whenever her eyes closed.

She needed help, and from the looks of Neve, she did too.

"I'll be honest with you." Chloe tucked a curl behind her ear and offered an insecure smile. "I've never had a coworker who wasn't listed on my birth certificate, so this will be a learning experience for us both."

The subtle offer of employment hung in the air, waiting for an acknowledgment.

"Thank you." Neve's shoulders relaxed for the first time since walking through the door.

"You're welcome." The words came easier than expected.

She offered Chloe a hesitant smile. "Not that I'm looking to be replaced any time soon, but you should talk to the paper about your ad next time. The words were so garbled I almost couldn't figure them out."

Heat crept into Chloe's cheeks. With a wince, she recalled

the stuttered voice mail she'd left on the local paper's free employment hotline. "Yeah, I'll do that." Free editorial service her foot. At least now she didn't have to wonder why Neve and a man who didn't exactly speak English had been her only applicants.

"So when would you like me to start?" Neve gave her an expectant look, the kind a stray animal gave the unwitting person they had adopted.

Chloe had thought she could send Neve on her way and think things over before making a commitment. She hadn't counted on hiring Neve right off the bat, let alone putting her straight to work, but something in her tired and strained face won Chloe over. She was too familiar with the desperate need for relief to turn someone away. "I…don't know. When's good for you?"

Dipping a hand into her purse, Neve withdrew a crinkled brown paper bag and gave it a shake. "I brought lunch." She shrugged when Chloe's eyes widened. "I had two more interviews lined up after this one. Just in case."

"Then I guess you start now?" Her stomach cramped, so she rested her palm across it. This was nothing to get nervous about. This was good news. Neve's determination to find work meant she needed the job in a bad way. So she should be a model employee. Chloe hoped.

"Great." Neve tucked her food away and set her purse behind the counter. "Do you mind if I make a few phone calls first?"

Chloe's upset stomach tightened. *Please let this be the right decision.*

As if reading her uncertainty, Neve supplied, "Like I said, there are people expecting me to show up later today. I'd like to call and cancel if that's all right with you." She blinked. "You did say I had the job, right?"

"Oh." Neve's courteousness reassured her. "Sure, go right ahead. Things won't pick up around here for another thirty minutes or so anyway."

Tucking the same stubborn curl behind her ear for a second time, Chloe pursed her lips and read over the damp application clutched in her hand. Several fields were left blank, the spaces for Neve's address and previous address among them. What little information she had filled out looked promising, though. "It says here you have cashiering experience."

Neve nodded.

Chloe chewed her lip in consideration. The till was low after last night's safe deposit. Even if the fifty-odd dollars she kept on hand for change went missing, she wouldn't be out much. She made her decision. She would keep an eye on today's sales, make sure her profits didn't walk out the door at shift's end, and give her new employee a chance.

"Okay," Chloe said. "Let's start you out on the register and go from there."

Within minutes, Neve had tamed her straw-blond hair into some semblance of order and made fast friends with the cranky vintage cash register. Her easy smile telegraphed an eagerness to please that put the upset flutters in Chloe's stomach more at ease.

Something told her hiring an essentially blank slate to work in her store might not be such a bright idea, but beggars couldn't be choosers. And she figured at the age of twenty-nine, she was due to take a leap of faith in someone.

"Chloe?" Neve's voice brought Chloe's head up. She stood

in the office doorway and indicated over her shoulder. "You have a visitor. He says his name is Wayne Durst, from Magazines Unlimited. Are you expecting him?"

"No." She groaned. She hated confrontations, but dealing with this guy had been a mistake from the get-go. While his invoices showed up every month on time, her order didn't. His product had a short shelf life, and the magazines she ordered from him often arrived well past that expiration date. "Send him in."

Before Neve could turn, the wiry man slipped past her.

"Ms. McCrea," he said as he extended his hand. His palm was damp and his grip tight. "It's been too long."

One of her eyebrows rose, but she played along. "Mr. Durst, it's nice to see you again."

He took the seat she indicated, then pulled a folded paper from his shirt pocket.

"Now, I won't waste your time today." He flashed a smile. "I know you're a very busy woman." Concern crept into his tone. "But there is a serious business matter we need to discuss."

She took a steadying breath and braced herself. "What seems to be the problem?"

He smoothed the creases from the paper he'd pulled from his pocket and scanned it over as if he'd never seen the information before. "Well, I have this letter. My boss sent it over this morning, and he asked me to get to the bottom of it. It says you don't want to continue your business with us." He shook his head in disbelief. "But surely that must be a mistake."

"It's no mistake." She kept her tone light. "I've canceled my contract with your company, and I've requested a full refund for the orders I never received."

He refolded the invoice, then pointed it at her. "To be honest, I'm concerned for you. Piedmont is, after all, a very small community with such limited resources." His polite veneer slipped as he leaned forward. "Let's not make a rash decision. We both know you'll be hard-pressed to find a replacement at our price or with our distribution."

"Mr. Durst, if you ever answered your phone or your e-mail, you would know I contacted you before making my decision." Chloe sat straighter and tried not to fidget. "I'm afraid my customers won't purchase at full price material they've had access to for several weeks, and I'm not interested in paying out of pocket for materials I only have a chance of selling on clearance."

His jaw flexed. "You have to understand this kind of thing happens." The paper crinkled as his fist tightened around it. "I have your order out in my truck, so there's no cause for pulling your account." He tried a smile, but it showed too many teeth. "Mistakes can happen."

"Yes, and if you make enough mistakes, then you lose business because of them." She laced her fingers in her lap. "I've gone with another, more reliable company, which is why your account with McCrea Books was canceled. You'll have to contact one of your other vendors and see if anyone is interested in taking those boxes off your hands at a discount." She stood and gestured toward the door. "Now if you don't mind, I have other business matters to attend to."

His expression darkened. He shoved off the armrests of his chair so hard that it toppled over when he stood. He made no move to pick it up, just stormed from the room. She hoped stomping his feet made him feel better, because her frayed nerves jangled with his every step.

"What was his problem?" Neve stepped in and righted the chair before Chloe reached it.

Chloe gave her a weak smile and leaned her shoulder against the door frame. "I dropped his company from our supplier list." Then she added, "If you see anything from Magazines Unlimited come through, mark it 'return to sender,' okay?"

"Sure thing." Neve nodded.

On the heels of Mr. Durst's hasty exit, a pair of women pushed through the front door. Chloe recognized them and smiled. Neve sidled past her and into the store before she took a step.

"Welcome to McCrea Books," she said. "If you need any help, just let me know."

While it might have looked as if Chloe lingered to watch her new employee at work, the sad fact was, her legs were too rubbery to carry her back to her desk. Her eyes closed for a moment, a smile playing around her lips. She'd done it. Handled a confrontation and not lost her cool. Now, if the feeling came back to her legs sometime before lunch, she'd be set.

Chapter 3

Nathaniel kept his expression impassive as he studied the cards in his hand. Around the table, expectant faces stared back at him, waiting for him to make his move.

"Are you in or are you out?" Saul's wings rustled as he leaned forward to survey the chips mounded at his elbow.

"Last chance to place your bets," Reuel said before he bit into a slice of pizza.

A few men shuffled their cards before pushing their chips forward.

The newest harvester to join their ranks, Abel, blinked rapidly and cleared his throat for the second time in as many minutes. He'd already worried a hole in the fabric of his wings by rubbing the thin material between his fingers. If he lost another hand of cards, he might be walking home tonight.

After turning his attention back to the game, Nathaniel did some quick math. So far he'd won enough money to cover the drained beer bottles and empty takeout boxes littering every surface in his home. He drummed his fingers in consideration.

For the past several months, these weekly poker games outlasted his enthusiasm.

Today was different, though. He needed to be here. His gaze slid over to Saul. His brother needed him here.

"I'm out." Nathaniel folded his cards and slapped them facedown on the card table.

The ringing of the doorbell interrupted Reuel's last call. No one at the table so much as glanced up. Nathaniel took his cue as host and stood. "I guess I'll get that."

"Expecting someone?" Saul's words were soft around the edges. Considering today was the anniversary of Saul's mortal wife's death, Nathaniel was impressed he was still vertical even if it was before noon.

The other players ignored him as he made his way across the living room. He pulled open the door, glimpsed his nephew, and cursed. "Now is not a good time."

Bran shouldered his way into the room. "I'm here on official business." He took in the smoke-filled room and beer-drinking harvesters with a twist of his lips.

"In other words"—Saul paused for a sip from his longneck bottle—"Delphi needed his gopher to pop its head out of the hole."

Nathaniel sighed in his brother's direction. "Could you stop being an ass?"

"I don't know," Saul chuckled. "I've never tried."

A muscle in Bran's jaw flexed. He angled away from Saul and addressed the rest of the small gathering. "Delphi has two collections he would like completed as soon as possible."

The room fell silent as if the harvesters feared a refusal would somehow reach Delphi's ears.

Saul glanced up, undeterred. "I swear Delphi has a fun

meter. When it senses fun, it must ding or flash lights or something." He stood and waltzed right up to Bran. "Then he dispatches Bran the Buzzkill to swoop in and break it up before anyone gets a chance to enjoy themselves."

"Bran is just doing his job." Nathaniel ran a hand over the stubble of his skull-shorn hair.

"You're always just doing your job, aren't you?" Saul jabbed Bran's chest with his finger.

Bran took a step back. "Don't touch me."

"Or you'll what?" Saul followed his retreat. "Get good old Uncle Nate to slap my wrist?"

"You need any help over there, just let me know." Reuel kept right on playing his hand.

"This is a family matter." Saul shifted his glare onto Reuel. "So fuck off."

Reuel didn't miss a beat. "Like I said, Nathaniel, you need me, I'm here."

"Thanks." Nathaniel sighed. "Bran and I can handle him."

"Whatever you say." Reuel went back to his game and Nathaniel was grateful for it.

"No one is *handling* me." Saul shoved Nathaniel. "I am not a child."

"Then stop acting like one," Nathaniel snapped.

Bran touched Nathaniel's shoulder. "Delphi is waiting."

Nathaniel returned to the card table and rapped his knuckles. "Everyone out. I'm heading to work." He arched an eyebrow. "Who's with me?"

The other harvesters found ways to appear busy while they avoided his gaze.

"There's one more collection due." Bran raised his voice over the discontented murmurs. "You all know the rules.

One collection made per harvester per day. That means one of you has to step up and—"

"I'll take it." Saul leaned toward Bran. "You've killed any chance for fun anyway."

"I don't think so." Bran scrunched his face. "Your breath could peel paint. How much have you had to drink?"

"Maybe you didn't hear me." His voice lowered. "I said I'd take the job."

"Enough." Nathaniel separated them, exchanging a look with Bran that said to humor Saul while they sent the others packing. Saul was a dirty fighter when he drank, and Nathaniel wasn't in the mood to clean up the mess afterward.

"Never a dull moment around here." Reuel caught the glance too. He stood and stretched his arms overhead. "If you're, ah, headed out for the night, then you won't mind if I…" His gaze lingered on an open pizza box and a picked-over basket of hot wings.

Nathaniel shook his head. "Take it." He glanced at the others. "Same goes for the rest of you. Take whatever you want."

By the time he got home, food would be the last thing on his mind.

Reuel took point and divvied up the spoils with good-natured ribbing. The same sleight of hand that earned him the dealer spot week after week also made his take-home pile grow taller with each helping he dished out. His hijinks earned him a rare smile from Nathaniel.

"All right, boys, let's leave the men to their work." Reuel shook out his wings and lifted his takeout boxes in salute. "This cute little thing moved into the apartment next to mine. I think I'll see if she's interested in a little 'welcome to the building' dinner for two. Hey, you got any more beer?"

"There's another case in the fridge." Nathaniel waved him on. "Help yourself."

Reuel disappeared into the kitchen. He strolled out with a wink, a quart of chocolate ice cream, and two spoons. "You were done with this, right?"

Nathaniel sighed.

Reuel executed a shuffle step on his way from the room.

Leftovers clutched in hand, the harvesters ambled onto the second-story balcony. They formed a loose line from habit and took turns unfurling their membranous wings and leaping into the open sky. Soul cloth billowed in the air, clinging to bone where feathers and flesh once grew.

Once in the air, each harvester made a concentrated downward thrust, slashing open a rift with the copper dagger from their belts.

The individual portals swallowed them down, leaving Nathaniel alone with Saul and Bran, or as he had come to think of them, between a rock and a hard place.

The two were a study in opposites, and each was a bone of contention in his relationship with the other. The pair even stood at odds. Bran with his spine ramrod straight and shoulders back, Saul with a hip leaned against the sofa. Though today, it might be the only thing propping him upright.

Saul grunted as he straightened. "Let's get this over with."

Nathaniel pushed him back down. "We can't let you go out like this."

Red-rimmed eyes glared back at him. "I said I'm fine."

"No, you're not." Bran exhaled on a tired sigh. "You can barely stand. You're in no condition to harvest."

"Don't tell me what condition I'm in." Saul's head swung his way. The thick shame in Bran's voice ignited Saul's temper between one heartbeat and the next. "You have no right to judge me."

"I have *every* right." Voice crackling with old fury, Bran pitched fuel on the fire.

Chest heaving and teeth bared, Saul challenged, "You have no idea what it's like—"

"You're right, *Father*," Bran cut him off. "No one could possibly know *your* pain because you're the only one who's ever lost everything. Thank God you found salvation in the bottom of a beer bottle." His jaw clenched and his voice graveled. "You were *not* the only one left alone. You are *not* the only one she left behind."

Nathaniel grabbed him by the arm. "Don't do this."

But Bran wasn't listening. "You didn't even visit her grave. My flowers were the only ones there." He shoved Saul's shoulder. "How can you say you loved her so much, yet deny her even that small show of respect?"

"Because her soul isn't there," Saul bellowed as he rounded on Bran. "I have no use for a handful of bones and dirt. That is not my Mairi." Saul launched his fist at Bran. "Your mother is not in some fucking hole in the ground."

Nathaniel intercepted Saul and his jaw popped from the punch meant for Bran.

"Damn it." Saul shook his hand. The sharp pain cut through his drunken haze, and his eyes cleared enough to focus with accusation in their depths. "What the hell did you do that for?"

"You didn't have to do that." Bran pushed Nathaniel aside. "I can take care of myself."

"I know you can." Nathaniel ignored his brother but met his nephew's wounded gaze. "You just shouldn't have to." Not when being half human and half angel meant the Nephilim was no match for his father, for any of them, physically. Nathaniel rubbed his stiff jaw while keeping an eye on Saul. "You have had too much to drink. Go home. Sleep it off."

He shook his head. "Yeah, maybe you're right." He lifted a hand in Bran's direction. "Sorry, kid." Gingerly, he made his way to the balcony and disappeared over the edge.

With his hands shoved in his pockets, Bran stared at the space his father had occupied. "You ever get tired of breaking us up?"

"We're family." Nathaniel clasped him on the shoulder. "We're all we've got."

Bran's pained expression spoke volumes about his feelings on being lumped in with Saul.

"What do you want to do about a replacement?" he asked at last.

"I can ask if Reuel wants to earn his leftovers." Nathaniel scratched his scalp. "I should have asked him to stay when I had the chance. He went straight home, which means he's with his flavor of the week by now." Saul wasn't the only harvester who used a mortal woman to while away his hours, which meant he and Bran had few choices, and none were appealing.

Exhaustion made Bran slump while old grief turned him quiet, introspective. Conversely, the argument with Saul left Nathaniel wired on adrenaline. "I'll handle them both."

"It's against the rules," Bran said with less conviction than before.

"It's not the first time a harvester has covered someone else's collection." Nathaniel doubted it would be the last. "We've wasted more time arguing than it will take to do the work."

"If Delphi asks…"

"He won't have a reason to." Nathaniel reached for the shears at his hip. "Once darkness falls, the soul pits will have their donations and I'll be home in bed."

Bran gave him a tired look. "One day you'll have to stop covering for him."

"I know." He'd been telling himself the same thing for ages.

Chapter 4

THE RIFT SPAT Saul above a rainy field in North Scotland. Through the haze, he spied a gnarled tree reaching its spindly branches over a small graveyard. Bran wanted him to visit Mairi's grave, so visit Mairi's grave he would. He'd been here once before, a long time ago. He wondered who had died that three headstones rose from the muck. Daffodils marked the smallest grave as hers.

Mairi's dutiful son had left her bones an offering. How quaint.

Bran didn't understand. No one understood. That mound of dirt was nothing, meant nothing.

Saul's head fell back on his shoulders. Cold rain pelted his face as he glared heavenward.

There was his Mairi. Her soul was trapped behind Aeristitia's golden gates.

His fists clenched. If it took the final breath of his existence, he would see her freed.

He was close, so close to finding a way to bring her back. A willing body to house her soul could be found with ease. Obtaining her soul...tethering her soul...those were the hard parts. If Nathaniel allowed him to borrow the shears, Saul could...But Nathaniel would never say the words to transfer their power to him or use them in any way except the manner Delphi intended.

Time, a smidgen more time was what he needed. He wasn't prepared for Mairi yet. He could wait a little longer. One day Nathaniel would need help, and Saul would be there. He'd be ready.

Through the film of alcohol numbing his brain, Saul decided to leave Bran proof of his visit.

Evidence guaranteed to send his darling son tattling to his dear Uncle Nate.

Crossing to the headstone bearing Mairi's name, Saul kicked it hard enough the stone split in two. He hefted the top portion and threw it as far as his strength allowed, then snatched the roses and beheaded them. When that wasn't enough, he ground them into the very dirt Bran seemed to believe represented his mother. Panting through the rush, he stared at the other two headstones. It shocked him to read his name engraved on one and Bran's upon the other. Fitting, he supposed.

All Saul's dreams had died with Mairi. He only wished he could say the same for their son.

"I grow tired of waiting, Saul."

Saul clamped his hands over his ears. *"Get out of my head."*

"I will not wait much longer for results," the mental voice hummed. *"Come to me. Now."*

"I'm in the middle of—" A lightning bolt pierced Saul's shoulder, dropping him to his knees.

"I bade you come, and you will heed my call."

Their connection crackled into silence. Saul braced his forehead on the ground until he could breathe again. How the hell Azrael had learned to tap into the harvest bond, Saul didn't know.

Then again, he was sure being the Angel of Death came with perks.

Saul's wings unfurled and hung limp around him. Holes gaped in the fabric. He'd be lucky if his wings held him now. Perfect. He hissed a curse when his wing crackled as they opened.

"*Saul.*" The single word rang with warning.

Saul palmed his knife and carved a rift. He tumbled headlong into Hell, the one place Azrael couldn't reach him telepathically or otherwise. Oh, he'd pay for this indiscretion. He always did.

Today it was worth the punishment awaiting him once he returned topside.

The crack of whips faded, their stings healed. Knives, ropes, chains all left wounds he could heal. Eventually. What he was about to see was worth the price soon to be taken from his flesh.

Scalding air ripped his first breath from his lungs. His lips chapped, tongue dried as he panted. His eyes itched and burned. He blinked. It didn't help. Once his vision adjusted to the heat mirages cast about him, he began walking. He used the black mountain range in the distance as his guide. When he reached the base of the northernmost peak, he slid through a tight crevice.

His ache for Mairi clouded his thoughts until he knew only one sight would appease him.

He entered a valley ringed by mountains. A cave loomed

ahead with an arched entryway. From its mouth poured pale-skinned creatures. Their eyes were the same bloodred as the skies overhead. They had all been human once. Their souls had been mortal as well. No more. They were immortal, ravenous beasts with a single thought—to feed. Flesh or souls, it didn't matter.

Azrael had done this. Saul had helped.

The angel was building an army.

Saul, well, he was learning the process. If souls could be stuffed into corpses and reanimated to make this army, then a soul could be placed within a host body and Mairi could be reanimated.

Resurrection was possible. These creatures were proof of that. But Azrael's process was flawed. Saul rubbed his face. He was missing something; a vital ingredient had been overlooked.

Azrael allowed Saul's experiments. Saul demanded perfection while Azrael was pleased with the slavering beasts. Saul had agreed to help Azrael on the understanding Azrael would teach him the secret to reviving Mairi. Though Saul followed the steps he'd been taught, he suspected a few were missing. Was Azrael holding out? Did he not know? Centuries later, Saul still wasn't sure.

Anger boiled within his chest. He was so close, but this was not the way. He would not let Mairi be reborn into the horror of this form. She would be revived as perfect as she had been in life.

"Come to see your handiwork?" a cool voice called from a ledge overhead.

"Has there been any change?" Saul glanced up, catching the ruffle of black feathers.

"None." The seraph confirmed Saul's fears. "This batch has soul-lust, just as the others do."

"I would not use that crevice if I were you," a second voice warned. "It has been far too long between feedings. Your wings are in no shape to save you should your creations decide your soul is on the menu." He paused. "Mention that to Azrael. We will guard only as long as we are safe."

"Have there been more escape attempts?" Saul hoped not. He'd hate to thin their numbers.

"One a day," the first seraph answered. "They are testing the valley for weak spots. We rest here because this is the only entry or exit. This is where they will come. Your scent lures them to us now."

His twin spoke. "Leave us. Your despair is a fine wine they grow drunk from scenting."

That, Saul could believe. He reeked, with alcohol and desperation, and he knew it.

Soft chuckles rained from overhead. The twins spoke as one in that creepy way Saul hated.

"We smell ozone." They studied his tattered wings. "We suggest that you return to Azrael of your own free will and accept your punishment. You do not wish for him to send Zared after you."

Saul suppressed a shudder. Zared was a cherub. Where Azrael found him, Saul didn't want to know. What their twisted relationship was, well, Saul didn't want to know that either. "I plan to."

"Remember." They spoke over one another again. "Feed the prisoners or lose the wardens."

"I'll see that it's done." Even though it meant Saul had to skim souls from the pits.

A shriek pierced the air as one of the creatures spotted Saul and charged.

The seraphs flitted from their perch into the valley, swords at the ready. "Leave. Now."

Saul did as he was told. Screams followed his retreat. The creature had bought him time. The blades the seraphs carried could kill the things. Once its soul was released, its brethren would frenzy.

They would fall upon its carcass and feed, but Saul had no time to watch the show.

He had a date with an angel to keep.

Chapter 5

W HEN THE PHONE on Chloe's desk rang, she tucked the receiver between her cheek and shoulder, leaving her hands free to sort invoices. "McCrea Books, Chloe speaking."

A familiar breathy voice replied, "I am so sorry to have to call you like this."

Between one breath and the next, Chloe broke out in a nervous sweat, making the phone slip down her face. "Mrs. Marshall, is something wrong?"

"It's Beth." She paused, and Chloe heard sniffling. "She ran off with that Jenkins boy." A small sob filled the line. "I told Harold we had to keep an eye on those two, but he didn't listen. He never listens. Now our baby has run off with a no-account farmer."

Pointing out the fact that the Marshalls were also farmers, who had lived on acreage bordering the Jenkins family for several generations, seemed like a bad idea at the moment. So she offered condolences instead.

"I'm sorry to hear that." And she was. No mother should have to wonder where her child was. Her own mother had said so often. Usually as part of her argument against Chloe going out with a friend, the few times she'd had one.

As ashamed as she was to admit her guilty pleasure, Chloe had lived vicariously through the tidbits of gossip Beth shared about her whirlwind romance with quiet little Osgood Jenkins. Hearing about their torrid affair was as close to experiencing the drama of high school as she'd ever come.

When it came to the teenage social scene, this home-schooler had definitely gotten the short end of the stick. Even if boys *had* sniffed around her, and they hadn't, Mom said dating was out. By the time boys were in, Chloe was too set in her routine, too painfully shy around the opposite sex, and too frumpy to make a good impression on anyone not looking to settle down with the librarian type.

"You're so kind to say so, dear." Mrs. Marshall cleared her throat. "Regardless, I wanted to let you know so you could make other arrangements. I know she does your gro-cery shopping for you, but that won't be the case now."

Chloe's eyes closed. "Ah." She hadn't connected those dots. Beth bought her groceries, ran her errands, did sev-eral things Chloe couldn't do without leaving the book-store.

She wouldn't starve to death in the meantime. If nothing else, the pizza place delivered.

"Oh." Mrs. Marshall sucked in an excited breath. "I have to go. Harold said someone at the market saw them heading toward Louvain. The Jenkins have a hunting cabin up that way. If we leave now, we'll catch them before it's too late."

In the background, Chloe heard Mr. Marshall's resigned sigh.

"Good luck," Chloe said. They'd need it. It wasn't every

day a person discovered what loving thy neighbor looked like firsthand. "Let me know when you find them."

"I'll do that." The call ended with a sharp click.

With her elbows propped on her desk and her forehead braced in her hands, she stared down at a spiral notebook and vowed to practice reciting the help-wanted ad she would have to place before calling the paper this time.

"Chloe?"

Her head jerked up with a start. "Yes?"

"It's after twelve o'clock. I didn't want to bother you." Neve covered her stomach with her hand. "But I skipped breakfast. Would you mind if I took my lunch break now?"

Shaking her head to clear the numbers from her vision, Chloe stood. "Do me a favor and flip the sign out front? I close from twelve to one daily." She stretched. "If we run late once, I doubt anyone will notice."

"Thanks." Neve picked at the tail of her shirt. "I noticed there's a picnic table around back. If you're taking off too…want to join me?"

"I can't." It would mean going outside, and that hadn't happened in months. Not since the dream where her nightmare man stumbled across a hiker in the woods…Remembering the man's screams, and the specter's fury, made her grateful she hadn't eaten yet.

It was definitely not a good day to go outside.

"Okay." Neve drew out the word. "I guess I'll see you in an hour, then. I'll be under the elm if you need me." With a wave tossed over her departing shoulder, she left Chloe alone in her office with only the gruesome memory for company.

In need of more comfort than her calculator could provide, Chloe headed upstairs to her apartment, grabbed a book from the coffee table, and then prepared her lunch. Her small table crowded the breakfast nook and overlooked the rear of the building. Her window framed the picnic table where Neve sat, nibbling her sandwich while flipping through the battered pages of a paperback novel.

She dropped to the window seat and took a sip of iced tea before folding her legs beneath her. A twist to the left angled her toward Neve, and she pretended they sat across the table from one another. She lifted her book, then lowered it as a thought occurred to her.

Tapping her nails on the cover of her book, Chloe decided a book club of two would be nice. Meetings over lunch, discussing favorite heroines, and teasing each other about heroes they would each add to their fantasy harem could be fun.

When Neve's head rose as if she sensed herself being watched, Chloe flushed and lifted the book she'd started the night before. As she took a bite of her salad, she smiled to herself and enjoyed the rest of her lunch with Neve.

Several minutes later, the antique clock mounted across the room chimed a new hour.

A shiver coasted down Chloe's spine as she realized there were only four hours left until closing. Only six hours left until dark. Her skin prickled with the knowledge of what awaited her in the night. Sentient, menacing, her nightmarish visitor was always hungry for her slumber in ways she couldn't understand and really didn't want to.

Nathaniel stepped into a dingy kitchen as the rift sealed on his heels. Fluorescent light buzzed overhead and cast his shadow across the floor. Extending his senses, he sought out his mark. His head snapped to the right, and he slid into shadow as a middle-aged man shuffled past the door. It took seconds to verify they were alone. Good. He could handle his business and leave this place.

His pendant hung heavy around his neck. Once he removed it, he felt lighter as the familiar mantle of invisibility settled about his shoulders. The shears hummed with eagerness in his grip.

One step, then two, and the harvester bond snapped into place with his prey.

"Come Friday, I'm buying some concrete. Dirt floor that's tore up looks suspicious."

Nathaniel waited while the man stripped in front of his washing machine, hating the way his gut pitched as memories poured inside his head and he relived the crimes that had earned this visit.

"I could use a new shovel too, an ax. It's been six months since I bought the last ones."

His mark padded into the kitchen wearing stained boxers and a white T-shirt with holes.

Nathaniel approached, trailing a finger over his mark's left breast pocket. Eager thumps met his fingertips as he slid spectral fingers through dense muscles and gave the man's racing heart a squeeze. His face paled and his breathing labored. He deserved death, and Nathaniel wanted it done.

"Hello?" The mark stared straight ahead while Nathaniel was wrist-deep in his chest, and he saw nothing. He tried for a jolly smile. It looked too practiced and insincere. "Is anyone there?"

Nathaniel withdrew his hand. Sometimes a man's final moments on earth were the most telling of his character. Alone, people slipped free of their masks. Nathaniel witnessed transgressions that twisted the thin thread of his hope for humanity into silken knots of despair.

This man, for instance, was no longer the red-checked grocery store clerk who made young mothers blush and offered their children lollipops as they passed through his line. A friendly man who gave select customers a memento, unbeknownst to them, that he fully planned to recollect.

Behind his mask was a man who had taken a low-paying job where the most taxing question he would ever ask was, "Would you like me to double bag?" Because the grocer shared the same block as the local elementary school, and he wanted to work close enough that he heard the bell ring.

Jerking his gaze from the empty kitchen, the man circled toward the doorway to his right. He chuckled as if to reassure himself. "Damn storm must be blowing shit around." He rammed his shoulder against the side door until the latch caught; then he chained and bolted the door shut.

With that task handled, the man went to the sink and scrubbed his hands. He was meticulous as he cleaned his nail beds. White suds turned pink as he scrubbed his hands and up his forearms.

The sinking sensation in Nathaniel's stomach worsened. He staggered toward the counter. It was then he saw the man was holding a pink plastic ring, the kind that cost a quarter in a gumball machine. The man smoothed his thumb across the rose on top and brownish flakes fell into the sink basin. Using a toothbrush, he scrubbed it clean, then set it on a wrinkled paper towel to dry.

Despite this mark's preference for girls, a child was a child, and all Nathaniel saw was Bran. The fight with Saul, the hurt on Bran's face, the desperate longing for Nathaniel to be the father Saul couldn't be, all crashed over him. That thin cord of restraint snapped and Nathaniel snarled.

Staring into this man's eyes, Nathaniel saw only satisfaction in the murky, green depths. The kind of sick contentment no amount of time spent in a cage or with a counselor would cure. After all, if rehabilitation had been possible or deserved, the man wouldn't have found his way onto Delphi's list.

Anticipation made Nathaniel's hands shake as he donned his pendant and his human façade.

"What you've done can't be forgiven." His voice boomed in his ears. The mark jumped back a step, clutching his chest. He gaped at Nathaniel as understanding registered across his features. Blood drained from his face. Indecision froze him to the spot. Nathaniel advanced on him and placed his palm square over the man's wildly racing heart. "You've taken innocence not yours to have."

His fingers, no longer incorporeal, sank into the man's chest.

Horror rounded the mark's eyes. His mouth fell open on a primal scream.

Nathaniel relished the sound, let it feed the darkness welling inside him.

No. He gritted his teeth. *This is not me; this is not who I am.* Taking his pendant, he wrapped it tight around his wrist. The mark whimpered when Nathaniel's hand vanished before their eyes.

"Please." The man panted while he pawed at Nathaniel's wrist. "I can change. I can."

"No. You can't." Nathaniel pushed his fingers deeper. "You're a rabid dog that must be put down for the good of those who would lie ahead of you and all those you've already left behind."

There, to his right. Nathaniel closed his hand around the oily swath of soul and gave it a tug.

The man's protuberant eyes widened even farther. Even his bulbous nose quivered.

"Enough," he said to himself, and ripped the man's soul free of its mooring. The mark's body hit the ground with a hard thump.

Nathaniel stuffed the soul into his bag and slumped against the counter. When he could breathe again, he tore paper towels from the roll and cleaned his hand. Then he mopped his forehead and staggered from the kitchen.

One more collection and he could go home, scrub his skin raw, and forget tonight happened.

Nathaniel stepped from worm-eaten planks onto the glossy tile of his second mark's bathroom floor. He shook his head to clear the tendrils of connection with his previous mark. It didn't help. His addled mind was swamped with sensation, and his hand shook around his shears.

This taste of psychic burnout must be why Delphi kept harvesters on a strict one-harvest-per-twenty-four-hour schedule, but it was too late to turn back now. Already the bond sought his new mark. She lived alone in an apartment over her bookstore, and she was sleeping soundly in the next room.

The deeper he probed their connection, the faster his heart raced. Tension coiled in his chest. The heady thrum in his blood drew him from her cheerful sea-blue bathroom into the living room.

Something about that brush of minds made his palms sweat, his throat tighten.

The mark lay on her side, her face pressed into the back of a long couch. The setting sun's rays poured through a small window behind her television and glinted off her chestnut hair.

He paused, wondering why he even noticed. Marks were nameless, faceless to him. Their crimes rendered them inhuman in his eyes, so he stopped looking, ceased caring. Yet he couldn't pry his gaze from her. He was mesmerized by the play of sunlight on her hair, the gentle rise and fall of her back as she slept. Peace enveloped him as he watched, utterly captivated by the mortal's slumber.

Chloe. Her name was Chloe. He wished their bond hadn't supplied a name for her.

At the edge of the couch, he knelt and pulled his pendant over his head. Tucking it safely away, he braced for what lay beneath her apparent innocence as their connection sparked to life.

"What are you waiting for?"

Nathaniel blinked at the unexpected question. Marked souls exhibited various levels of awareness. It wasn't impossible for hers to recognize what his arrival meant.

She reached through their bond and spoke again. *"Get it over with."*

His fingers rested above her spine, and he imagined the fabric gave beneath his hand. He shook his head. Forget Saul—he must have had too much to drink. Marks didn't talk back, and the spiritual couldn't touch the physical. Hadn't he just proved as much with his earlier collection?

Ignore her, do the job, then go home. Maybe when this was over, he'd ask Bran about taking some time off. Get his head on straight. The past several months had scoured his already-frayed nerves. The more he thought of it, the better he liked the idea. He doubted Delphi would care.

Forcing his mind back to the task at hand, Nathaniel returned his attention to his sleeping mark. He sank his hand deep…with resistance.

She tensed and sucked in a hard breath. *"Just do it so I can wake up."*

Her bizarre thoughts confused him, so he blocked her out and began his search. Her breathing turned shallow and her heart accelerated.

Nathaniel's fingers contacted the tendril of awareness nestled behind her heart. It felt strange. Slick but not in the way he'd come to expect. Almost like…silk.

He snatched his hand back. "It can't be." Jumping to his feet, he leaned over her, staring. Flushed pink from sleep instead of pale from the cold, he recognized her face.

With a much lighter touch, he located the root of her soul. It strained to escape him, the same as before. He slid his hand down its length and found a coarse patch marring its silken texture.

"It hurts." She stirred on the couch.

He withdrew his hand and swiped it down his face. Heaven help him, it was the same woman who had consumed his thoughts since he left her by the roadside months ago. What he had meant as a gift had damned her. His spirit was stained with his guilt and his sins. Where their souls meshed, his had tainted hers over time.

She would be barred from Aeristitia now. Only Dis accepted souls like his, like *theirs*, which meant she was Hell bound.

"Thank you," her mind murmured to his. *"I was getting tired of dying."*

His chest constricted. He chanced communication with her, uncertain why or how it would work. *"What do you mean?"*

Her thoughts grew irritated. If he pushed much harder, she would wake. *"I want to sleep."* She snuggled under her blanket and deeper into the couch cushions.

"I'll let you rest if you answer a question for me."

The mental equivalent of a sigh brushed through his mind. *"All right."*

"Why did you say you're tired of dying?"

"Because you've killed me every night since—"

"—*the accident.*" He completed her thought and lapsed into stunned silence.

She burrowed into the blanket until only the crown of her head remained visible. He reached out to stroke her hair, amazed to feel the gentle waves fanned across the seat cushion.

Though his pendant enabled his physical form to hold on to spiritual matter once freed from its host, the spiritual should only ever contact the spiritual. In this form, he shouldn't have been able to touch her, yet he could. The caress soothed him, another unexpected facet of their bond.

What horrors she must have witnessed. All because he hadn't let her soul follow its charted course.

Now what to do? Whether natural order, his tarnished soul, or a higher power was to blame, her end had come.

If Nathaniel didn't collect her soul, Delphi would throw him into the hottest pit in Hell and pass her collection to the next harvester.

Bran was also a consideration of Nathaniel's, because Bran's mortal half put his soul in as much jeopardy as hers had been. Nathaniel acted as his tether, and love for his nephew promised Bran's soul the journey home his would never make again.

"Still here?" Her words slurred from sleep. Their bond hummed between them, unbroken by her death.

"For a few more minutes." He reached for her again, caught himself, and dropped his hand. He remembered her skin as soft and cold, but now it glowed warm from sleep.

Before he gave in to temptation, to touch, he donned his pendant and left her to the peaceful dreams he owed her.

His life, and her death, had just gotten more complicated.

Chapter 6

THE VAGUE RECOLLECTION of something peculiar about last night drifted along the edge of Chloe's thoughts. Her dream had been different somehow, but the one time she wanted to recall the details, they were hazy.

She'd fallen asleep with her book in hand, and the same awareness of being in a dream had blanketed her. A small taste remained of the usual death and violence, but she'd also dreamed about sorrow. She'd woken lonely, aching from the loss of something she couldn't put a name to.

As if she had found something she'd been searching for, and the rush of relief, belonging, was heady. Then she awakened to the same empty bed, in the same room from her childhood, and whatever she imagined she had found proved as insubstantial, as elusive, as always.

She gave in with a sigh. She lacked the time to overanalyze this morning. Besides, this dream would give her something new to tell her therapist. She could imagine how that session would go.

She could imagine Dr. Carmichael smiling at her coolly.

"Has anything changed since your last appointment, Chloe?"

"It's odd you should ask. That nightmare man I've been dreaming about? You know, the one who tortures me the second my eyes close? Well, it's like this…I don't think he's all bad. I think what he's doing makes him sad, and he takes that out on me. What do you think about that?"

Yeah. Dr. Carmichael would have a field day with her diagnosis—a patient who experienced Stockholm syndrome with the voice inside her head.

But the man of her nightmares seemed so real, so terrifyingly *there*. Shoving a hand in her pocket, she took comfort from the sliver of pill wedged in the bottom seam. The grainy remains of the other half still soured her tongue, but it was progress. Half was better than whole.

Her dreams might spin out of her control, but she would master her waking hours. The accident had made her aware of how fleeting life was, and she wanted to live hers to the fullest. She wanted to be a glass-half-full kind of person. An optimistic, embrace-the-moment kind of woman her father would be proud of, instead of one who wore her smile like a shield and hid behind it. It would take time for her to work her glass up to full from, well, empty, but she would get there.

Dressed and ready to start her day, Chloe took the stairs down to her store. She spotted Neve on the porch, holding something and waiting to be let inside. "Hey, come on in."

"You sound chipper this morning." She reached inside a paper bag and shoved something warm into Chloe's hand. The smell of fresh baked blueberry muffins drifted up to tickle her nose.

"I slept last night." She scooted aside while eyeing the bluish and splotchy muffin.

"You rebel, you." Neve bit into her own muffin as she headed toward the register.

After peeling down the paper cup, Chloe nibbled tentatively until she got a mouthful of the kind of pure bliss that screamed homemade. "You made these?"

A frown tugged at Neve's mouth. "What gave me away?"

"The taste did." Chloe took another bite. "This is delicious."

"Thanks. I bake when I get nervous." She offered a weak smile. "I don't have much in the way of a kitchen at the moment, but one day I'll show you what a good case of nerves can do to me."

Chloe could sympathize. The soothing weight of a hardback calmed her almost as much as the mental escape hidden between the pages. Some sources of comfort were irreplaceable.

"Shoot." Neve fumbled her muffin, and it crumbled on impact with the hardwood floor.

Something in her expression made Chloe think she didn't believe in the five-second rule. "Is there anything—" A shrill ring interrupted her. "Let me grab that right quick." Leaning over the counter, she answered the phone. "McCrea—"

The same breathy voice from the day before cut her off. "You won't believe it."

"Mrs. Marshall?"

"They're *married*." Her wail of despair rattled Chloe's eardrums.

"I'm…sorry?" She gave a concerned Neve an apologetic smile.

"You would think even if she had no respect for her father, or *me*, she would have at least considered you."

"I…" Chloe didn't know what to say to that.

"It's all right to be upset, really. Beth knows you can't even feed yourself. She left you high and dry, and her father and I are appalled by her behavior."

Chloe's cheeks burned. Even if it was easier to heap blame than acceptance at this point, she wished her name hadn't cropped up. She had a good idea of how her patrons viewed her, and she didn't need the reminder they saw her as the shopkeeper who was nice, but…

"It's fine, really." She made all the proper placations. "I'll take an ad out in the paper. There are plenty of high school students looking to earn a little extra cash." That much she could count on. "I'll find a replacement. Tell her I wish her all the best."

"I'm sure you're right," Mrs. Marshall said. A heavy sigh huffed in Chloe's ear. "I suppose this was inevitable, what with graduation and all. I just wish she had given us a bit more notice."

The line crackled into silence as their conversation faltered.

"Do you have an address for her?" Chloe grabbed a pen and a stack of sticky notes. "I'd like to send her a little something to celebrate her marriage." The quiet grew tense. "That is, if you don't mind."

Appeased, Mrs. Marshall rattled off an address similar to the one where she'd mailed Beth's paychecks. She must be living on the Jenkins farm, at least for the time being. With that out of the way, talk dried up again, and this time, she had nothing left to say.

"Well," Chloe said at length. "I appreciate the call. I'm sure everything will work out given time."

"You're kind to think so. I'm sure I'll see you around." She cleared her throat. "I mean, the next time I need a book or something." She paused. "You know what I mean."

"I do." In other words, Beth had been the only thing they had in common. With her gone, there was nothing left for them to talk about. Their short-lived, quasi-friendship ended with a sharp click and the steady hum of disconnection.

Feeling depressed despite herself, she turned her attention back to Neve, who was scraping a fuzzy adhesive smear from the countertop with her thumbnail.

When she glanced up, her eyes held a question for Chloe. She ought to have known she could play normal for only so long.

She'd lasted twenty-four hours longer than expected.

"Go ahead," she said. "Ask me."

Her new employee gave her a look that said she was weighing what she wanted to know against what she thought Chloe's reaction to being asked might be. She licked her lips and must have decided it was a safe enough topic to broach.

"I heard what you said about placing an ad." She went back to picking at the old tape line. "I thought yesterday went well. I mean, if there's something you'd like me to improve on, I will."

"No, it has nothing to do with you." Chloe rushed to assure her. "Yesterday was great—*you're* great. This is something else entirely."

Neve exhaled and lifted a hand over her heart. "Is it anything I can help with?"

"I'm not sure," she said slowly. "I paid a local high school student to help me out two days a week. She did my grocery shopping and ran errands for me. Paid bills and shipped orders, that kind of thing." She pointed toward the phone. "That was her mom calling. Yesterday Beth ran off and married her boyfriend."

"Been there, done that." Neve brushed her fingernails against her pants. Shaking her head, she didn't expand on her thoughts. "If it's just two days a week, I can help out. I mean, if you don't mind." Her voice lowered. "I could use the money."

Relief made Chloe light-headed. "If you want it, the job's yours." She felt a happy dance coming on. She wouldn't have to live on takeout after all.

"I have, um, a couple of obligations at home." Neve fidgeted. "What will the hours be like?"

"I can let you work half shifts on those days." Having the store to herself for a couple hours every week was no hardship for Chloe. "That way, you'd still get off around the same time."

Her hand, and all pretense of cleaning, dropped. "That would be great."

After checking her watch, Chloe asked, "I know this is short notice, but Beth left me hanging yesterday. Do you think you could swing shopping today if I let you go after lunch?"

"No problem." A red tinge spread across Neve's cheeks. "I can probably cover the bill, but I'd need to be paid back today." She cleared her throat. "Or maybe tomorrow."

"I wouldn't ask you to do that. I have a rechargeable gift card tied to Donor's Grocery. You can use it."

"Great." Neve's relief was palpable. "That would work much better for me."

"Let me grab my purse, and I'll give you my list and the

card." She dashed to the office and back, then dug out her notepad. When she pulled out the list, a crisp prescription sheet stuck to its back. A refill Dr. Carmichael had left with her last week. One Beth wasn't around to fill.

"I forgot to mention one more thing. Beth also handled my prescription refills." She tapped the paper across her palm. "Do you think you could drop this off at the pharmacy?"

"Sure." Neve shrugged. "Just tell me where it is."

"It's in the front of Donor's Grocery, so you won't have to make two stops. Ask for Miss Pat and tell her you're my new aide." She glanced away. "Because the pills are narcotic, she'll have to fax me some paperwork to have you added to the authorized list of people able to make the pickup for me." Her hand shook when she held out the paper. "Is that okay?"

"I don't mind." Neve must have seen her nervous trembles. "Are you feeling okay?"

Chloe squeezed her eyes closed. "I'm fine." *I'm not crazy*, she almost added, though she wasn't sure which of them she meant to convince. "I have an anxiety disorder."

Her shoulders hunched as she prepared a defense against more questions, or worse, the sympathetic tone people used that all but screamed *there, there* with false compassion.

"Is that all?" Neve laughed as she took the prescription and added it to the pile. "These days, I can't say I blame you." She checked the wall clock. "I think I'll grab something from the deli for lunch while I'm there. Would you like me to bring you back a plate so you don't have to cook once I get back?"

"Yeah." Chloe braved a smile. "I'd like that. I'll have whatever you're having."

"Good deal." Neve tucked the card and papers in her purse, then headed back to work.

And that was it. No sidelong glances. No uncomfortable silence.

Almost as if she were normal.

Nathaniel growled low in his throat as the overhead lights flipped on and seared his eyes.

He'd been sitting in the dark for a reason. Not that Saul had asked before blinding him.

"What do you think you're doing?" Saul sniffed the air as he rounded the arm of the couch. "Holy hell, what have you done?"

He'd tried to numb his conscience with alcohol and failed. "I haven't done anything."

"So I heard." Saul grimaced. "At length, from Delphi." He waited for a response, but the best Nathaniel could give him was a bleary stare. "He's got a quill up his ass because *some-one* came in short last night." He rubbed at the bridge of his nose. "Only two collections were issued. Word to the wise, it won't take him long to connect the dots."

Guilt churned Nathaniel's stomach. Never had he failed in his duty to Delphi, and this first exception had potentially catastrophic consequences. One thing was for certain. No one could say he ever did a half-assed job. He raised a glass to his lips and swallowed. "I'll take care of it tomorrow."

"You won't have time." Saul perched on the arm of the couch and flexed his left wing. The dark fabric framed Nathaniel's television almost perfectly, and the local forecast was visible through a gaping hole in the lowermost portion. "It's the first of the month, and you, Weaver, have a job to do."

He couldn't argue. Last month's work was already deteriorating, obviously.

Even fresh souls had a limited shelf life, and decaying wings posed a flight risk to the others. Soul cloth was thin and fragile; harvesters were not. There was nothing for it. Weaving couldn't be postponed. Harvesters needed fresh wings, which meant Nathaniel needed to weave fresh cloth for those wings. That also meant sharing space with Delphi when that was the last thing he wanted to do. Thank Heaven, there could be no harvests made while he wove, which meant his greatest mistake would remain secret for a while longer.

"Then I'll take care of it the day after." Once he had formed a plan.

"Delphi would skin you alive if he caught you like this." Saul's voice took on a thoughtful tone. "We've all heard rumors you're having some sort of breakdown."

Saul's face wavered in Nathaniel's vision. "What rumors?"

"That you're fraying around the edges." Saul's gaze raked over him. "You're short-tempered and defensive when you're usually a paragon of fallen virtue. Should I go on?" He stared at the sheath strapped to Nathaniel's thigh. "If you were anyone else, I'd say you'd done something wrong and were afraid of getting caught."

Nathaniel choked on his drink and wiped his mouth with the back of his hand. This was no time for confessions. Not here, not now, and not with Saul. His brother had enough trouble staying on the right side of Delphi as it was. And, as much as it pained him to admit it, he didn't trust his brother with his secrets. That realization shook him to his core, and he was grateful the alcohol numbed the worst of his shock.

After a moment's careful pause, where he seemed to gauge

Nathaniel's reaction, Saul said, "I also heard you were taking some time off."

"That much is true." He cleared his stinging throat. "I'm burned out. I spoke with Bran about arranging a few weeks for recovery. He's gone to Delphi for his approval. I'm waiting for Bran to return with an answer."

"I doubt you'll have to wait long for your answer." He snorted. "You never do."

"Look, I had a long night." To occupy his hands, Nathaniel poured himself another round. "I'll be better company after I've had a few hours' sleep." He swirled his glass and listened to the ice cubes clink.

"I know a brush-off when I hear one." Saul ruffled his wings. "Whatever you've gotten yourself into, there are ways around it." A small smile teased his lips. "Delphi's power is not absolute."

Nathaniel's glass slipped in his hand. "What is that supposed to mean?"

"It means we were cast out of Heaven. Did you never wonder if he hadn't been as well? I mean, who volunteers to leave paradise for purgatory? No one, that's who." His smugness irritated Nathaniel. "He fought in both the holy wars, and it's been said his loyalty to Aeristitia might have finally cost him the ultimate price—his very existence. It's said a holy sword impaled him, which would have fatally wounded his immortal soul."

"You must be joking. You can't believe Reuel's tall tales." Nathaniel gave his brother an incredulous glance. "His version of the battle for Hell is as reliable as a compass without a needle. He'd lost so much blood by the time he was found in the borderlands, he was delirious."

Saul remained emphatic. "Seraphs are twins, always. It's said one can't survive without the other. If one brother fell, then Heaven would lose her greatest champion and her greatest politician in one fell swoop." He wet his lips. "Reuel saw Delphi mortally wounded and he saw Gavriel claim the body, but they didn't return to Heaven. Ask yourself why that is."

"No." Nathaniel fixed him with a measured stare. "He saw Delphi injured and his brother carry him to one of the nearby triage camps, where he was healed." He sighed. "Gavriel was always the studious one and Delphi the more proactive twin. It made sense to give control of Dis to some-one with the drive to hold it."

"Think about it." Saul warmed to his topic. "Delphi couldn't retain rank if he were fallen. Yet he can't enter Aeristitia. If he could, he wouldn't need Bran to deliver those idiotic journals to Gavriel. He would meet and dis-cuss things with his brother himself. For that matter, he can leave Dis for only short periods of time." He paused. "I think Reuel's memory is better than you give him credit for. I think Delphi was killed and Gavriel brought him back somehow."

An inkling of foreboding wormed its way through Nathaniel. "Resurrection is forbidden."

"But it is possible," he countered. "Someone in Gavriel's position would have access to the very spark of creation. Even Delphi retains his divine talents. You're wearing the proof of that now." His attention returned to Nathaniel's shears. "Delphi gave you an extraordinary gift. Those shears mean you're the only fallen who can slice a rift and stroll down the streets of Aeristitia. You could go home." His eyes lifted.

They were dark with deep thoughts and hungry with a pain Nathaniel almost tasted. "Think of what you could do."

"No," Nathaniel snapped. "We're not having this discussion. I don't want to hear any more speculation about Delphi. The shears are a tool, not a gift, and it's my life if they're misused." He tried to soften his tone, but still his voice rang sharp in his ears. "I know you're not homesick for the landscape. You have something in mind. Something I won't even say aloud for fear someone would hear it and think for a second I was fool enough to help you."

As Nathaniel's temper flared, the shears sparked to life and reached hungrily for his essence to fuel their awakening. For once, he was grateful Delphi had the forethought to create them with a fail-safe. Forged with Nathaniel in mind, they were nothing but sharp blades with handles until they siphoned energy from his particular soul.

His brother leaned closer, his gaze lowered to the shears. "Mairi is there," he said. "I know she is."

So were innumerable other souls. "It's where she belongs."

Saul's mutinous expression said he disagreed.

Nathaniel dreaded Saul's reaction if he ever learned of his indiscretion. His actions with the mortal woman skirted the line, but she had been alive when he saved her, though her grip on life had been slipping. What Saul proposed, after Mairi's centuries of insubstantiality, would mean finding a new host to accept her soul. He would either scavenge a body or, worse yet, harvest a fresh one for her. How Saul thought to conjoin the two, Nathaniel couldn't begin to imagine.

While Saul continued to glare at him, Nathaniel's patience wore thin. "Say I took you there—and make no mistake, I won't—you'd have to find her, one soul in millions. Then you'd have to tether her, revive her, and unless you've been hiding a halo in your pocket, you don't have the power or the knowledge to do either. Or access to anyone who does."

Otherwise, Saul would have completed this fool's errand by now. "So, if by some miracle you made it that far, when you failed to tether Mairi, her soul would evaporate over time. She would be reabsorbed into the heavens and would cease to exist in any recognizable form." Nathaniel sighed. "You can't want that for her."

With a low growl, Saul rose. "I will save her, with or without your help." His wings snapped out behind him as he opened them.

"This is your grief talking," Nathaniel said.

"No," he replied softly. "I'm talking; you're just not listening." Saul sliced a portal and launched himself through it with a thrust of his wings. A rush of air scattered newspaper sheaves and empty food boxes onto the floor.

Lacking energy to much care at this point, Nathaniel let his head fall back against the couch cushions while he considered his own woman troubles.

His plan had backfired, and his mark's extension on life had run out before she could choose a different path. It made no sense, even all these months later, that she had no loving relationship with another living person. For whatever reason, she chose emotional isolation rather than involvement with her fellow mortals. A mistake she would pay for if some compromise couldn't be reached.

He'd seen her soul, held it. She deserved the gift he had given her, but she had still failed to make use of it. Her waste of his good intentions tempted him to go back. He wanted to shake her shoulders until she woke up to the truth. He wanted to demand her reason for squandering her second and final chance at ensuring her soul's salvation.

A mental picture of her sprung to his mind. She wasn't flawed in any obvious way, but his time harvesting had taught him well that beauty was skin deep and a pretty face sometimes masked hideous intentions.

Not that he thought she was beautiful, exactly. Her soul was, certainly. Her person…recalling her tumbled curls and the warmth of her skin made his cheeks flush. He set his drink aside and blamed the alcohol for the rush of heat spreading low through his gut.

Chloe was such a simple name for such a complex problem.

There was no choice. If he backed out now, she would pay a harsher price for his interference. More than his earlier impulse to help, he owed her now. Besides, how much time could it take to assess her situation and his risk? Not long at all. A day or so of observation would tell him what he needed to know.

So he would watch her. Find an excuse to talk to her.

He spoke with Nephilim often. How much harder could it be to talk to a full human? His hand went for his drink. Not hard. He could do it. Lifting the glass to his lips and draining the liquid, Nathaniel found himself recalling the room where he had found Chloe.

She lived above a store carrying her last name, McCrea Books. Nathaniel searched his memory for clues about the building from the last time he'd walked through downtown Piedmont. The front steps had seen better days. One of the windows had been boarded over, but how long ago? He couldn't recall. It could have been last week, last year, or ten years ago. He hadn't passed through that section of Georgia much since Reuel moved out of Atlanta.

Nathaniel's trade had been carpentry for centuries before the modern era made living on his investments a simpler matter. He had once labored among mortals, earned whatever currency they dealt in, and hoarded his shares until he proved to Delphi he could afford to live in their midst. After all, Dis had been no place to raise a child with Bran's fragile health. Later, he'd discovered he enjoyed his taste of freedom, his view of the sky too much to return to Dis.

Nathaniel sat up, braced his forearms on his knees, and stared into his glass. All the stores downtown were old. Only a handful had been renovated and none of them recently, though he couldn't remember the particulars. Maybe Chloe was in the market for a handyman. Lucky for her, Nathaniel knew someone perfect for the job.

Chapter 7

Fury made Saul soar as he glided over the crumbling ruins of a forgotten castle. The turret jutted proudly amid scattered stones. He circled it, his nerves winding tighter the higher he flew.

The base of his skull tingled. Another mind brushed against his in warning.

"Keep your shirt on," he muttered.

Around him, the air charged and crackled. Lightning flashed spiderwebs across the sky.

Saul took the hint and descended.

Below him, a golden cherub sat perched on a rock at the base of their master's feet. Zared. He didn't lift his electric-blue eyes or bat his white-blond lashes. His full, red lips parted, but the rich words rolling from him belonged to the angel at his shoulder. "How fares your brother?"

Saul lit at the base of the stone and knelt. He tried not to stare at the angel, but the chains glinted and drew Saul's eye time and again. *Focus.* He cleared his throat. "He is well."

"Has he been swayed to our cause?"

"No." Saul modulated his tone. "He is, as you said, show-ing signs of stress. It is my belief he will join us soon. If he continues on as he is, his mind will break, and he won't risk that." His fists tightened. "Bran means too much to him. He would never risk leaving the boy in my care."

Stiff laughter shook the cherub's shoulders. "His devotion to the child is noteworthy. That's what makes him the war-rior Delphi covets most. Nathaniel is selfless, loyal." That remark stung Saul's pride. "But if you command those he loves, then you command him. It is…his weakness."

Fresh anger sparked at the reminder that Saul was but a pawn in a greater game on a larger board than he could con-ceive of. "Why use me?" Must he always be second best? "Why not use Bran?"

More laughter came. "Bran's loyalty cannot be bought. Yours, however, can." The cherub shifted to face him but maintained his indifference. "There's also the fact that your brother fell from grace for you. He loves you. He's watched you deteriorate, year after year, and it gnaws on his bones. If he thinks for an instant you can be saved, he will leap at the chance without thought."

"You overestimate his naïveté." Tonight his eyes had lost that spark when he looked at Saul.

"It makes no difference." The cherub scowled. "You will continue on as you have been."

"Nathaniel requested some time off," Saul pointed out. "I doubt he invites me to join him."

The cherub made a thoughtful sound. "Interesting. I won-der…" Several moments of silence passed. "Follow him. This might be the chance we've waited for. When you aren't har-vesting, you're tracking Nathaniel. Understand? I want reports nightly, where he goes and who he sees."

"I will do as you ask." He had no choice if he wanted to remain on Azrael's good side.

"See that you do." The cherub grinned in the vicinity of Saul's feet. "Soon the gates of Hell will swing open for us. Our time is coming. Accomplish this task and your reward will be great."

"If I fail?" Nathaniel was more stubborn than Azrael gave him credit for.

"Then you will learn the steps of resurrection through experience." Zared snarled Azrael's message. "Your soul is mine. I will not relinquish it, not to Delphi and not through your failure."

Saul ducked his head to hide the hate burning in his gaze. "I'll keep that in mind."

"See that you do." The cherub smiled, and it was a cold thing. "Now, I believe we have one final matter to discuss—your failure to appear at my summons." He leaned close. "You were in Dis. I smell the sulfur on your clothes. You visited with our creations, then? How do they fare?"

"Soul-lust is riding them hard. They're rabid, starving." Zared grinned as Saul said that. "The seraphs think the creatures should be fed more often." Saul agreed with their assessment. "They also said if conditions in the valley deteriorate much further, they won't act as wardens. The creatures are antsy. Escape attempts are escalating. It would only take one escape for Delphi—"

"Fine," Zared hissed. "Alter their feeding schedule. We can't afford to lose the seraphs."

"I'll inform the twins." Saul clenched his fists. Yet another task left for him to do.

His schedule ran tight enough as it was. He alone could

access the soul pits, so that meant he had no choice but to do this job. At least he didn't have to worry that Delphi or the others might notice a few extra souls gone missing. Saul used pits that had been sealed after the harvester who filled them snapped. Those were checked every few decades, giving him time to cover his thefts.

"You are upset with me." Zared conveyed Azrael's amusement. "Anger is fire for the soul."

"I knew the price of ignoring your summons." Saul's skin crawled to think of it.

"Good." He nodded. "Do you resent me for exacting the cost of insolence from your flesh?"

"No." Not when Saul tallied every lash, every cut, and every ache.

He vowed Azrael would one day suffer every ounce of pain he'd dealt him.

"Carry on, then." The cherub waved his hand. "Let the punishment commence."

Zared licked his lips and Saul knew the cherub had regained control of his body.

His eyes glazed as Saul removed his shirt and pants, headed for the thick wooden post set in stone. He grasped the handles, one to either side, and held on tight. Air stirred as the cherub lit at his side. Zared ran the whip down Saul's flank. Saul bit his cheek to keep from crying out when the crack of leather split the backs of his thighs open. Blood ran down his legs, pooled at his feet.

All the while, Saul counted. He let his mind drift to that dreamy place where Mairi was alive. She'd tend his wounds, kiss his mouth, tasting of paradise. His love for her tightened his chest.

Too soon, the cherub fisted Saul's hair and ripped his head backward so their gazes locked.

Zared was panting; his hands trembled. "Thanks for that." This time, his voice was his own.

"My…pleasure," Saul said through gritted teeth.

Leather tickled his side. "No." Zared dropped the whip with reluctance. "But it was mine."

Saul rested his forehead against the whipping post, and who but an angel too long gone from Earth would conjure one? Slowly the haze subsided, leaving him the agony of his shredded skin.

"You may go now." Zared's voice was once again deep, rumbling, Azrael's.

Glancing toward the rock, Saul winced. The cherub turned its back. The angel didn't move.

Saul wasn't sure if he *could* move. All those chains kept Azrael's wings locked against his spine. His arms were bound against his sides and his feet were shackled. A cloth sack covered his head, and thick rope gagged him, stuffing the coarse fabric in his mouth. Since the angel used a proxy, Saul couldn't place his voice. With Azrael's head in a bag, Saul couldn't place his face, either.

He had only Zared's word that the captive angel was Azrael, but it hadn't mattered to Saul at the time. Only that the angel knew the secrets to life and to death that Saul had failed to uncover.

Pain faded. It always did. Wasn't Mairi's freedom worth a little pain? Yes. It was.

She was worth all of this and so much more. She was worth anything, everything.

Chapter 8

CHLOE COULDN'T SHAKE the uneasy feeling of being watched. It started in after she opened the store this morning and the sensation hadn't let up yet. Glancing around, no customers picked through the sales rack or milled around her. No one paid her any attention at all, to her relief.

A shiver worked its way down her spine. Her imagination did enjoy playing tricks on her.

Last night should have left her rested and relaxed. Two dreamless nights in row, no nightmare man in sight, it should have been heaven. Instead, so much sleep made her anxious.

Shrugging off the uncomfortable sensation, she went in search of Neve and found her bent over by a pair of armchairs. When Neve straightened, Chloe spotted a dark leather wallet in her hand. Much too chunky for a woman's, it must belong to the young man she'd noticed reading in that spot earlier.

Her stomach dropped when Neve cracked it open, thumbed through the contents, and made a withdrawal. Before all Chloe's insecurities could escalate, she saw Neve snap the wallet shut, then head for the register. Neve stuck the wallet in the back of the cash drawer, then held up a card and dialed a number. She was all smiles and warm laughter while on the phone. She even patted the register before she ended the call. Without hearing a word, Neve's message was clear. The wallet was safe and ready for pickup whenever the owner could manage it.

Chloe exhaled on a sharp breath full of relief...and a smidge of guilt. Trust had been as easy as breathing when her parents were alive. Now she struggled with the concept. She'd never really had to protect herself or judge another person's trustworthiness all on her own. Without Mom's prodding questions or Dad's silent observations, Chloe felt out of her emotional depth.

Neve caught her staring and waved, no doubt uncertain why she was the center of her attention. Chloe waved back, content everything was as it should be. Then she hefted a box of new arrivals from the storage room and lugged it to the sales floor. The oversized travel books were backbreakers. And the hefty titles never failed to belong on the top shelf.

After a quick check of the author names at nose level, she rose on her tiptoes and tapped her way down the spines until she found the letter she was looking for on the second shelf down.

"I was wondering if you could help me," a deep voice asked from over her shoulder.

"What the—" She jumped and then turned toward the unexpected sound. Her shoe caught the box's edge and she tripped. Hands thrown out, she braced for impact. Instead, she got a handful of man as the customer caught her against his chest. Her palms slapped his shoulders, fingers bunched in the flannel of his shirt. She gasped as his hold squeezed the air from her lungs.

"Are you all right?" His full lips twitched into a hesitant smile.

Chloe's mouth ran dry. The reply perched on the tip of her tongue? Gone.

Their gazes locked. "I'm fine." She had never seen eyes like his before. They were a brilliant shade of blue, as clear as the Caribbean waters featured in the books at her feet.

His eyes crinkled at the corners while she stared, dumbfounded, right into them.

He probably knew from experience women had trouble talking when he looked at them that way.

She hissed as a sudden headache made her vision waver from pain. *I need some aspirin.*

"Would your friend have something you could take?" His large hands rubbed circles against her lower back.

"I don't know." She rubbed her temples. "I have some in my office." Her head snapped up. Had she said that first part out loud? Her skull throbbed as the cascading discomfort built.

He dropped his arms and the terrible bubble of pressure burst, ringing through her ears.

"You look pale," he said. "Do you need help getting up?"

What did he mean up? Chloe glanced around. When had they sat on the floor? And...*oh snap*...what was she doing sprawled across his lap?

She scrambled across the hardwood planks and leaned her back against a bookshelf while he chuckled softly at her expense. Unfortunately, the ground didn't do anything helpful, like open up and swallow her whole.

"I'm looking for Chloe McCrea." His leg bent while he waited for her answer.

Trying not to choke on her tongue, she replied, "I'm Chloe." His broad hand appeared in her field of vision. She took it and he pulled her to her feet. "What can I help you with? Are you looking for a particular title or author?"

"No." His smile made her insides quiver. "I'm looking for you, in particular."

She hadn't realized they still held hands until he pumped her arm as he introduced himself. "I'm Nathaniel Berwyn, with Handel's Handymen. I noticed the porch out front could use some work, and I thought I'd offer my services."

The size of his hand wrapped around hers distracted her. "I, ah, appreciate the offer, but I don't think I'm in the market for repairs at this time."

He tipped her chin up so their gazes collided. "Are you certain I can't change your mind?"

His thumbs were at it again, smoothing over her cheek with easy familiarity that really should bother her. She was sure it would. Any minute now.

When dots swam in her vision, she realized she hadn't taken a breath since their gazes met. "No?" With doubt thick in her voice, she wasn't surprised when he pounced on her indecision.

"What if I make you a deal?"

Chloe found herself leaning forward into his touch as his hand slid away. No longer distracted by the coarse texture of his fingers, she shook the cobwebs from her thoughts. The store did need work, but she had skipped the contractor in favor of hiring Neve since one could wait and the other had waited long enough. Still, she wondered at his offer. "What kind of deal?"

"I'll write up an estimate and we'll negotiate terms."

She frowned. "That's not a deal; that's standard practice."

"I'll cover the up-front costs. I'll do the work and let you approve it before accepting payment."

His offer wasn't too far off base from what other contractors had done for her. Usually, it was a half-now-and-half-later kind of deal. If he was willing to cover the cost, then he was offering a solid guarantee on his work. She respected that. She also recognized the company's name. Handel's was a local company, so Nathaniel's boss was a phone call away if he gave her any trouble.

"If I'm not pleased with the quality of work completed?" she asked.

"Then I won't charge you a dime."

"Can I get that in writing?"

"Of course." Nathaniel's smile said she was hooked and he knew it. "Would you like me to start with the estimate first? See where we go from there?"

"Sounds like a plan. I'd like to know what kind of expense I'm looking at." She risked a smile. "Well, assuming your work is up to par."

His answering grin made her heart stutter. He turned and walked toward the door, then pulled a pencil and pen from his back jeans pocket. She bit her lip as she took in the view.

A week ago, she would have tossed him out on his mighty fine assets. Heck, two days ago she would have spun him on his heels and watched him walk away. Grinning, she admitted she would have enjoyed every step of it too. So why was today any different?

Maybe having Neve around made the difference. She wasn't alone anymore. Funny how that made her heart lighter just thinking it.

How had she gone from *no thanks* to *what harm could a look-see do*?

Nathaniel glanced over his shoulder at the last minute and caught her looking. That right there was the harm in a look-see. She'd looked, and he'd seen her do it.

Her cheeks tingled with embarrassment while his eyes glimmered with what had to be amusement.

Way to go, Chloe, she chided herself. She'd seen more handsome men before, probably. Though this was the first time a stranger had walked in off the street, given her a sinful smile designed to curve his full lips to perfection, and made her melt at his feet.

His touch made her want to curl up in his lap while he stroked those long fingers of his through her hair. She couldn't stop from walking to the window and staring out after him.

But my, oh my, what a view.

Chloe McCrea. Nathaniel made a show of checking the bookstore's porch for rot while his mind was otherwise occupied—namely by the curious face peering through the window as she tracked his progress.

He glanced up and met her gaze through the glass. Her lips parted as if on a gasp. Holding her gaze for a few heartbeats, her cheeks pinked and she stepped back into the shadows of her store.

His recent contact with her soul proved she still had no bonds in place. He sighed through his disappointment. After the better part of a year, she was no closer to salvation than the first time he'd met her. Or was she?

The lean blonde working the register seemed protective of Chloe when he asked for her. A friendship might start there, and those ties were sometimes the strongest. If she began to care for Chloe, then his problem would be solved.

Chloe's soul could be harvested, and he could pretend ignorance about the stain he'd caused on it and approach Delphi with the issue. Instead of the soul pits, Delphi would summon his brother, Gavriel, who would escort Chloe's spirit to Aeristitia for processing.

A neat plan wrapped up but for a lie. He would need some reason for how his soul became tangled with hers, but he could think of a believable excuse.

Nathaniel picked absently at the handrail, disturbed by how quickly the solution had come to him.

"Well?" Chloe stood in the doorway, palms braced on the casing.

Her nearness made their bond jolt to life as it had in the store. Her thoughts streamed into his head. Her memories were a pool of information glittering outside his periphery, one he could tap into if he chose. He hesitated to dig through her mind, hating the idea of violating her further, so he blocked her out until her mental voice was a bare whisper.

"You see this?" He lifted a warped post cap and the wood crumbled.

"How bad is it?" She craned her neck for a better view.

He held his hand out toward her. "Come here and I can show you."

She backed up a step. "Can't you just tell me?"

"It won't take a minute if you come here and look."

"That's okay, really. I knew it needed repairs. I was just hoping later rather than sooner."

He tilted his head to one side and watched as her face inched into shadow. The only part of her left in the sunlight was her hand, where it curled around the doorknob in a white-knuckle grip. Then it vanished too.

Curiosity got the better of him. Forcibly invading her privacy might not appeal to him, but he was willing to eavesdrop on any thoughts she broadcasted.

"Get it together." She released a mental groan. *"It's three steps, maybe four, and just onto the porch. I can do this. If I don't, this guy will think he can walk all over me. No matter how good-looking he is, I can't afford that. Neve's watching too…Damn it."*

"I'd prefer you have a look before I get started," he called, pushing her to make a decision.

Her head popped around the corner and her teeth worried her bottom lip.

While she debated her answer, he drank in the sight of her. Her soft reddish-brown hair was braided in a tight line from her widow's peak down the rope of hair brushing below her shoulder blades. Her shirt was starched and her pants pressed. No makeup, but he liked her bare face.

She had freckles dotting the bridge of her nose and speckling her cheeks. She gave him a strange look, as if wondering what he found so interesting, and damn if he couldn't help but smile at her.

"Why are you looking at me like that?" A frustrated line puckered her brow.

"I'm only being polite." He chuckled as one of her eyebrows cocked in disbelief. "I'm trying to sweet-talk you into giving me a job, remember?"

"How could I forget?" She tried staring down her nose at him, but it didn't work well, given the foot and a half in height he had on her five-foot-nothing frame. "You're laying it on pretty thick."

"You're here, talking to me." He flashed his teeth. "That must mean it's working."

Chloe rolled her eyes, appearing calm and collected, but inside her head, her thoughts were a black jumble of uncertainty. *"Here goes nothing. I'll look, smile, and approve. It'll take five minutes, tops."* Her hand shook when she leaned out the door and reached for the porch railing. Once her fingers made contact, she exhaled as if that small feat had drained her.

Try as he might, Nathaniel couldn't figure out what the problem was. "Do you need help?"

She shook her head and took a half step. The toes of her tennis shoes rested on the porch while her weight balanced over the threshold. Her grip on the rail tightened and she pulled herself a full step onto the porch. When she glanced up at him with stark pride in her eyes, it was his undoing.

He met her halfway and tried not to spook her into retreating into the store. He offered her the post cap.

"Um, that's okay." She scrunched up her nose. "I can see just fine while you're holding it."

"The other posts are in the same shape." He backed off and gave her room to breathe. He descended the stairs, stood in the center of the bottommost step, and bounced a little. "You can see the steps are shot. The planks are warped. This can't be fixed." She flinched when he said, "It'll have to be demolished and rebuilt, all of it."

"I knew I kept putting it off for a reason." She sighed. "All right. How much is this going to cost me?"

"I need a few more measurements; then I'll call around and get an estimate on supplies."

"You can't give me a ballpark figure?" She was clearly bracing herself for the worst.

"I'd rather give you an accurate quote the first time." He needed time to acclimate himself. He hadn't done a project like this one in decades. The price of raw material and labor would have to be researched, so his estimate slid into that comfortable place between too good to be true and scalping her. Plus he didn't want to give Chloe a reason to dial up Handel's and discover Nathaniel was borrowing on the reputation of a local company to put her at ease.

"All right." She was back to nibbling on her lip.

Still unsure what to make of her odd behavior, Nathaniel tested his theory. "Can you hold the measuring tape for me?"

Panic widened her eyes. "I…I need to get back to work." She spun on her heel and bolted through the door. A second passed and then she shoved her startled employee through it.

"What did you say to her?" The blonde jumped as the door slammed shut behind her.

Nathaniel said dryly, "I asked her if she'd like to hold my measuring tape."

"Nice." The blonde snorted. "Will anyone do or was that a Chloe-specific request?"

"I was perfectly serious." Metal glinted in his hand when he wiggled the silver tape measure.

The woman didn't answer. She was too busy staring over her shoulder into the store.

"Should you check on her?" Tension radiated through his

bond with Chloe. Nathaniel was seconds from hunting her down if this woman didn't. He smoothed a hand over his scalp. "She seemed rattled. Is she okay?"

The woman's brows knitted together, but whatever occurred to her, she didn't share.

Suspicion tightened his gut, but she wasn't a mark, and her secrets were her own. Whatever she hid from him was none of his business. He grimaced. Unless it involved Chloe, then it was definitely his business.

His conversational skills with humans—or the opposite sex for that matter—were rusty. Still, he might learn something new about Chloe if he got her talking.

"You'll have to forgive me." He forced a smile. "I didn't introduce myself earlier."

"Nathaniel Berwyn." When his eyes narrowed, she added, "Voices carry."

"I'm sure they do." He would have to remember that. "And you are?"

"Neve." She didn't offer a last name or anything else of value. She was being cautious.

He would have to try harder.

"This place is falling apart." He slapped the post cap back in place, and debris rained onto the ground. "Chloe's lucky there haven't been any accidents." When Neve kept silent, he figured she must agree with him. Giving her a smile, he did his level best to be charming. "Would you mind helping out? I'd like to get this project approved and started as soon as possible."

She answered with an uncertain nod. "Sure." She walked over and took the hooked end of the tape and set it against the board where he indicated.

"Is Chloe always so…?" He cast about for the right word. "Skittish?"

"I don't know what you mean." Their eyes met and understanding passed between them.

She knew more than she let on, but her loyalty lay with Chloe, not with him.

Something about the firm set of her lips as she considered him made him think it was more than token concern making her comb him over with such sharp focus.

His skin had flushed under Chloe's assessment, but this woman's attention didn't stir his curiosity on a base level, only his desire to know more about her role in Chloe's life.

Since the women worked together in close quarters, Neve was his best chance at getting Chloe emotionally attached to someone. He was heartened by the fact that she appeared to care for her already.

His larger worry at the moment was she might not be the only one becoming attached.

Humans were fragile and finite. Chloe would die in time, even without his interference, and he would forget her. Glancing up, he caught her staring down at him from the second-story window with her small nose all but pressed against the glass.

His gut clenched. He would forget her all right, when Dis froze over.

Chloe plucked at the ruffled edge of Nathaniel's estimate until a layer of confetti covered her desk. Using the end of her pencil, she prodded the fist-sized chunk of wood he'd brought her as further proof she was doing the right thing. When she stabbed at the hunk, the lead sank clear through to her desk. Not good.

It was official. Her porch was crumbling.

Accidents happened, but ignoring this amount of decay would be negligent when customer safety was too important to begrudge the unplanned expense. Not to mention repairs were the responsible thing to do, and she was nothing if not pragmatic. Besides, it would only take one customer who paid more attention to their phone conversation than their footing, and she would have a lawsuit on her hands.

Pine porches lasted about a decade, so hers had outlasted its life expectancy. Hard to believe she'd been eighteen the last time the sagging frame saw a hammer and nails. Graduation loomed around the corner for her and Piedmont's other teens. Her parents had rushed the construction order after they hit on the idea of a lavish party for her thrown in view of the town.

Their intentions were good. Party in plain sight, lure in kids her own age with bright lights and finger food. But as fate would have it, they picked the same night as the local high school's senior prom.

Standing by the uneaten buffet had given Chloe a front-row seat for the parade of convertibles balling tires down Main Street. Prom princesses wore their sequined best while snuggling their tuxedoed princes. Thanks to the fifteen-mile-per-hour speed limit, she'd gotten an eyeful as life passed her by.

She hadn't thought of that night in years. Some combination of the porch and how Nathaniel looked standing there dredged up the unhappy memory. She would have given her eyeteeth back then for a guy like him to sweep her off her feet. But he wasn't her long-lost prince charming, and she was nobody's princess.

Focus on the problem, not the hot guy who would make a nice lawn ornament for a few weeks.

Okay, okay. She was focused. Repairs were a given. So…hiring Nathaniel would *really* be the responsible thing to do. And while he was at it, he could fix her busted window and make some much-needed repairs to the bookshelves. Tapping her pencil against her desk, she wondered if he knew anything about plumbing…

"Oh, ick." She recoiled as a bug climbed from the soft wood and scuttled across her desk. Taking off her shoe, she whacked it hard enough to draw Neve's attention.

"Everything okay in here?" She walked from the counter to the office and leaned a shoulder against the door.

"I think I'm going to have to add a pest control touch-up to my to-do list." Chloe held up her shoe with the offending bug mashed on its heel.

Neve eyed the bug, but her face held a faraway expression.

"Is everything okay?" Not that Chloe had any experience with giving personal advice, but she could listen. Sometimes a sympathetic ear would have made a world of difference to her.

"Yeah," she said at length. "I was thinking about something."

With the bug scraped in the trash and her shoe back on her foot, Chloe scooted forward. "Anything I can help with?"

"It's more that I wanted to ask you something." She glanced up. "Personal."

"Okay." Worst-case scenario, Chloe could always fake a potty break if the question was more than her limited life experience could handle. "Shoot."

"Have you heard of Dem Bones?" Neve prompted. "From down the street?"

"Sure." The place was a local barbeque institution. "What do you want to know?"

"I got some good news earlier today, and I kind of wanted to celebrate." Neve straightened and ran a hand down the front of her softly faded blouse. "I was wondering if you'd like to share an order of ribs or something."

Chloe could count on one hand how many times she had been asked to go out with a friend. This was number one in her adult life, and her gut ached with the hollow acceptance of the fact that she would have to say no.

"I can't."

She felt about two inches tall for begging off another invitation and knew from experience if she said no often enough, they'd stop coming. Stepping onto her porch was one thing, but the five blocks between here and Dem Bones might as well have been five hundred miles. Her palm scrubbed over her pants pocket and slid across the almost imperceptible bump nestled beneath the heavy fabric seam.

"I saw you earlier." Neve rocked back on her heels. "You didn't look comfortable going outside. Was it the handyman? Did he make you uncomfortable?"

Though tempted to lay the blame at Nathaniel's feet, Chloe resisted the urge. "No."

"Okay." Neve hooked her thumbs in the back pockets of her jeans. "Well, I was just thinking. You wouldn't eat outside with me yesterday, either. And you go through a whole lot of trouble getting groceries delivered. Not to mention the hoops you had to jump through before I could pick up your prescription yesterday."

The pill shattered as Chloe pinched it between her fingers. She struggled to keep the hurt from making her chest ache as Neve ticked off her shortcomings.

"It makes me wonder if there isn't more going on here. That bag from yesterday was heavy for one refill. So when I saw how you reacted to leaving the store, it kind of struck me. I worried you might have a condition I should be aware of, in case you ever need help." Neve's pale eyes considered her. "I'd rather ask you outright than dance around the subject, that's all."

Chloe's throat cinched tight over what she would have said.

"Look, I'm sorry if I was out of line." The toes of Neve's shoes tapped on the floor. "You don't have to say anything if you don't want to."

She turned to leave, and Chloe made a decision. If she didn't want to lose Neve, she had to give her what she wanted—the truth. No matter how uncomfortable the topic made Chloe.

"You're right. There is more." Neve faced her slowly. "I was in an accident almost a year ago. I already had a social anxiety problem, but afterward…" *The nightmares came.* "I started having these panic attacks and spacing out. They're not so bad here, at home, but I *can't* leave the store."

Both times she'd tried ended with her curled in a ball on the sidewalk until help came. Humiliating wasn't anywhere close to how ashamed those episodes made her feel.

"So you're agoraphobic?" Neve asked as if cataloging some strange, new breed of animal.

Hearing the word made blood drain from Chloe's face in a cold rush. "Yeah, I am."

"You know," she said softly, "if I had this setup, I don't think I'd ever leave home, either." As Neve rolled her shoulders, Chloe felt her burden lift too. "So anyway, about cele-brating, I was thinking—what if we call in our order, and I pick it up once we close shop for the day?"

Chloe blinked up at her. "You don't mind?" Her voice held an edge of hope she couldn't mask. "My apartment's up-stairs. We could eat there if you want to."

"Sounds like a plan." Neve's grin held not a single ounce of pity. "I'll start winding things down out here." She pointed at Chloe. "Be thinking about what you want."

Maybe for the first time ever, she would.

Chapter 9

AFTER LEAVING CHLOE with what Nathaniel hoped would amount to a job offer, he headed home to prepare for his night's work. The alley behind her store gave him cover enough as he sliced a rift and made record time, hopefully, with no one the wiser. He stepped from a lone tree's shade into a pool of ambient light.

"Where have you been?" a voice called from his living room.

Nathaniel's shoulders tensed and a hand went to his shears before he recognized the speaker. He forced himself to relax. "Tying up loose ends." From his tone, Bran had been waiting for a while. "What are you doing here?"

"Delphi sent me to escort you to Dis." His jaw popped as he yawned.

Raising an eyebrow, Nathaniel said, "I doubt after all this time I've forgotten my way."

Bran gave him a lopsided grin. "Your request was approved." He chuckled. "So it's more likely he wanted to make sure you showed up tonight and didn't take off early."

Relief made it easier to return his smile. "How much time did I get?"

"One month, in mortal time, scheduled to start after your weaving has been completed." Clearing his throat, he added, "I'm glad you realized you needed a break."

"Oh?" After his talk with Saul, Nathaniel imagined what came next. "If I hadn't?"

"Delphi had already authorized me to use any means at my disposal to convince you to take one." His expression turned sheepish. "I was really hoping it wouldn't come to that."

Nathaniel laughed. As if Bran would ever have to resort to force. All he had to do was ask and it would be given. Still, it might have been amusing to see him try coercion.

"I did want to ask you something, though." He leaned forward, elbows on knees, expression serious. "There's nothing wrong, is there? With you, I mean?" His forehead creased. "If there was, you'd tell me, right?"

For once in their lives, he couldn't. Even the thought of lying to Bran tasted of ash on his tongue.

"I need some time to myself." Nathaniel gave a terse shrug. "That's all."

Bran's relief was tangible. "Well, I think it's a great idea." He exhaled sharply. "You've spoiled the others by taking part of their workload onto yourself when you were never meant to do more than weave. It will be good for them to step in and pick up the slack." He smiled, but there was steel behind it. "I'll make certain no one bothers you while you're resting."

He meant Saul, and he ought to know by now nothing attracted his father quite like the forbidden.

Nathaniel rolled his shoulders, wishing his mind relaxed as easily as other muscles.

Bran needed no encouragement to discuss his father's shortcomings, so bringing up Saul's grief-stricken ramblings would start an argument on the spot. Considering they were expected elsewhere, and it was old ground they'd covered numerous times, he decided it wouldn't hurt to wait until he'd handled the situation with Chloe. Then he and Bran could decide if things with Saul had progressed to the intervention stage. He hoped not. They'd held Saul together this long.

Stretching as he stood, Bran asked, "Are you ready to go?"

Nathaniel patted his hip. "I have everything I need."

Bran headed for the balcony. "I'll meet you there."

He closed the sliding glass door, then lowered his eyes in concentration. A second later, the hungry whoosh of fire igniting filled the compact space as wings crafted from holy fire blazed from behind him and fanned a sweltering breeze. His expression smoothed and became one of utter bliss as the white flares surrounded and consumed his body.

Nathaniel waited until the light faded, taking Bran with it.

He remembered a time when he'd kept a sword of the same material tethered at his hip where his shears now resided. His gaze dropped to the sooty footprints burned into the concrete.

Unsheathing his shears, Nathaniel made his slice and stepped through the rift into Dis.

He coughed as heat sucked the air from his lungs, burning his nose and throat. Bran walked several yards ahead, striding toward the towering white monstrosity where Delphi resided.

Bran reached the arched entrance to the mansion well before Nathaniel. The guards to either side of him narrowed their eyes at his approach. All six sets of their wings twitched in agitation.

The seraphs hadn't fallen or been cast down. They had chosen to travel with Delphi as his private guard, and their loyalty to him was absolute. Instead of the golden hair and pale iridescent wings of their birth, both were as coal black and dull as their eyes now.

Nathaniel's heart stopped as two silver blades crossed not an inch from the tip of Bran's nose. The guards holding those blades seethed.

Even across the distance, he heard their taunts and winced as each barb struck home.

"What are you doing here, Nephilim?" the seraph to Bran's right asked.

The seraph to his left sneered. "You should know by now to use the pet door in back. All the other mongrels do."

Bran kept his gaze forward. "I've brought the Weaver as Delphi requested."

Trates lowered his blade until the tip dug into Bran's chest. He stood on the left side, closest to Bran's heart. "Well good for you. It still doesn't explain why you think you have the right to waltz through the front door." His lip curled. "You're tainted."

"Nephilim have as much right to be here as you do." Bran's chin lifted. "We're all blood of the same creator."

Arestes lowered his blade to a point on Bran's body Nathaniel couldn't see. Bran's shoulders tensed, though he didn't step away or make a comment. On a man whose birth was considered an abomination, their target was an easy guess.

As he continued forward and his angle shifted, Nathaniel

saw the point of Arestes's sword aligned with the zipper of Bran's jeans.

Nathaniel fought the urge to charge the steps and crack the twins' skulls together. Anger shook his hands until he shoved them into his pockets, protecting the pair from his fury and, in turn, from Bran's wrath.

He stepped from baked clay to marble, but Bran and the seraphs still blocked the entrance. Bran's eyes narrowed a fraction when he glanced Nathaniel's way. He gave a slight shake of his head to indicate he'd rather be left with the twins than have his uncle step in on his behalf.

Heaven forbid he be allowed to publically support his nephew. Bran would see it as Nathaniel being overprotective instead of endorsing his one-man campaign for Nephilim rights.

Furious with the situation, and Bran's stubborn pride, Nathaniel snarled, "Do you mind?" He gestured toward the door with a jerk of his chin. "The others are waiting on me."

The twins spoke as one. "Our apologies, Weaver. Of course, you may enter."

Nathaniel glanced to his right where Trates dug his blade into Bran's chest until a red stain bloomed. "Watch yourself or you'll put your eye out with that." To his left, the second seraph snickered. "The same goes for you. Does Delphi know you're hassling his guests?"

Arestes hissed, "This one isn't a guest."

Nathaniel had interfered as much as he dared, and still he knew Bran would hold a grudge. "Suit yourselves. Delphi requested my immediate arrival and commanded *this one* to act as my escort." He struggled against the desire to slice them from ear to ear and scrawl Bran's name in bright red across the pristine white walls. He was a person, damn them, and he had a name. "I suppose when he asks where *this one* is, I'll tell him to check his own front porch."

With that, Nathaniel shoved them aside. A pained grunt and several cruel chuckles followed him down the hall. The urge to look over his shoulder made his neck twitch.

Bran shouldn't be left alone. He should be forced to accept help and made to stop being stubborn and prideful. Nathaniel had tried reasoning with him before, several times, but he wouldn't listen.

After he had caused so many deaths, a small part of him whispered these could be two more added to his tally. He wondered if the seraphs' coloration reflected the state of their souls. He hoped it did. He knew well how to handle moral decay.

He bit the inside of his cheek until it bled, but nothing blunted the agony of knowing he'd left Bran on his own, yet again. He walked through an open doorway into a cavernous room filled with his kin. His gaze zeroed in on Delphi, hoping the master seraph prized his emissary enough to intervene on Bran's behalf.

"Weaver, glad you could join us," Delphi said as Nathaniel entered the weaving room. He sat on a simple chair behind a plain desk where he sometimes observed the proceedings. The quill pen in his hand wavered. "Where is the Nephilim?"

"Ask your guards," Nathaniel said with as much calm as he could manage.

Delphi's eyes hardened as his gaze swept over Nathaniel and rested down the empty hall at his back. His hand struck out and toppled the bottle of red ink by his journal. *"Erseeh tesahiel."*

His dark wings quivered, then tucked against his spine as if they were afraid of his anger. He stalked from the room with the thin journal tucked under his arm, leaving his quill and ink abandoned. The deafening sound of ancient oak doors meeting their frames rang through the room as the doors slammed shut on Delphi's heels.

Nathaniel's heart raced. Delphi had made him a promise. *They will pay blood for blood.* It was an oath, the closest he ever came to swearing, and Nathaniel would help measure had he been asked.

His attention lingered on the sculpted silver doorknob until someone cleared their throat, a warning.

Cold metal had filled his palm. Nathaniel glanced down, surprised as his knuckles popped from their tight grip on the shears. He jolted when a heavy hand landed on his shoulder.

"He knew not to use the front door," Saul said. His calm demeanor grated on Nathaniel's already frayed nerves. But then, their earlier argument could hardly be continued around so many perked ears. "He's got a stubborn streak a mile wide and he has to learn to play by the rules."

"Like we did?" Nathaniel shrugged free of his grip.

"It's not the same thing."

"I know." Nathaniel walked toward the line of waiting harvesters. "We had a choice in what we became. Bran didn't."

"You say that like it's my fault. It was an accident."

Nathaniel spun on Saul, and his fury lashed at his brother. Grabbing Saul by the throat, Nathaniel smashed his brother's head into the wall as his fingers bit into Saul's skin with crushing force.

"He wasn't an *accident*. He was a child." Fury threatened

to choke him as surely as the hand he wrapped around Saul's neck. "He *is* your son."

Saul covered Nathaniel's hand with his, but he didn't try to dislodge it. "You're right. He's my child, my responsibility." He swallowed as best he could. "But if he's going to survive, he has to learn to stop pushing his luck because one day it will run out." His gaze traveled toward the door. "It might have already."

"Don't say that." Nathaniel released Saul, then braced his palms against the wall. His knees threatened to buckle under his weight and his surgeon-steady hands shook with fine tremors. "He's fine. He has to be."

Saul stumbled out of range. "It's his own fault." His voice was hoarse. "He's a grown man who knows better than to provoke the seraphs. He's been told to ignore their taunts often enough. Yet he incites them." He rubbed his throat. "He might get off on the pain for all we know."

"Or he might think he has something to prove," Nathaniel snarled. "You fight your way out of everything. That's the legacy you left your son. Every punch he takes is one he's seen you stand up from and ask for more."

"Blame me all you want, brother." He snorted. "You're his idol. He might take punches like his father, but the martyr act he pulls is one hundred percent classic Uncle Nate."

Before Nathaniel grabbed for Saul a second time, the chamber door swung open on Delphi's return. He brushed a strand of his ebony hair from his face, marring the pale skin of his temple with a crimson smear.

Nathaniel prayed the blood was seraphim.

The weight of Delphi's stare swung between Nathaniel and Saul. Their chests heaved and foreheads sweated. Saul had struck a defensive pose while Nathaniel let the wall support him. Their connections to Bran were well known, as were their heated arguments on his behalf.

Delphi dismissed Saul with a soft rebuke. "Unfortunately, the child often pays for the sins of his father." His dark eyes focused on Nathaniel. "The Nephilim is in good hands."

Nathaniel bowed his head in silent thanks while Delphi stared at him with the intensity of someone eyeing a bug. As if undecided whether crushing it was worth the effort. "I expect your disposition much improved when you return next month."

Without waiting for a reply, he returned to his desk, righted the bottle of spilled ink, and blotted the excess with a handkerchief from his pocket. Pen and ink in hand, he said, "You may begin." His gaze touched on every harvester present. "I trust the rest of your night will be uneventful."

The benign words were a threat, and the best course of action was to offer silent agreement, which every man in the room did.

Tension from Delphi's departure thickened the air. Nathaniel ignored the quiet and walked toward the center of the room. Smoothing a hand across the frame of his loom, he allowed himself a smile. The white ash wood shone. Its finish preserved all this time by his gentle care.

The loom resembled those used by humans for making fabric. His performed an identical task, but there the similarities ended. Rather than spun wool, his yarn came from a rarer source.

"Who's first?" Any other time, the harvesters would have flocked to him. Now they divided their attention between his face and the shears in his hand. "Is no one here in need of mending?"

For a full minute, no one moved.

"I'll go first." With a derisive snort, Reuel shoved his way forward. "I remember having to draw straws last month and tonight we're taking volunteers?"

A few of the others chuckled with unease.

"I am oldest, you know." Reuel puffed out his chest. "I deserve a few perks."

"You know what they say, 'age before beauty,' " Saul said dryly.

Reuel flipped him off, which earned a round of heartier laughter.

Dropping to his knees before Nathaniel, Reuel spread his wings wide. "I don't envy the judge of that contest. This lot has some of the damn ugliest mugs I've ever seen."

Nathaniel pressed a hand between Reuel's shoulder blades. "Hold still." He used his shears to snip away the tattered remnants of soul cloth stretched over Reuel's wings. By the time he had finished, the heavy bones stretched out like skeletal fingers into the room.

Satisfied the frame was cleaned, Nathaniel passed over the detritus to a waiting harvester, one of the newer arrivals, for disposal. The man blanched as the strips wriggled in his arms.

It was easy to spot the newest faces added to their rank. Their white wings turned black within a few hours. Then, even those began to molt. Before long, the skin melted away, leaving dense muscle tissue twined around bone.

It was as much a statement as a punishment. It said these men were no longer of the light, and any who dared break the rules risked the same set of consequences.

If anyone had asked if Nathaniel mourned the loss of his wings, he would have said no. Although the agony of his exchange with Delphi still radiated through his back, he'd rather have the shears than the grisly reminder of what he no longer had fused to his spine.

His fingers worked the familiar ties at his hip and freed his soul bag. He plunged his hand into the blistering pit to scour for a candidate and landed on an oily patch, which he ripped free of the portal. The black expanse slithered up his wrist, flaying his skin with its scalding temperature as it sought freedom. His lungs filled with the stench of burned flesh and sulfur.

Soul in hand, he sat at an ancient spinning wheel, the mate to his loom, and pulled fibers from the dark mass with practiced ease. Once he tied a fresh leader and threaded the orifice, he spun the wheel clockwise then treadled until the twist came up the leader and grabbed the fibers in his hand. He pinched and guided the wound length until he filled a bobbin with glistening black yarn.

Seating himself at his loom, he started his task anew. Soul cloth took several hours to weave, and his line of customers circled the room.

Seasoned harvesters settled in for the long wait, prepared to amuse themselves. They drew straws, made bets, and wagered for the next spot in line, knowing if they were among the first, they could earn a few hours of freedom from their duties as the others waited their turn.

Harvesters learned quickly that time moved slower in Dis. Twelve hours topside equaled seven days here. Though mending every set of wings present would take the better part of a week, at the end of that time, Nathaniel would go home to his own bed and wake to the morning after he arrived in Dis.

Delphi thought by forcing the harvesters into fellowship, confining them here, they would embrace the values most had disavowed and devote those long days to contemplation.

He was wrong.

If anything, the fallen angels resented their new positions as harvesters. They had gone from guarding gentle spirits in paradise to ripping corrupt ones from their mortal hosts on Earth. Their punishment was gruesome, and not all who fell could handle the job.

Some fell even farther, and they were imprisoned in the very pits they'd helped fill.

Nathaniel adjusted his position, then leaned forward and scanned the woven fabric for dangerous imperfections. His loom glowed with muted light, holding the writhing yarn immobile until he finished his task.

When he had enough cloth to reupholster Reuel's massive wings, he fit the length of fabric to the bony limbs and pulled the copper spool and hooked needle from his pocket. He stitched for several hours before tying his knot and signaling Reuel to rise.

"Ah." Reuel thrust his wings downward. "That is much better." His feet cleared several inches above the floor before he lighted. "Well done, Weaver, as always." They clasped forearms; then he left with another slice of his broad wings through the air.

Nathaniel straightened while the muscles in his back protested the long hours spent hunched over his workstation and Reuel.

"Ready for round two?" Saul asked as he settled at Nathaniel's feet.

"Shouldn't you let some of the younger ones go first?" They were the most annoying. Hopping from foot to foot, flittering their wings like butterflies caught in a net. "They're more impatient than the ancients."

"So am I." Saul twisted to face him. "Hasn't it occurred to you the only 'safe hands' in Dis are attached to seraphim arms?"

He shredded the soul cloth still in his hands. "We don't know for certain where Delphi sent Bran." One of two places, but he could only guess which. Dis was unsafe for Nephilim, but Delphi often underestimated his kind's hatred for half-breeds. Whether it was done on purpose or in an attempt to force an accord was anyone's guess. "Do you think he's with the Order?"

Bran had founded the Order of the Nephilim as a safe haven for his kind. Since they had a small medical staff at their compound, it would be the best choice for his care.

"I can't be sure." Saul glanced toward the door. "Delphi could have kept him here, in the seraph's quarters. Do you really want to chance that?"

Seven days at the mercy of the twins and others like them. Nathaniel couldn't risk it. "Turn around." He rested a hand below Saul's shoulder. "Hold still."

For once, his brother did as he was told.

Chapter 10

Saul strolled through the double doors and stepped out into the hallway that led to Delphi's quarters. Arestes and Trates kept rooms to either side of his, and if Saul had to guess, they would have had Bran brought to another seraph's quarters. It wouldn't do for Delphi to hear them play.

With a sigh, Saul picked up his pace. If the boy was hurt—well, hurt worse—Nathaniel would blame him and Saul wasn't ready to lose his brother's goodwill yet. Not when he'd be trailing him for the next few weeks. Better to deliver Bran to his home and let the Nephilim handle him.

Saul strained his ears but heard nothing. His foot hit and slid on his next step. Streaks shone dull across the glossy black marble floor. He knelt and let his fingers trace the outline of a boot.

They came away red-brown. Old blood. Dried blood. *Bran.*

Following the smears to a room at the far end of the hall, Saul pressed an ear to the door.

"…won't last the week…"

"…father doesn't care where you are…"

"…Weaver can't save you, mongrel…"

Pressing his forehead to the door, Saul dismissed the odd tightness in his chest. He exhaled, eyed the door, then kicked it in. Wood splintered. The door hung from its hinges. Six seraphs jumped to their feet and faced him, scowls plastered on their faces. The tallest pair approached.

"What are you doing here, Saul?" they asked as one.

"Is twin-speak something all seraphs are taught at creation?" They cast him a confused look. Saul sighed. "Never mind. I came for my…for the Nephilim. I'm here on the Weaver's orders."

"Not as his father?" another seraph asked from the corner.

Ignoring the question, Saul entered the room. Bran was easy to spot. He was sprawled across a low cot. One of his legs was…wrong. His face was smashed and blood concealed his features.

The ball of rage in Saul's gut ignited. "Is he alive?"

"What do you care?" that same seraph asked.

If Bran died, Nathaniel would snap. The shears would be lost, the key to the gates of Heaven would be ripped from Saul's fingers, and he would lose his best chance to reclaim Mairi's soul.

"I'm taking him to the Order's compound." Saul shoved through the seraphs to reach Bran.

"He was given into our care—" the tallest pair said.

Saul spun on his heel. Except for their differences in height, these seraphs were all identical. All had lank black hair and dull black eyes. Each had six sooty wings attached along their spines.

He was outnumbered. His palm itched until he fisted his

blade. "If I called Delphi in here, I wonder what he'd think of Bran's condition. Is this how he left the boy? Perhaps I should go—"

"Take him." Agitated wings ruffled as the tallest pair cleared a path for Saul.

"That's what I figured," he muttered. Turning his attention to Bran, Saul was at a loss.

"Do you need help?" he heard from over his shoulder.

"No." Saul folded Bran's arms across his stomach and adjusted him on the cot so he could get a grip on him. Bran's chest rose and fell with wet gurgles. The prospect of holding his son for the first time since infancy made Saul's palms sweaty. When Bran's eyes cracked open and met his, he smiled. Or he tried to. Part of his mouth was frozen, his lips slack. Drool ran down his chin.

"Father." Bran's laughter brought blood to his lips. "Now I know...I'm dead."

Biting back his retort, Saul used his dagger to slash a rift, then grunted with the effort it took to lift Bran into his arms. He stumbled through the portal into an alley behind the Order's central compound. The center was shielded against portals and teleportation, so visitors had to enter the front door. Saul supposed it had something to do with the number of women and children inside.

The Order was situated on miles of land outside the city of Aurora, in Cloud County, Kansas.

He snorted as he always did and wondered if his brother or his son had picked the location.

It fit with their senses of humor.

Staggering under Bran's weight, Saul's knees gave and they hit the asphalt. For a minute, he sat there with Bran across his lap. Beneath the blood and swelling, Saul searched for a resemblance to Mairi. He found none. Bran looked like him, like Nathaniel. Perhaps Saul might have loved his son if he had Mairi's wide eyes or her sloped nose, her thin lips or sharp chin. But he doubted it.

Mairi's love for Bran had killed her. If she hadn't— He shut down that line of thought before he did something foolish, like snap Bran's neck and dump him on the doorstep. That Mairi loved their son more than she wanted to stay with Saul had shattered him. She had been his everything.

Saul shut his eyes, inhaled cool night air, and exhaled. He still had hope, and he clung to it.

Dumping Bran from his lap onto the pavement, Saul knelt over his son.

How many times had he stood over Bran's bed when he was a child and considered snuffing out that tender life? The longer he stared at that battered face, the louder the voice in the back of his mind whispered no one would know if their twisted relationship ended here, tonight. Pressure on Bran's throat where his windpipe was already crushed would quench Saul's thirst for justice.

He fit his hands around Bran's throat, paused. Nathaniel would hunt him down and gut him for this. If Nathaniel snapped, would he withdraw as Saul had suspected? Or could he be lured to Azrael's cause because he'd lost the person he loved most? Bran's loss would shatter Nathaniel.

Saul and Azrael could reform him while he was lost to his grief.

Slight pressure caused Bran to stir, his chest to rattle. That same odd pressure built behind Saul's breastbone until he scrambled backward, panting. He couldn't breathe, couldn't move. It was as if he were glued in place by the sight of Bran, by the knowledge of what he'd almost done.

Heaven help him. His stomach rebelled. He'd almost killed his last living link to Mairi.

"Hey, who's out there?" a husky feminine voice called.

"It's Saul." A flashlight shone in his eyes, blinded him. "There was an accident..."

She kept the beam of light trained on him as she approached. "What kind of accident?"

His voice broke. "It's Bran."

The flashlight lowered, illuminating Bran's crumpled form. The woman yelled over her shoulder, "Get Hannah out here now."

A second voice answered, "I'm on it."

The husky-voiced woman skidded to her knees at Bran's side and her flashlight hit the pavement. "Oh, Bran, what did they do to you?" Her gaze snapped to Saul's. "Who did this?" She reached for a knife at her belt and held it between them.

"Delphi's seraphs." Saul stood and forced his legs steady. "Nathaniel asked me to bring Bran here." At his words, the woman's shoulders slumped a fraction. Of course hearing that eased her.

"Thank you." Her hand shook where she touched Bran's cheek. "I just...thank you."

Saul inclined his head, sliced his rift, and left before he did something stupid.

Like stay and see if his son survived the night.

Chapter 11

THE NEXT MORNING brought a somber Nathaniel to Chloe's door. His cheeks were sunken, his eyes shadowed. Stubble covered his face and his enticing lips were turned down.

"You look like you had a rough night." Talk about an understatement. "What happened?"

A smile ghosted his mouth. "My nephew was involved in an accident." His brilliant eyes were empty of the teasing light from the previous day. "He isn't doing well."

She touched his forearm. "I'm sorry he was hurt." Coarse hairs tickled her palm, and the temptation to stroke him made her thumb glide over corded muscle. She dropped her hand before he noticed and stared at her feet, a much safer spot than anywhere on his body.

"I could have prevented it." His voice softened. "I shouldn't have let him go."

Busy staring at his large hands, she almost missed what he said. His fingers were long and tapered. His broad palms would engulf her hand if he held it. Forcing her attention to his face, she said, "You can't blame yourself. Once you get behind the wheel, anything can happen." She was living proof of that. "So don't beat yourself up over it. You did the same as anyone else would have in your shoes."

"You would think so."

His cryptic reply coupled with his tormented expression made her heart hurt. He must care deeply for his nephew to be so distraught. His pain softened her toward him, which couldn't be a good thing. Not when she had trouble keeping her hands to herself around him already.

Scrubbing a rough hand down his face, he left red marks behind. "I don't think I'm up to negotiating contract details with you today. Can we do this tomorrow?"

Happiness blossomed at the promise of seeing him again, but she hesitated to let him leave. "Would you like something to drink?" She licked her lips and he tracked the progress of her tongue. "Neve brought in some cookies. Homemade chocolate chip, if you're interested."

"Thank you." He stepped back. "But I should get going."

The pang in her chest took her by surprise, reminded her of every time she'd gotten her hopes up only to have them dashed. She almost laughed at how pathetic she must sound to him. This infatuation was one-sided like all the others. She really should know better by now.

"No problem." She resisted the urge to touch him again by balling her hands at her sides. "Get some rest. We can work out the details tomorrow, whenever you're feeling up to it."

He must have caught the glimmer of hurt in her expression as she turned.

"Chloe." He caught her by the wrist. "Don't look at me like that."

"Like what?" Her skin warmed beneath his and her pulse kicked up as he pulled her close.

His frown was endearing, and he appeared as confused by his reaction as she was. "I said something to hurt you."

"No, don't be silly." She put up a token resistance with every step he dragged her forward. "I know you were turning the cookies down, not me." Her struggle got her nowhere. "I mean, I know you're not interested in me, as a person, and I'm not interested in you either…"

She lost her train of thought when his hand slid down and linked their fingers. "You should go rest up." Heat spun low through her belly and made it quiver. *And I should go upstairs and take a cold shower.*

"Don't leave on my account," he said. "I'm already on my way out."

Chloe went limp in his hold. "How do you do that?"

"I'm not doing anything." His voice took a persuasive turn.

She swallowed hard and kept her thoughts together by sheer force of will. "Yesterday you asked me about Neve having aspirin, and now I was thinking I wanted to go upstairs and you tell me you'll leave so I can stay."

"There is a very simple explanation for both of those things." With less than six inches between them, they inhaled each other's breath and the closeness made her light-headed.

"Yesterday you were in an obvious amount of pain. I suggested your coworker might keep something on hand you could take." His thumb swiped across her cheek. "Just now, you tried to pull away from me, so I knew you wanted space. I didn't want you to leave because I made you uncomfortable."

"I guess." She was so warped. He was concerned about his nephew while she worried he could read minds, which was impossible. "You have an answer for everything, don't you?"

"No." He smiled fully for the first time since arriving. "But I'm flattered you think so."

His breath fanned her face, cinnamon sweet. She imagined a handful of Red Hots on his tongue and wondered if he kept a box in his pocket. He leaned in. When had he gotten so close?

"Maybe I shouldn't have said anything." She thumped his chest. "You're already too smug for your own good."

"I'm not smug. I'm…confident." He grinned. "There's a difference."

He moved faster than she anticipated. Dropping her arm, he traded his hold for her hips, dragging her across the few inches left between them. His head lowered, lips parted, and she squeezed her eyes closed.

His lips moved feather soft over hers in a slow claiming she felt from the crown of her head to the tips of her curling toes.

When he deepened the kiss, she jerked free and covered her mouth with her hand. "I don't do that."

"What, kiss?" He sounded skeptical. "Everyone has been kissed."

"Of course I've been kissed." She added a silent *once*. His eyes darkened in a way that should have unnerved her. "I meant I've never kissed someone I just met."

"Good." His relaxed grin returned. "You shouldn't offer your cookies to just anyone."

Chloe stepped back into the heat of his body and got right in his face. If she had an ounce more nerve, she would have kissed him again to prove her point, but she wasn't that brave. Not yet. "You are going to stop making fun of me if you want that job."

"Maybe I want you more than I want the job."

They both froze stock-still. Her eyes widened and she saw his do the same. Their flirtations, or whatever they were, had taken a neat step into dangerous territory.

The sound of running water filled the silence left by his shocking admission. Down the hall, a door clicked shut. "Did you guys come to an understanding?" Neve asked, walking into the room.

Chloe and Nathaniel jumped apart as an ice bath of reality splashed over them.

"Yes." She cleared her throat. "I mean, no, Nathaniel doesn't feel up to negotiating today."

"That's too bad. I hoped you guys would get the details nailed down so the repairs could be finished before fall gets here." Neve squinted as she walked past a sunny window. "Maybe by then we'll have cool enough weather to enjoy it."

"If you have time, I think we can work out the details." Nathaniel's gaze slid over her shoulder, toward her office door.

Chloe's palms dampened. "I thought you wanted to wait."

"I changed my mind."

Of course he had.

* * *

A moment alone in Chloe's office gave Nathaniel time to collect his scattered wits, or at least try. Rational thought eluded him while the taste of her lingered on his tongue.

A mark. His lips burned from kissing a woman marked for death, one who remained here only because of his bond with her. How could he frown upon Saul for his mortal liaisons and then indulge himself with someone who wouldn't live past the month's end.

He might have curbed his impulses before her soft hand rested on his arm, soothed him with hesitant strokes of her thumb. Her kind words had acted as a balm to his chafed soul.

Chloe was a perceptive woman. She would realize there was more to their connection than he admitted. But as far as he knew, there was no etiquette for telling someone their life had been saved, an irrevocable bond forged, and that he was charged with collecting their joint soul and ending that spared life.

His muscles tensed to rise, ready to seek her out if she took much longer.

The desire to touch her again was now a physical ache. Adjusting in his chair, he gave up on getting comfortable and braced his elbows on the edge of her desk, staring where she would sit.

This crazed obsession for her searing through his bones couldn't be a natural response. Their mingled essence must be to blame for this desperate attraction. Yesterday, she appeared wary and reserved. Today, she had moaned beneath him like a woman starved for what only he could provide.

He growled low in his throat, a hungry sound. Common sense told him he should know better than to pursue a relationship of any kind with her.

He had obligations. Her death was one of them. It was his job, his life, if he failed.

"You look like you're thinking hard about something." Chloe walked in and took her seat.

The band of discomfort cinched around his chest loosened, and he took a steady breath. She was here, safe. When had those things begun to matter? Sometime during his week in Dis when he could be certain of neither.

He fought the urge to bite his tongue against what he had to say. "I shouldn't have kissed you. It was unprofessional of me." In more ways than one. "I apologize. I had a rough night and I wasn't thinking clearly."

She shrugged as if she expected as much from him. "It was as much my fault as yours." Her polite smile was a pale echo of the one he'd seen, tasted, minutes earlier. "I guess hearing about your nephew made me emotional." She cleared her throat. "Obviously, I wouldn't have kissed you otherwise."

"Ah." Gone was the flush to her skin and the hesitance in her voice. She had moved on, given him the out he needed to excuse his behavior, yet his fists flexed in his lap.

She glanced up, dark eyes somber.

He'd hurt her, again, and it didn't sit well with him. Every time he tried to spare her pain, he made their situation worse. Their connection couldn't be undone, so he would be more careful. He ignored the tiny fissure of want for her that threatened to break his resolve.

He'd been alone too long, which explained why he craved her company. His loneliness couldn't get in the way of her salvation. He'd risked too much for his plan to fall apart now.

He would step back, let Neve bond with Chloe while he watched from a safe distance; then he could do his job and wash his hands of this debacle.

He should let Chloe take her chances with salvation. Instead, he might damn them both.

"So," she began, "I did some digging on the Internet, and the estimate you left with me seems fair." She scooted bits of torn paper around with her finger. The remains, he assumed, of the estimate he left with her the day before.

When their eyes met, she blushed, then dusted the bits into her trash can.

Despite his earlier resolve, he couldn't bank the amusement in his tone. "So you're interested in my proposition."

Her face reddened further. "I'm interested in having you work on my porch, yes."

"What else would I mean?"

Her dark eyes glared a hole through him. "You know." Her brows puckered. "Or I know what you meant. I'm not that naïve."

Her need to proclaim her experience made him think that wasn't the case. Part of him wanted to explore the sore spot he'd uncovered, but the larger part wanted to guard himself against her gentle invasion into his every waking thought. There were things he had to do, things that couldn't be done if this deadly fascination continued.

He leaned forward, all business. "How about we cut to the chase? You've seen my estimate and agreed to the cost and suggested time frame." He linked his hands in his lap so they didn't get away from him and do something foolish, like reach for her and cover her much smaller hands with his. "I can purchase enough supplies to begin work tomorrow." He paused. "Sound good?"

Blinking through her surprise at his abrupt change in subject, she nodded. "That sounds great." Rising as he did, she stuck out her hand. "I guess I'll see you in the morning."

As badly as he wanted to touch her, connect with her again, he couldn't risk it. He needed to check on Bran, and Chloe was a distraction he couldn't afford at the moment.

Instead, he tipped his head and sidled out the door. He didn't exit fast enough to miss rejection flash across her face, but he couldn't stay and make amends.

He left before he did something they both regretted, like kissing her until she understood how deep their connection was. How powerful his attraction was to her and how hopeless their situation would always be.

Chloe's hand lowered after Nathaniel left her hanging. He must have wanted out of her office in a bad way to move so fast. Dropping back into her chair, she traced her mouth and her lips tingled under her touch.

He had kissed her. Not a friendly buss on the cheek or peck on the lips, but with his *tongue*. She covered her stomach, but she swore butterflies were flitting around in there, bumping hard against her palm.

She licked her lips and tasted cinnamon. Caging her tongue behind clenched teeth, she prevented it from seeking the reminder of his flavor a second time.

Now if she only had a clue why he made his move, she could decide if she was excited by what happened or put out with him for slamming on the brakes when he initiated the kiss in the first place.

Frowning hard at the seat he had occupied, she jolted when Neve called her name.

"That's not a happy face." Neve's attention shifted between the empty chair and Chloe's face. "He didn't try to take advantage of you, did he?"

"No." At least not the way she meant. "His estimate was fair." Though now she almost wished his price hadn't been. "He's promised to pick up some supplies and get to work in the morning."

"Well, that's good news, then." She didn't sound convinced. "Anyway," she said, moving on, "I know it's not my place, and it's your call whether you go through with it, but I made some phone calls last night, and there's something I wanted to talk to you about."

Chloe winced. Yesterday, she'd gotten off the hook with Neve too easy, and she knew it. Today she would pay for the false sense of normalcy in unsolicited advice, like always.

People reacted to learning about her condition in one of two ways. They either outright denied the possibility of the disorder's existence, or they played Good Samaritan and tried to fix her.

Both routines proved equally frustrating for her, and them, because her problem wasn't something the wave of a magic wand could fix.

Hands splayed across her thighs, she waited for the other shoe to drop.

"It's like this." Neve pulled a wrinkled flyer from her pocket. She handed the paper to Chloe, who recognized the logo. "I called the chamber of commerce looking for a schedule of community events, and the clerk told me the National Fair is coming to town."

Chloe traced the familiar elephant and globe design. "They come earlier every year," she mused. "When I was a kid, Dad sneaked me out of the house on nights Mom hosted her quilting circle." She smiled. "I don't think we ever saw more than one act, but we ate until cotton candy and sausage dogs came out of our ears."

Mom never went with them. She had to have known where they were going, because she knew everything that happened under their roof. More than likely, the same anxiety that made it impossible for her to let her daughter go for eight hours during school or leave the house without Chloe's father had prevented her from enjoying the one childhood indulgence Dad refused to let Chloe go without.

Lowering the paper, she considered all the girls who grew up swearing they wouldn't become their mothers, only to wake up one day and realize it was already too late. She mentally added her name to the tally.

"It sounds as if you were close to your parents."

Concern radiated from Neve, but Chloe didn't want a therapy session. She got her weekly recommended dose of psychoanalysis as it was.

"We were very close." The memories of being wrapped in their love made her throat tighten. "Sorry, I didn't mean to get you off topic. What about the fair?"

Neve's face scrunched up as if she might argue, but in the end, she leaned over and flipped the paper. On the back, a whimsical logo, also familiar, decorated the center of the page.

"Did you draw this?" It was the McCrea family crest, the same one used in the sign over the bookstore. "It's beautiful."

Shrugging aside the compliment, Neve tapped a finger

on the words below the design. "I was thinking if you were interested, we could participate this year. The clerk said he waved fees for participants with educational materials. We could set up a literacy booth or something." Straightening, she added, "It could be fun and it would be good promo for the store."

She made her plan sound so easy, as if they could be a team. But they couldn't be, and Neve must realize Chloe couldn't venture out so far. "It's held at the fairgrounds on the other side of town, which limits what I can do to help other than sponsor you." She considered Neve. "Are you sure this is something you want to tackle alone?"

"I doubt there'll be a rush. I should be fine." She smiled. "Besides, I have helpers lined up."

Snap. Neve did move fast if she had already wrangled volunteers. "What about supplies?"

With a sheepish grin, she admitted, "I haven't gotten that far yet. I thought about asking the library to loan me some of their children's books. I might even be able to talk Mr. Donor into donating some face paints and brushes, that kind of thing. I'd probably have to add his store's name to the sign." She paused in her planning long enough to ask, "You wouldn't mind sharing the spotlight, would you?"

Chloe didn't answer for a minute. She was lost to her thoughts.

"Over the years, I've heard a lot of parents complain about the lack of a children's section at the library, so I doubt the library has much in the way of loaners." Here was an area where she could help. "How about this? I'll let you pick a dozen or so of the children's books I have in stock. At the end of the fair, you can donate them to the library so they'll be there to use again next year." Assuming Neve stuck around that long. "And if you want to paint faces, then we might as well go all out. There's a small party supply store in the next town over. I'll give you enough money to cover whatever you'll need to do that, plus a little extra if you want to pick up some favors or candy or whatever you think the kids would like."

"Wow, Chloe, thank you." Neve checked the wall clock, making Chloe smile. Her kind of excitement was infectious, and Chloe struggled not to get wrapped up in the same urge to hit the ground running and make their plan happen. A second later, Neve's expression tightened. "I promise this will be the last time you see me coming at you with my hand out."

"You asked to help promote my store, not for a handout." She softened her tone. "The money *I* decided to throw at you is going to a good cause. Plus, it will give me something to do. I can help make signs or stuff goodie bags to help you get ready."

"You're helping out enough as it is." Neve's smile widened. "But a girls' night in could be fun, if you're up to it."

"I'd like that." More than she could admit without sounding pathetic.

She'd already filled today's humiliation quotient by falling into the arms of a near-stranger, so she wasn't in a hurry to compound her embarrassment. If everything about Nathaniel didn't seem so familiar, she could have resisted him. Though she suspected she really didn't want to. The thought of him sparked a question. "Can I ask you about something?"

"Of course." Neve leaned her shoulder back against the door frame. "Ask away."

"You seem to have more experience with kids than I do." The sum of Chloe's personal knowledge extended only as far as the handful of mini-customers who left her pages sticky with fingerprints yet still managed to charm her out of stickers on their way out of the store.

Neve shifted, seeming uncomfortable with the subject. "What is it you want to know?"

"What's the going rate on a 'get well' gift these days? I mean, I always got a stuffed toy or a new doll." To lighten the tense shift in the atmosphere, Chloe added, "I'm guessing it's different for boys?"

Perking up, Neve smiled. "Yeah, boys are more into electronics or sports." She shook her head. "Kids are so hard to pick for these days. I think gift cards are the way to go if you don't know the child personally. Maybe add in a few balloons and a card to top the whole thing off."

"Oh, I like that idea." Chloe wrote a note in the margin. "I'm sure the florist can work with me on the details." She reached into a drawer and pulled out the phone book. "Thanks for the suggestion."

"Who's feeling under the weather, if you don't mind me asking?" Neve laughed. "There I go again, sticking my nose where it doesn't belong." She held her hands up, palms out. "I promise I'm not usually so nosy. I used to volunteer a lot back home. I guess I have a case of idle hands since the move."

Chloe smiled. "You're fine. I'm not used to having someone to talk to. It's nice." Heat crept into her cheeks as she prepared an answer for the question. "Nathaniel's nephew was injured in an accident."

"Oh no. What kind?" Neve asked.

"I...um..." Chloe groaned. "When I heard *accident*, my brain filled in *car*, but he didn't correct me. I don't know if I got it right or if he didn't want to seem rude. He was really upset about it, so I thought I'd do the 'get well' thing to try and cheer them both up."

Neve appeared thoughtful. "Now that you mention it, he did seem tense today." Leaning over the desk, she snagged a square of sticky notes and scribbled down a phone number. "Don't worry about calling the florist. I think I'll hit that party store you mentioned tonight, so it's no problem if you'd like me to pick up some stuff for his nephew while I'm there." She tore off the top sheet and passed it over. "Here's my cell number." She sounded hesitant. "I forgot earlier or I would have given it to you already."

"That would be great." Prying the paper from her tight grasp, Chloe began thinking there was good reason she hadn't been given the number initially, and the personal information came with an unknown burden of trust. "Are you sure it's no trouble?"

"No trouble at all." The tinkle from the bell suspended over the front door made Neve turn. "Give me enough time to make it across town after we close up; then I'll give you a call and let you know what they have." She tugged down her limp ponytail, then finger-combed it. "That way you can choose what I pick up." She winked as she rebound the pale strands. "Personal touches are important when you're trying to make a good impression."

"I'm not trying to impress him."

Neve gave her a doubtful look, which Chloe pretended not to notice.

"I'm doing what anyone would do in my situation."

"If you say so." Hearty chuckles followed Neve out the door.

Chloe's gaze slid back to the chair across from her desk. She wasn't trying to impress anyone. She was trying to do the right thing.

Sure she was.

Chapter 12

Sunlight reflected off the dozen Mylar balloons fisted in Chloe's hand and made her squint. Sleep hadn't come easy last night. For once, her unrest had nothing to do with nightmares and everything to do with why her sweaty palms caused the strings to slip through her fingers.

Give or take another ten minutes and Nathaniel would be here. Hopefully, before any customers arrived. Otherwise, she might look odd standing in the foyer with the balloon bouquet held in one hand and a plush bear in the other.

Even though Neve cautioned her against going plush, Chloe couldn't pass up the little guy's description. He was a ball of fluff with a ball cap pulled low over one eye and a blue and white jersey bursting at the seams. In his paws, he held a gift card sleeve that said "I hope you can run home soon." The gift might be too babyish, but she had waited too long to change her mind now.

Her shirt stuck to her back and made her wish she hadn't chosen a square of sunlight to make her stand. Phew, she was getting downright steamy in here. She fanned herself, which stirred the balloons and made a few bounce off her forehead.

She jumped when the door's bell tinkled in protest and a person stepped inside. All she saw was the silver backsides of the balloons. The person's steps were heavy, sure, and headed her way. She swallowed hard and tasted fear and plastic.

The footsteps halted.

"Is Chloe under there?"

Her shoulders snapped back as the timber of his voice jolted her nerves.

"Yes." Her voice squeaked like two balloons rubbed together.

"Can I help you with those?"

"They're for you." She thrust the gifts at him with her arms outstretched as far from her body as possible.

He accepted them with confused grace. "Thank you?"

The balloons bobbed as if with amusement and the paper crinkled to cover…a chuckle? She couldn't see his face. Couldn't tell if he was laughing at her or not. She had a funny feeling he was. He seemed to do it a lot.

"You said your nephew was hurt." She retreated a few steps, hoping to put the counter between them as if distance would lessen the hurt if he rejected the gift. "I wanted to do something nice, I guess."

The room stilled. Even the balloons quit jostling one another.

He broke the silence. "You did this for Bran?"

Was that his nephew's name? It must be. "Yes, I did." A few more steps and the relative safety of the counter would be between them.

The mass of *get well* paraphernalia took a few steps to the right, where a pair of club chairs marked off a small reading area. He set the armload down and straightened, staring at the jumble as if he had never seen anything quite like it.

She couldn't blame him. It was an overwhelming display for someone she hadn't met. Blast it, she *had* wanted to impress him, but his confounded expression said she had tried too hard.

Her eyes closed for a second to brace for his reaction. When they opened, Nathaniel's face filled her vision. "How did you—"

His mouth descended, crushing her words between their lips. His thumbs slipped into her belt loops and yanked her closer. Her body crashed into his and their kiss never paused, never ended.

"You are a miracle to me."

Chills broke along her spine because she couldn't breathe and wondered how he managed words when her brain barely registered thought. Breaking free of him, gasping, she placed her palms against his chest. She didn't push him away, though she should have.

"Didn't we do this yesterday?" she asked, breathless, voice hitching.

"Yes." His warm lips traced the line of her jaw. He forced her back until her spine hit a bookcase and pinned her in place. Her skin rippled with awareness. Anyone could walk in and see how she'd fisted his shirt in her hands as she tore at the fabric with impatience.

"Skin." She craved it. *"I need to feel skin. Just once, please, let me touch you."*

Her fevered thoughts failed when he jerked his shirt free from his low-slung jeans and placed her palms against his hard stomach.

Warm muscle tensed beneath her palms. Her nails scored the sleek contours of his abs, and his stomach quivered in response.

This was insanity. Here in the front of the store, they could be seen by anyone who stepped through the door. She really should care if they got caught.

If she had a customer, she could stop. Sure she could. No problem. If someone entered the store, she would make sure this didn't go any further.

Nathaniel's teeth grazed the underside of her jaw.

If someone walked through that door…she might have to kill them.

"You said…" He nipped her collarbone and her vision faded. "Oh God." *Focus.* She needed to focus. "This was a mistake yesterday, remember?"

He hummed against her throat. It might have been an accusation since she had agreed with him, said she didn't want him, or this, the day before. Shoving Nathaniel back, she earned a few inches of space between their heaving chests. Cupping his face in her hands, she forced him to look at her. "What's going on here?"

His dark lashes rested against his pale cheeks. "I can't seem to help myself around you." When his eyes met hers, amusement danced in their depths. "I wonder why that is?"

"Don't try to blame this on me. I gave you a present and you—"

"You gave me a greater gift than you know," he said simply.

To keep sane, to keep from tearing at his clothes, she dropped her hands and braced them on the bookcase behind her. "I couldn't even pick all that stuff out on my own." She wished she would keep quiet and take the credit, but the words popped right out of her mouth. "Neve went to Donor's and picked up the balloons and the bear." She glanced away. "I did help with the card."

"Whose idea was this?"

She couldn't meet his gaze. "Mine."

"Who knew Bran had been hurt and wanted to make him feel better?"

"I did."

"So why shouldn't you take the credit?"

"I don't want to talk about it, okay?" She couldn't move him. He was too big, too tall, and too much arrogant man to be brushed aside.

"Is there a reason you couldn't pick up the gifts yourself?" His curious expression asked her to confide in him.

"I had my reasons." Though she was tempted, she kept them to herself. When his mouth opened on his next question, Chloe cut him off. "I hope Bran likes his gifts."

"I'm sure he will." Nathaniel's brow wrinkled, giving her the impression he was trying to figure out something. She really hoped she wasn't the puzzle he wanted solved. "What matters is that you thought of him." The lingering sparks of sexual tension lightened as he pulled her into his arms for something she had gone years too long without—a hug. "Thank you."

The need to return the gesture made Chloe's grip release. She held his hips, but it didn't feel right. It didn't feel like enough.

His skin called to her fingertips. Toying with the hem of his shirt, her thumbs snuck beneath the fabric to stroke the hard muscle rippling in response to her touch.

"Aww. You guys are so sweet."

Chloe dropped her hands, then knocked Nathaniel aside and stepped in front of him. As if such a short woman had a hope of hiding such a tall man behind her.

Neve glanced between the two of them. "I guess this means Nathaniel approves?"

Chloe's mouth wouldn't work. Never in her life had something like this happened to her. Neve knew what she had interrupted, and amusement at that knowledge was written all over her face. Chloe couldn't think up a single excuse for how they had been found. She was caught with her hand in the cookie jar, and they all knew she had crumbs left on her fingers.

Nathaniel's shirt was untucked. His full lips were roughed from her kisses. The flannel shirt he wore was shoved from his shoulders and he hadn't tried to cover up his involvement.

Neve tapped the base of her throat. Chloe patted her collar and found the buttons of her blouse opened clear to her navel. She spun on Nathaniel, whose unrepentant grin made a five-alarm fire race up her neck and flare across her face.

"I have work to do. I should get to it." Her fingers flew over the buttons as she refastened them. She couldn't meet his eyes. "You have work you should be doing too."

"I'll get right on it." He spun her around and, before she thought to stop him, tilted up her chin and stole a kiss. "You have a decision to make." His head lowered a second time. "About where this goes from here." Then he strolled toward the door. "Until then, call if you need me."

Aware she still held Neve's undivided attention, and how bad this must look, Chloe retreated behind an all-business façade and tried to save face. "What I need is the porch you promised me." The words came out breathy and soft instead of as the order she'd meant. "Remember, it's your money on the line if I don't approve."

She ran a hand over her hair and loose strands met her palm. The diabolical man had undone her hair and her blouse, and she had been too busy counting the ridges of his abdomen to even notice.

The smile he turned on her said he didn't give a damn about the money, and that frightened her. A man like Nathaniel didn't do things without a reason. Now she had to wonder what his was.

A thick splinter bit through Nathaniel's hand as he unloaded boards from the bed of his borrowed truck. He grimaced through the sting and glared at his work gloves where they sat on the tailgate, unused.

All the while coming to accept the fact that he was doomed in all matters concerning Chloe. She bent the iron will honed during his existence, dulled the razor-sharp edges of his reality. His common sense checked itself at the door every time he walked into her store.

The hardened Weaver of Souls, collector of the debts mortals owed to the divine, had shirked his duty, broken his oaths, failed in his loyalties, and lacked the sense to be terrified of the repercussions. Maybe after an eternity of service, he should have expected the breakdown.

Centuries spent punishing the sickest members of the human race had left him exposed to infection from their corruption. Humanity's ills afflicted him, and he feared Chloe was the only cure.

His original plan no longer held any appeal. If he stood on the fringes of her last days, he would never sample more than the small dose of pleasure she had meted out to him. Her innocence melted his resolve. She was in life as he knew her while on the cusp of death—passionate, willful, and a vibrant reminder of the reason Delphi took harvesting so seriously. He believed Earth should mirror Aeristitia's purpose, and harvesters should be the ones to shape those core beliefs until mortals embraced those same values. Honor, integrity, decency, she had all those virtues in spades. Was it any wonder he couldn't resist her?

He tossed a hunk of wood against the sidewalk. Without his interference, and the dark scrap of his soul meshed with hers, she would already be dead. His jaw shouldn't pop or his teeth clench with anger at the thought of her life ending. She was mortal, and all mortals died. No love burned strong enough to tether a human soul in the sort of spiritual limbo where harvesters existed, and when an attempt to chain the fading spirit failed, loss of that magnitude shattered all those involved.

He knew, because he'd once witnessed it firsthand.

Although Chloe was unlike any woman he'd ever met, he couldn't risk losing himself after her death. Bran still needed him to act as his tether, would continue needing him unless he and his father reconciled. Even then, there were no absolutes in a harvester's life. The more protected he could make Bran, the better.

His nape stung with irritation. He wiped the sweat from his brow and glanced toward the bookstore's windows, expecting Chloe or maybe Neve, but he saw neither. His guilty conscience must be kicking his imagination into overdrive.

Turning his mind toward a lighter subject, Nathaniel imagined Bran's face when he presented him with Chloe's gifts. He chuckled at the thought of the centuries-old Nephilim holding the fluffy bear. His only presents came from Nathaniel, and nothing he'd given Bran had ever been soft or feminine.

Chloe gave them each a gift without realizing how much her action meant. Her acceptance and concern for Bran translated to acceptance and concern for Nathaniel. If he could form cohesive thoughts where she was involved, it would terrify him. No mortal should have so much control over his happiness.

Armed only with the knowledge a child had been hurt, she found Bran worth comforting. Not because she knew him, but because basic human decency thrived in her where it failed in others.

She had no reason to care for Bran, yet she did. By reaching out, she assured him his health and happiness mattered to someone other than Nathaniel. It was a refreshing change for someone so used to safeguarding the fragile child Bran had been. Someone who struggled to see the hardened man he had become. One who witnessed the dark side of humanity too often.

Neve also surprised him. She had gone out of her way to help Chloe make her grand gesture, showing deeper affection than he anticipated so early in their relationship. Relief at the unexpected realization should have loosened the tense knot in his chest.

His plan was working. Due to the unforeseen twist of adding himself into her life, Chloe had reached out and Neve had stepped in. They were becoming fast friends, which was what he wanted. He crushed the tiny seed of jealousy that she hadn't called on him instead. She needed Neve, not him, he reminded himself. Maybe if he reminded himself often enough, he might believe it in time.

He would give them space, for now, and make the most of what moments he could steal with Chloe. In the meantime, he would gut the porch and show her some progress.

A quick glance at the sun helped him gauge the hour and estimate how far his deconstruction would go before lunch. Then he threw himself into his task, stacking his supplies neatly to one side of the bookstore's entrance, then hauling a set of temporary stairs to the other. Taping a sign on the door and a few to the brick façade, he directed patrons around to the side entrance used by delivery drivers.

After he emptied his truck bed, he palmed a crowbar and set to work prying up rotted boards and tossing rusted nails into a widemouthed can.

Hours passed with nothing but the sounds of light traffic and faint music. The jazzy notes floated down the street from where a local barbeque joint had thrown open its patio doors. The upbeat tempo lured sweltering patrons into its chilled interior. His stomach gave an appreciative growl as a scalding breeze carried the scent of mesquite.

He wouldn't budge until Chloe came for him, though, if for no other reason than to hear her call his name. His damp shirt stuck to his skin, plucked at his arm hairs where it dried in places. Frustrated, he grabbed the hem and tugged it over his head. Salt burned his eyes as he dried his face, then tossed the shirt to dry on a section of railing.

The same spot between his shoulder blades itched. He scanned the streets for signs of life, but he stood alone at the curb. Unease settled around him. Someone had an eye on him, and whoever it was didn't mind getting close enough for him to sense their presence.

No one of power would be so careless. If they suspected him of wrongdoing, he would be a scorched patch blackening the sidewalk long before the first hair prickled on the nape of his neck. So his watcher wasn't Delphi or another seraph. Another harvester would have approached him by now unless he had orders not to engage him, though that option seemed unlikely.

Another possibility could be a younger Nephilim from the Order's compound. Nathaniel's visits with Bran sometimes resulted in a few of the more curious tailing after him. He allowed it because many of the first-generation Nephilim grew up fatherless. Their mothers were casualties of a handsome face and a lover who vanished when the sun rose. The women were left alone to birth extraordinary children they didn't understand and couldn't control.

The later generations were especially curious about the part of their heritage they lacked. Some mistook Nathaniel for Bran's father, a misconception Bran allowed to flourish. The result was a false sense of safety in approaching him. They assumed he wouldn't mind their interest since he embraced his half-breed son instead of treating him with the same disdain so many harvesters doled out to their offspring.

The mental picture of Chloe curled up in a wingback chair reading to blue-eyed boys and brown-haired girls staggered him with its clarity. It was a dream she wouldn't live to fulfill and it pained him. Such an odd thought for him. He wondered whether the flash came through their bond or if he'd dreamed the notion himself. He hoped for the sake of his sanity it was the former.

Children weren't an option for him and hadn't been since he fell. His physiology had been altered to forge the bond with his shears.

The best he could do was continue loving the child his brother had given him and safeguard the woman who was quickly becoming every bit as critical to his happiness as his nephew.

A swarm of darting swallows drew his eye toward a neighboring church's bell tower. They chirped their annoyance at an unseen disturbance, then descended on the nearby power lines. Seconds later, the snap of leather unfurling echoed from across the street and left him with little doubt as to what type of visitor he'd had. Another harvester had Nathaniel under surveillance. Now if he only knew what they wanted.

Wiping his brow with the back of his wrist, he resolved to wait. He couldn't risk pursuit until he knew who watched him and why he was of sudden interest to them.

Chloe was safe. His brethren, even on Delphi's orders, wouldn't dare claim a mark from under his nose.

His teeth bared in a feral smile. Let them dare to try.

Chapter 13

CHLOE STOOD AND stretched before leaving her office. Her stomach rumbled a lunchtime reminder even before she checked her watch. "Are you ready for a break?"

Neve pushed aside her crossword puzzle. "Definitely. I thought lunch would never get here." She covered a yawn. "I guess business will be slower than usual until Nathaniel finishes up out front."

"Probably." She frowned. "At least until customers realize we're still open."

Hesitant steps brought her to the door. When she looked through the glass panel, dirt and chunks of old concrete caught her eye. The skeleton of the old deck haunted the sidewalk, but the planks were pried off and buried under rubble in the bed of his truck.

"Wow." Neve bumped shoulders with her. "Someone's vocation has been very kind to him."

"What do you...Oh my." Nathaniel's shirt hung limp from the handrail, a crumpled casualty of construction. "Why don't you...um"—she forced her attention from the fluid curve of his bare spine—"take some money. From the register." What was the mark on his shoulder? "And wait on food."

"Hon, you need to step away from the glass." Neve grabbed her shoulders and twisted her around. "Can you try that again, in complete sentences this time?"

"Sorry." A step back did wonders for her concentration. "I think the glare distracted me."

Neve snorted. "Yeah, that glare is something else all right." Even after she covered her mouth, her shoulders still shook. "Before the sun got in your eyes, what were you saying? About lunch?" She squeezed Chloe's arm, encouraging her to share in the laugh.

"Oh." She had mentioned lunch. "I ordered takeout for three from China Doll. Mei's Mongolian beef is fantastic. I was going to ask you to keep an eye out for the delivery while I made a quick phone call." Neve opened her mouth, probably to protest the free meal, so Chloe spoke over her. "We can make it a working lunch. I have a couple of ideas for the store I'd like to bounce off someone, and while we're at it, we can iron out the details for the literacy booth."

Neve gave her a look that said she didn't buy Chloe's excuse for a minute.

"Knock, knock." Chloe peeked around Neve and found a lanky teen standing on the side staircase while craning her neck to ogle Nathaniel. "Whoa, Ms. Chloe, the scenery has definitely improved around here. Piedmont should award you for hiring him and beautifying the city."

"*Lin*. He'll hear you." Chloe blamed the rush of heat in her cheeks on a gust of humid outside air. Swallowing her mortification, she asked, "How's summer vacation treating you?"

"My days are numbered." Her lips thinned. "Mei is sending me to visit Nai Nai next week. Summers are supposed to be fun. Scrapbooking with Grandma? Not so much."

"Thanks for the quick delivery." Chloe exchanged a handful of bills for the bag of food.

Lin shoved the cash into her jeans. "Sure thing." With one last appreciative glance at Nathaniel, she trotted up the alley and across the street, then pushed her way inside the restaurant.

"Oh, man." Something warm and sticky oozed through Chloe's fingers. "I must have tilted the containers when I took the bag. There's sauce everywhere."

"Here, let me take that. I'll run upstairs and get the food plated." Neve stuck a tissue in Chloe's hand. "Should I set three places?"

"I'm not sure." She rubbed at her palm. "I didn't exactly ask either of you before I ordered." And now she could kick herself for it. "He may not even like Chinese."

"Well, there's only one way to find out." Neve walked past. "Go ask if he's brave enough to join us." She chuckled. "And remember to use your words…in complete sentences."

Chloe steeled herself as she turned. Surely she could keep her tongue rolled up off the floor long enough to ask him a simple question. After all, he was more than a sweaty body. He was special, even if she couldn't put her finger on the difference in him. It could have been the way his eyes sparkled when he laughed or darkened when he was frustrated. Or sad as it might seem, it could be the way he looked at her like maybe she was special too.

Every sappy movie ever filmed said a person *just knew* when they met their soul mate. Everything clicked into place.

Birds chirped, music played, the sun shined. Every ounce of their being said *this one is mine.*

Chewing on her thumbnail, she admitted none of those things had happened to her. Little wonder since she had only known Nathaniel a grand total of three days.

With a groan, she admitted this was why she shouldn't have hired him. One kiss—okay, a few kisses—and she was trying on his last name for size. For someone who hadn't attended high school, she sure had the right mentality for it. If she didn't watch herself, she'd start doodling on her receipt books and drawing hearts with his name in their center.

One calming breath later, she pushed every single girly thought aside so she could ask him about his lunch plans and keep a straight face. Approaching the glass front door, she found him sitting on the tailgate of his truck. Shirtless.

Her forehead met the cool glass as she watched, fascinated by the way sun glinted off his sweat-dampened shoulders and pale chest. The way his throat flexed and necklace shifted as he raised a bottle of water and took a deep drink.

He glanced up then and caught her staring, of course. He gave a small wave, which she returned shyly, then tapped his forehead.

Oh. Her nose was still pressed against the glass.

He slid from his perch and navigated the wreckage-lined curb. The door opened and heat filled the cool interior of the store.

"Did you need something?" He traced the top button of her collar with his finger.

Her tongue stuck to the roof of her dry mouth. Luckily, the scent of man and sweat made her salivate. "Are you hungry?"

He dropped his arms and bent down, trailing his nose

along the column of her throat. "If I am?" His teeth closed over her pulse and his laughter vibrated through that contact. "What did you have in mind?"

"L-lunch." Her knees might as well have been wet noodles for all the good they did her. She leaned into his strength to keep herself upright. "I thought you might be hungry. For food."

"I didn't notice the time." He cradled her against him, so close their heartbeats matched rhythms, then kissed the top of her head. "I'm sorry. I shouldn't have assumed you'd made your decision."

She found the notion of her brain working while in his general vicinity laughable. Her gray matter leaked out her ear whenever he crooked his finger. "I don't think I follow you."

"I'm wounded you've forgotten my offer so quickly." He hummed with amusement and she soaked up the delicious vibration working through his chest into hers. "I guess this means you'd rather keep our relationship professional."

His attempt at leaving didn't get him far. Her arms, linked around his waist of their own accord, held him in place. "I didn't say that."

"So you do want more?"

"I didn't say that, either." More meant opening herself up to the probability of getting hurt. Meant as badly as she already wanted him, she would be accepting an invitation to pain.

After Nathaniel left, and he would leave once his job was done, Chloe would be alone again, emptier than ever. Every day the sight of the porch Nathaniel had built would drive a nail deeper into her heart.

"I'm being impatient." He shook his head and stepped back. "I won't push you again."

"You're fine." Better than fine. "It's not your fault I'm more of a looker than a leaper." She caught his arm before he headed to his truck. "Do you want to join me and Neve for lunch?"

His lips curved in a pleased smile. "I'd like that."

"It's nothing fancy, some Chinese from across the street."

"I'm easy to please."

Lately, so was she. "My kitchen is on the small side." The daydream where she sat across the table from a half-naked Nathaniel evaporated. "We could eat in the living room, I guess. The coffee table is probably big enough for the three of us."

"No, don't put yourself out. I should probably eat outside as it is. I've already gotten you sweaty, but furniture is harder to clean than a shirt." He stroked a finger down her arm. "Besides, I stink."

She bit her bottom lip. He smelled spicy, exotic...edible.

"I'll wash up around back if you don't mind."

"No problem." She pointed over his shoulder. "Head down the alley. The faucet's around back and there's a bench under the elm tree. If you'd like to eat there, Neve can bring your food out to you."

"Thanks. I think I'll do that." Gravel crunched underfoot as he left, giving her a perfect view of the silver mark on his shoulder. *"And why, I wonder, won't you bring my food, meira?"*

Her mouth opened, then closed. Instead of helping him understand, she held her secret locked in her throat. If he hung around long enough, he would discover her condition eventually. If he didn't, then she saw no reason to tarnish his memory with her reality.

While Nathaniel splashed water on his face and hands, a

chill swept up his spine. Ingrained fight-or-flight reflexes swamped him with adrenaline he would have once used to power his liftoff. Now it made him anxious for his shears. Their absence from his hip made him antsy.

He closed the faucet and waited. His visitor didn't take long to make his presence known.

"She's very pretty." Saul stepped from the shadows, and sunlight glinted from the silver pendant lying against his chest. His wings were a glittery outline, visible only to their kin.

Foreboding tightened Nathaniel's gut. "I suppose." He remained neutral as they strolled toward the picnic table.

Reaching the bench first, Saul sat in the deepest shade. "Is she yours?"

The simple question had such a complex answer. "Not exactly."

"I knew something was up. I said to myself, 'Self, Nathaniel never does anything without a reason.' " He dusted the tabletop with a swipe of his hand. "I couldn't figure out what yours could possibly be."

"So you followed me." Nathaniel sat at the far end of the opposite bench, where sunlight could warm his chilled insides. "Next time, try not to go for the obvious." He grinned through the uneasy feeling of having a harvester so close to Chloe. "The church's bell tower, really?"

"It was high and cool. Besides, you've known me long enough to sense when I'm near." Saul rested his elbows on the table. "So, tell me. Why are you here, really?"

"I've already told you, I'm burned out." Nathaniel should have expected Saul wouldn't let the matter drop without further argument. "I wanted a break, a little normalcy for a while."

Saul drummed his fingers. "So why not stay at the Order's compound?"

"I wanted a change of pace."

"Fair enough." His gaze soaked up their surroundings. "This is a nice spot for a vacation. Quiet. Two pretty women to keep you entertained." Saul smiled. "I didn't know you had it in you."

Nathaniel's fingers curled into his palms. "It's nice enough."

A woman's low singing halted their conversation.

"Chloe said to—" Neve paused as she glanced between them. "Oh, I didn't know you had a guest." She flashed Saul a hesitant smile. "Should I divide this up?"

She set a simple plate on the tabletop with a tall glass of sweet tea beside it.

Saul stroked the back of her hand as she withdrew. "No, pet, I'm not hungry." His eyes said otherwise as they roved appreciatively over her body.

Blood drained from Neve's face. "I should get back to Chloe. Let me know if you change your mind."

Saul ran his finger along the rim of Nathaniel's glass. "Yes. I think that's a fine idea. I'll keep my brother company. Don't you worry your pretty little head about it."

Neve's knees seemed locked in place.

"Are you all right?" Nathaniel touched her forearm and she flinched.

"I think it's the heat." She laughed in easy dismissal. "I haven't lived here long enough to build up immunity to it."

He didn't believe her for a minute. "Would you like me to walk you inside?"

"Oh no, you have company. Enjoy your visit." She left with a brittle smile poised on the breaking point.

"Pity she's too skittish for my taste." Saul speared a piece of beef with Nathaniel's fork, then popped it into his mouth. "So," he said around a mouthful of food, "what are you doing here? I take it the blonde isn't the one holding your attention. The brunette, then?"

"I've taken a job here." Working in plain sight had invited Saul's interest, which was unfortunate. Nathaniel owned up to part of his reason for being here, hoping the other part remained private.

Saul almost choked. "You're joking." His eyes widened. "What is she paying you?"

Nathaniel didn't answer.

"She is paying you something, right?" The fork fell from his hand. "Money? Sex? Her firstborn child?" He paused. "That last bit was a joke, by the way."

Still no answer.

"I can't believe this. You're building a mortal woman a porch?" He took a drink. "It's a supreme waste of your time and talent."

"It's my time to spend."

"True enough, but still. There has to be more to this story than you're telling me. Since when are there secrets between us?"

On Nathaniel's side, this was the first.

"Interesting." Saul glanced up, drawing Nathaniel's attention toward the upper windows. "Why hello there." He waved at Chloe.

She frowned down at Saul, and the look she gave him disquieted Nathaniel.

"You know," Saul said thoughtfully, returning her stare. "You could have prettier women for far less work than this one."

Chloe's imperfections, her personality quirks, made her attractive. Her stubborn, too-sharp chin and the sparkling intelligence in her wide-set eyes captivated him.

"You haven't done something foolish, have you?" Saul wiped his mouth with the paper napkin stolen from beneath the now-empty plate.

Cold sweat trickled down Nathaniel's back. Few knew him and how to interpret his silences as well as Saul. Fewer still had his brother's nose for ferreting out gossip.

"You have." Saul gloated. "Well, well, this day wasn't a total wash after all. My brother—enamored of a mortal." He stood. "I never thought the day would come."

Neither had he and he couldn't afford to admit to it. "Have you seen Bran today?"

It was not the most subtle change of topic.

"I saw him this morning." He brushed lint from his shirt. "He's still stable, isn't he?"

"Yes, he is." Nathaniel refrained from pointing out if Saul had visited Bran, then he wouldn't have to ask about his condition now. How easily the lies fell from Saul's mouth. When had Nathaniel started counting them? Worse, when had he started expecting them? "When I called the Order earlier, Hannah told me Bran has nerve damage, but the extent is unknown."

"Pity." Saul stood and tensed his shoulders, fanning warm air when his wings outstretched. Curiosity sated, at least for now, he withdrew his dagger and fingered the blade.

A stark cry pierced Nathaniel's mind. His head snapped up. "Chloe."

"What is it?" Saul's wings snapped shut, and his stance widened. His eyes darted left to right in search of danger.

Finding none, he homed in on Nathaniel, who jumped to his feet. "The woman?" The dangerous edge of interest crept back into his tone. "How do you know?"

"It doesn't matter." Nathaniel strode toward the building's side entrance.

"The hell it doesn't." Saul grabbed his shoulder.

"She needs me." Nathaniel jerked from beneath his hand.

"Fine. I'll go with you."

"No." He snapped his teeth shut over the word. The last thing he wanted near Chloe was a creature capable of collecting on her mark.

For a long moment, Saul met his gaze with eyes that saw too much. "All right, then. Go. I'll catch you later."

Nathaniel tried not to read too much portent in the words.

Chapter 14

THE SHEARS GLEAMED on the nightstand at Saul's hip. He traced their handle with his finger. They were cold and smooth, but no power zinged through them. They were lifeless, useless, until his brother gave the verbal command to transfer their power. Walking away took supreme effort.

He could count on the fingers of one hand the number of times they'd been left unguarded.

This time made two.

After making a slow circuit of Nathaniel's bedroom, Saul strolled into the living room. If he got caught, he had several excuses handy. Few would question him. He gave them no reason to.

A series of high-pitched beeps split the silence. Saul froze, listening.

Heavy footsteps swung his head toward the kitchen. An alarm? No. A microwave timer.

He readied his story and prayed it wasn't his brother, come home for an afternoon snack.

"What are you doing here?" Reuel strode toward him with a takeout box in hand.

"I could ask you the same thing." Saul sat on the arm of the couch.

Reuel made a scissoring motion with the chopsticks in his hands. "I came for the food."

"I came to pick up something for Bran." The lie came easy to Saul.

"I heard about that." He glanced up, chewed, then swallowed. "I heard the seraphs messed the kid up pretty badly. Not that I'm surprised. They're nasty bastards. Arestes and Trates are the worst of the lot." He took another bite as if waiting for Saul to chime in. "Heard you saved him."

"Bran?" Saul's voice cracked. Memories of Bran's battered face made Saul's gut clench. "I took him to the Order's compound and left him with his own kind."

"Who better to understand a half-breed than another half-breed, huh?" Reuel turned the box upside down at his mouth and drummed his fingers on the bottom. "Did you even stay long enough to hear whether he was going to survive?"

Glancing away, Saul's gaze lit on a bookshelf. "Look, I'd love to stay and chat, really, but I have somewhere to be." He walked to the shelf and skimmed the titles. "Ah. There we are. I'll just swing by and drop this off—"

"Cut the bullshit, Saul." Reuel pointed a chopstick at him. "We both know you don't give a damn about Bran."

Saul narrowed his eyes. Not much he could say to that, and Reuel knew it. So what was his angle?

"If you'd said Nathaniel sent you for something, then maybe I'd have bought that." Reuel shrugged. "The thing is.

He knows you. Knows you'd screw around because whatever favor he asked involved Bran. That tells me Nathaniel would cut out the middle man and handle it alone."

"What are you trying to get at?" Reuel wasn't usually so astute.

"Why are you really here?" Reuel frowned. "Does your brother even know you're here?"

Reaching into his pants pocket, Saul lifted a ring. "I have a key."

"Cute." Reuel chuckled. "When was the last time you used a key? Do you remember how?"

Saul thumped the book in his hand. "I have what I came for."

"Hold up." Reuel's grin turned sharp. "You might have said your piece, but I haven't said mine."

Impatience simmered along Saul's nerves. "I don't have time—"

"Delphi sent me." Reuel set his trash on the coffee table. "He wants the missing soul."

Though Saul was tempted to snap *I don't have it*, he said, "I'll handle it."

If Saul turned in Bran, Nathaniel would cover for him. If he turned in Nathaniel, no one would believe him over his gilded brother. It was easier to say Saul had made a drunken mistake than to consider Nathaniel had made a conscious one. How had he lost the soul? Was such a thing even possible? Saul didn't know. He would have thought the mark would tether Nathaniel to the thing.

"See that you do." Reuel gave him a measuring look. "I did you a favor by having this chat topside. Delphi's spoken to you once, personally. That's once more than most folks get. Word to the wise, I've been authorized to use whatever means necessary to get that soul into Hell where it belongs. That means Trates and Arestes, topside. I don't think either of us wants that to happen."

"No." Seraphs were like bloodhounds in that sense. It was part of the reason Azrael retained his pair to guard their creations. If one were to escape, it wouldn't make it far. If either of those seraphs were set onto his trail, Saul wouldn't make it far either. "Let's not be hasty. I need time."

"You've had days to set this straight." He glanced aside. "I can give you a week."

"Thanks." Good to know how much time he had left.

Reuel scooped up his trash, crumpled it. "When that time runs out, I'm coming for you."

"I wouldn't expect anything less," Saul murmured.

"It's either you or me, and it's not going to be me." Reuel glanced at the kitchen. "Bran's a better man than I am. This job is a pain in the ass. *Delphi* is a pain in the ass." He made a shooing gesture. "Go on now. Visit your son. Get him well, out of that bed and back on the job."

Turning and heading toward the fridge, Reuel rolled his shoulders as he went.

Responsibility made Reuel twitch. It always had. Saul guessed that was why Nathaniel made fast friends with the other archangel. Reuel was content to follow like a good little soldier. Nathaniel was content to lead, as always. Their friendship had fallen into a familiar pattern.

Now that pattern had expanded to include Saul.

His head throbbed. What had Nathaniel done with the missing soul? Could Saul afford for it to come out that Nathaniel and Bran had organized that second collection?

No. He couldn't risk Delphi learning that unless there was no other way. If Nathaniel were found guilty, then he would be stripped of his rank and of his shears. Then what would Saul do? After all this time, those shears were still the only way he knew of getting into Heaven.

Well, there was Bran.

But those fiery wings of Bran's might only have strength enough to carry one. Besides, his son hated him. No, there was no help there. Without leverage, Bran would never aid him. Not surprising since Bran was content to worship the mother he had barely known at her graveside.

"Time's wasting," Reuel called.

That much was true. If Saul wanted answers for Delphi, he'd better start asking questions.

Surveillance of Nathaniel hadn't turned up anything new, much to Azrael's displeasure. For all the time Saul had sunk into trailing his brother, all he had to show for his efforts was the grim satisfaction that Nathaniel would experience the same loss he had. Saul wouldn't even bother to break up the happy couple. Let them spend time together, age together; then death would shatter them.

Knife in hand, Saul sliced a rift. Something about Nathaniel and his mortal bothered him.

How had Nathaniel sensed the woman's distress and known that she needed him? If such a connection were possible between a harvester and a mortal, Saul would have had such a bond with Mairi. He'd loved and cherished her for years, but the only bond they'd shared was in their hearts. If Saul had only known that Mairi needed him…

His jaw clenched. He shut down that line of thought. Time was wasting. He could wallow in guilt and misery later.

Now he had to save his own neck by finding the lost soul, and that meant he had to pay his brother another little visit. But first he needed to return to the old church's bell tower and watch the show. If Saul gave Nathaniel enough rope, perhaps he would hang himself.

And when he did, Saul would be there holding the knife to cut him down. For a price…

Chapter 15

NATHANIEL BURST INTO the bookstore. Skating over the polished floor, he stumbled to a stop at the base of a wide staircase. Chest heaving, eyes wild, he searched for signs of Chloe. He was up the stairs and in her apartment before he heard Neve's crooned reassurances.

He charged through the somewhat familiar layout, running until he found the kitchen window where he'd last glimpsed Chloe and where the source of Neve's voice originated.

"What happened?" He pushed Neve aside and knelt.

Chloe lay on the floor curled on her side, shivering violently and unconscious.

"I don't know. We were getting ready to eat. She went to the window. A minute later, she collapsed on the floor." Neve's voice broke. "I'm calling nine-one-one."

"Not yet." Chloe's pulse raced and her eyelids fluttered. He needed to open their bond.

"Are you sure? With the medication she's on…" Her lips pinched together.

His chest tightened until he couldn't breathe. "What medication?"

Neve shook her head.

"This is not the time to worry about her privacy." His teeth bared in a snarl. "What did she take and why?"

"Anti-anxiety medication." Her chin lifted. "The reason is none of your business. If you want to know, you can take it up with her."

His focus sharpened on Chloe. He should have known living with the burden of knowledge she carried would drive her to seek help. "That explains a lot." Her shyness and the state of her soul could be direct results from it as well. Even her hesitant touches should have hinted at inexperience rather than indecision on her part.

He ground his teeth at his own foolishness as he set to work unfastening the restrictive collar of Chloe's shirt. Then he spread the halves so she could breathe easier.

"I don't think it's her medication." He feared it was something much worse, an ability she could have only through contact with him. "It's probably this heat."

He lifted her and shivered with relief from the simple contact. The quickest way to find out would be to ask Chloe, but first he had to get rid of Neve. She paced the kitchen floor, too wound up to stand still. She needed something to keep her busy and he needed her gone.

Standing took effort. Heat mixed with fear kept him off balance. Once on his feet, with Chloe secure in his arms, he turned to Neve. "Can you bring her a cup of ice chips and a cool washcloth?"

Neve wasted precious minutes frozen in place. "I don't think her freezer makes chips."

"Go down to my truck. There's a hammer on the tailgate. Put some ice in a plastic bag and smash the hell out of it."

After a jerky nod, she broke away and ran from the room. He followed as far as the living room, where he nudged pillows aside and tossed the blanket to the floor to make room for Chloe. Dropping to his knees, he settled her in and propped her head up on the remaining pillow.

He fumbled her limp hand in his, wanting a physical connection to tether him. Relief made him press his lips to her knuckles as he tapped into their bond with surprising ease.

"Chloe?"

She whimpered in response.

"Shhh. I'm here now. You're safe."

"Never safe." A choked sob. *"He always comes. I knew he'd be back."*

"No, meira, *he didn't come for you."* Though Saul would if he learned what she was.

She squeezed his fingers past the point of pain. *"I don't want to die."*

His eyes crushed tight against her plea even as her words stabbed through his heart.

"I saw him…"

"I know you did." He stroked her cheek with his fingertips. *"He's gone now."*

"He had wings. Like a bat. They were black glitter and bone." Her thoughts turned frantic. *"He came for me. I know he did. He always does…"*

"Enough. Try not to think about it." Never one to follow his own advice, his mind churned over the fact that her terror was meant for him, although owning up to it now would be disastrous. *"He's gone now and I won't let anyone hurt you."*

"Nathaniel?"

If he answered her again, he risked revealing himself. Part of him wanted her to know, to have his crimes spread out between them and let her judge him as he had judged so many others.

Their bond was growing roots, deepening their connection. If she could see Saul now, when souls were invisible to mortals, then what other talents might she develop in time? She used the harvester bond between them unconsciously, but with ease. Could she channel other harvesters as well? He doubted she would live long enough for them to find out.

Warmth spread through his hand from the small one curled in his grasp. The notion of losing her made his every fiber rebel against the inevitability.

He couldn't save her. Delphi's scales demanded balance, and her soul was the weight they required.

From downstairs, he heard a series of dull thumps as Neve used his hammer to make a bag of crushed ice. Hurried footfalls brought his head up in time to see her crest the stairs. Forget smashing ice; he should have sent Neve to a gas station to buy some, anything to steal a few more minutes alone with Chloe.

"Will this do?" Neve hefted a bag as she approached.

"It's fine." His focus had already returned to Chloe.

Neve knelt beside him and pressed the back of her hand against Chloe's forehead. "She's not feverish. Give me a second and I'll grab a towel to wrap this in." Clutching the bag of slush, she vanished into the kitchen where he heard drawers slide open and closed. She reemerged with towel in hand. Its center darkened as the melting ice spread through the cloth. The damp strands of Chloe's dark hair were pushed aside to make room for the cool compress.

"She looks better already." Neve sounded relieved. "Are you staying with her awhile?"

"I'd like to." Though he didn't need Neve's permission, he asked, "Do you mind?"

"It's not my place to say. You make that call." She exhaled. "Look, I can't leave the store unattended. Let me finish up with the customers we have, and I'll lock up for the rest of the day. Can you hang around that long?"

"It's no problem." Neve would have to drag him out if she wanted him to leave.

"All right." She turned to go. "I'll be back as soon as I can."

"Take your time." There was that word again, *time*. They had so little of it.

He didn't bother watching Neve go. There were more pressing matters on his mind. Bent over Chloe's couch while he watched her sleep, he couldn't help experiencing a moment of déjà vu. He had been foolish to think Saul wouldn't become curious as to his whereabouts. The danger to her now was greater than it had ever been. He groaned through a spike of exhaustion. *"I should leave."*

"No." Chloe stirred, cuddled against his thighs. *"Stay."*

His resistance crumbled with every sleepy stroke of her thumb over his shin. Her loose limbs dangled as he lifted her and settled on the couch, situating her across his lap. Tucking her close, he whispered placations in the language of his creation. Rusty from disuse, the melodic words came hard to his tongue.

While her even breathing signaled her descent into deeper sleep, he indulged his need for reassurance by inhaling the sweet scent of her apple shampoo, then tracing her features with his fingertip.

Beautiful and gentle, Chloe was stronger than she realized. She was his *meira*, his light, and he would kill anyone who dared attempt to extinguish her brilliance.

Chloe woke to a throbbing ache in the back of her head. She groaned, shifted her weight, and felt something too soft to be floor and too hard to be couch beneath her. Her eyes opened and bright sunlight sent shafts of pain stabbing through her temples.

"Ouch." She blinked up at Nathaniel, who didn't look happy. She pasted on an I-feel-perfectly-normal smile from reflex. "What's with me and your lap, huh? I mean, it's comfy, but I do own chairs."

The worry lines on his face relaxed and his grip loosened, but not by much.

"I was worried about you," he said. "Are you okay?"

"Me?" Her voice trembled. "Oh, I'm fine." She was home. She was safe. And whatever creature she had imagined lounged beneath her elm tree was just that—her imagination. The shaking moved into her hands. "I should get up." *Quick.* "I need something to drink." In case this new manifestation of her nightmare man paid her another visit. Wings, really? They only made him more terrifying.

Refusing to let her budge, Nathaniel grabbed a water bottle from the side table at his elbow and handed it over. "Here you go."

"Thanks." The cold bottle was sweaty from the warm room. "I should probably still sit up." She cleared her throat. "I don't want to choke." She patted her pocket. *"Or let you see me lick a crushed pill from my fingertips."*

His eyes darkened in an unnerving way. His jaw set and instead of helping her out of his lap gracefully, he sat her upright like she weighed no more than a child. One of his large palms spanned her lower back and kept her balanced on the width of his thigh. An air of expectancy surrounded him, but he couldn't know how much she needed him to look the other way.

She dropped hints the best way she knew how, but he didn't pick them up. Being around him made it all too easy to sink back into his warmth. Let him stroke her back and press hot lips to her forehead.

Fear of reliance pushed her from his lap. "I could use something to eat." Her fingers worried the crescent shape on the outside of her pant leg until it drew his notice. "I didn't get much lunch down me before…" She winced. "Well, I'm hungry anyway. I saw you had company. That plate probably wasn't enough to fill up two guys your size. How about I make some sandwiches?"

"Are you sure you feel up to it?"

Her head was killing her, but she had to get a pill down her throat before she had another episode. "Oh, I'm fine." She headed for the kitchen.

His voice trailed behind her. "You said that already."

"Well, you keep asking me the same question." Desperation made her snappish. "So, I figure you must want the same answer."

"In that case, I apologize." The corner of his lips hitched to one side. "I really was worried about you. I didn't know if the heat, or something else, might have caused you to black out."

The way he said "something else" made her bristle. Unsure how he could know, but equally certain he did, Chloe experienced a sinking feeling in the pit of her stomach. "You sound like you think it was more than the heat."

He found a sudden interest in the tasseled fringes of her couch pillow. "I used the restroom while you were sleeping." His hand fell into his lap and still he wouldn't meet her eyes. "I thought you might want something for a headache when you woke up, so I opened your medicine cabinet."

She winced. "And found a pharmacy."

His cheeks creased in a smile as he rose. "Something like that."

Somehow she ended up in the kitchen with a tie in one hand and bread slices in the other. The counter bit into her stomach and her knees bumped the lower cabinets. She was as far away from Nathaniel as she could get without climbing in the sink and crawling down the drain.

Heat encased her back from shoulder to hip as he crowded her with his large body. His chin rested atop her head. His arms wound around her, trapping hers against the countertop.

"I'd like to know more about you," he said, "in case something like this happens again."

Complete truth wasn't an option. The last thing a sane man wanted to cozy up to was a crazy woman. But he did seem concerned, so a brief explanation might do the trick.

"I have these episodes." Her nails poked holes through the soft bread. He took the ruined slices from her, covering her hands with his. Protected by a wall of Nathaniel, she pushed her trust further. "They're, um, panic attacks?"

"What triggers them?" His lips brushed the shell of her ear. "So I'll know what to look out for."

Low and deep, his voice drew the words right out of her.

"I was in an accident last year." Heated breath fanned the column of her throat. She swallowed hard. "And when I see things that remind me of... Well, it triggers an attack."

"So there's something on your porch that bothers you?" Moist lips trailed down the back of her neck.

She tilted her head and was rewarded with a string of kisses across her jaw. He mumbled something against her skin. "What did you say?"

"You wouldn't come outside to inspect the porch." He nipped her chin. "I wondered if something about it bothered you."

"The porch is fine." It was the world surrounding it that made her twitchy. "Can we discuss the price of lumber or the going rate on nails?"

His cheek came to rest against hers. He supported her as she leaned against him, made her feel his acceptance clear to her soul.

"I'm here if you ever want to talk. No matter what you have to say, I won't judge you." Lower, she heard him say, *"I don't have the right."*

She worried he did have rights to her, too many for comfort.

Chapter 16

Mᴉɴᴅꜰᴜʟ ᴏꜰ ʜᴇʀ wishes, for now, Nathaniel rubbed Chloe's arms and changed the topic. "Your air conditioner hasn't kicked off since I got here. It feels like it's blowing hot air."

"I'm not surprised." She stepped away long enough to gather supplies for their sandwiches. "The upstairs unit is pretty much shot."

"The store runs on a different circuit?" Several of the older, larger buildings worked that way.

"Mmm-hmm." She sliced into a tomato and layered the thin circles between pale turkey slices. "My parents moved here right after they got married. The apartment was leased separately from the space below while my grandparents owned the place, so all of the utilities were divided. Even after my parents took over the business and moved in, they never changed things over." "Anyway," she carried on, "I had the downstairs unit serviced a couple of years ago. I opted to wait and purchase new units once I'd saved up some more money." She shrugged. "I just never got around to doing it."

And now she paid the price for it. "You could have mentioned it to me."

"We negotiated for a porch, not a renovation." She frowned into the jar as she scraped mayonnaise dregs from the bottom. "It would have been unfair to take advantage of you just because you're here."

"I know my way around most units." He ought to, since he helped Bran with the compound's maintenance often enough. "It wouldn't take but a minute for me to find out if I can patch them until you make the service call."

"It's not that hot." She laughed. "I'll turn on a fan or something."

"Where are the units? Out back?"

"Yes." She shook her butter knife in his direction. "And you are not to touch them unless we come to some kind of understanding."

He understood perfectly. She was uncomfortable, so he was going to fix the problem. "All right." He tore his gaze from the window and its view of the back alley. "I can respect that." He just wouldn't abide by it.

She popped strips of bacon into the microwave. "I'll call and see if I can't get someone out here Monday morning. I'd rather wait out the weekend than pay for a padded service call." Her lips moved in time with the countdown and earned him a blush for noticing. "Why don't you sit down while I finish these up?"

Following her orders, he sat in one of the two chairs crowding a small table in the breakfast nook. Sun glinted off the window and made him glance away. Through the glass, he saw the elm's dusky green leaves and the picnic table's edge, which explained how she had glimpsed Saul.

"Here you go." Chloe plunked down a white plate with raised seashells ringing the outer lip. A glass of sweet tea in a matched glass came next.

He took a bite, watching to make sure she did the same. "It's very good."

"I can manage a halfway-decent sandwich." She wrinkled her nose. "I just prefer not to."

"Well, I appreciate your efforts." He smiled where she couldn't see it, then indulged his curiosity. "You'll be closing up shop in a few hours. Do you have any plans for the weekend?"

She pried a tomato from her sandwich and nibbled it. "Not really." Her smile almost hid behind it. "Neve asked me to sponsor a literacy booth to run at the fair the week after next." She set her sandwich down. "So we're going to hang out maybe tonight or tomorrow and stuff goodie bags."

"That sounds nice." Bonding was good. The more Neve turned to Chloe for companionship, the safer her soul became. "I hope you both enjoy yourselves."

"How about you? You're off until Monday." Her dark eyes held an undetermined emotion. "Got any plans?"

"I'm visiting Bran." He would spend the rest of his time with her, if she let him. "If you're not too busy tomorrow, I can pick you up for a lunch date. Off the clock." Uncertain whether the porch was a trigger for her or not, and assuming the table was out, he added, "We could dine in at that barbeque joint up the street."

Her face lit up and lips parted on what he thought would be acceptance. "I'm sorry." She started picking the crust from her sandwich instead. Shame thickened her voice. "I can't."

Corresponding shame radiated through him. Whatever her problem was, he was the root of it. "There's something you're not telling me."

She hid her hands under the table, making him wonder if she was toying with her pocket again and exactly how many of those pills she kept there.

"I didn't agree to the relationship thing, okay?" Her voice rose. "I told you something I *never* tell anyone. Why can't that be enough for you?"

"I want to know you." His tone lowered. "I want to understand you."

Her eyes shone with anger. "You don't have to understand anything about me to collect a paycheck."

"It's not like that and you know it."

"You don't get it, do you?" She shoved from the table and started pacing. "Men like you don't show up and sweep women like me off their feet. It's not real. It doesn't happen."

"It must happen." He stood and followed in her tracks. "Because I'm here now and you're the reason." He flinched at the double edge to his truth. "Look, I care about you. If I can stop another day like today from happening, I'd want the chance to do it. That's all."

"Why do you care?" Brushing past, she snatched her plate and tossed it into the sink. "Why are you here, right now? Really?"

He didn't answer. He couldn't.

"Did you want a job? Need the money?" She braced her hands on either side of the sink with her back facing him. "Expect me to roll over easy? What?"

He stopped by the table, grabbed his plate and cup, and then set them on the counter. She refused to face him, and he was man enough to admit the slight hurt. He pressed a quick kiss to her cheek and turned to leave.

At the doorway, he stopped. "I care because you make my world a brighter place." His voice roughened. "I wanted to spend time with you. I thought we could both feel normal, feel something, for a little while."

Then Nathaniel left her apartment, snatching Bran's gift on his way out of the store.

The rim of the sink pressed cool and damp against Chloe's forehead. She swallowed convulsively and tried not to lose what lunch she managed to eat before her showdown with Nathaniel.

His words cut her to the quick because he was right. She wanted normal and he gave that to her. More than that, he made her happy.

Her insecurities had built a neat bridge between her and the rest of the world a long time ago. It boggled her mind that a man like him seemed determined to be the one who crossed it. Much to her surprise, he was making good time, if she didn't run him off first.

She turned her head when a light hand touched her shoulder. "You okay?" Neve asked.

"I'm fine." Or she would be. "I think Nathaniel was right. I got too hot."

"Is everything okay with him?" She gave an amused smile. "He almost popped the balloons jerking them through the door on his way out."

"I think I screwed things up." Chloe hated the thought. "He asked what I was doing this weekend and instead of being civil or acting like a normal person, I attacked him for wanting to help me." She stared at her feet, wiggled the toes of her shoes. "I'm used to being ignored by men. Being invisible I can handle, but Nathaniel shines a spotlight on me. He looks at me and I…worry what he sees."

She thumped her forehead on the metal rim of the sink for emphasis.

Neve chuckled. "I doubt one little spat will run him off. You should have seen the way he charged up the stairs and ran right to you. He wouldn't even let me get close."

"Really?" She liked the idea more than she probably should. "I must have screamed bloody murder for him to hear me all the way from out there."

She laughed but Neve didn't.

"You didn't scream," she said slowly, as if only now realizing it. "You went to the window and you passed out. The next thing I knew, he was coming up the stairs and taking charge." She glanced at Chloe. "I wonder how he knew?"

"I don't know." He always seemed to know too much where she was concerned.

Neve's frown relaxed. "Oh. I forgot. Nathaniel's brother must have changed his mind. I told them to call me if they wanted another plate fixed. Nathaniel must have come looking for me when he found us in the kitchen."

"Yeah." Chloe suppressed a shudder. "That must be it."

The man had luck on his side for sure, and a boatload of convenient answers. He hadn't mentioned a brother, either. Though it made sense they would meet to discuss concerns for Bran.

"Speaking of the weekend…" Neve leaned an elbow on the counter and grinned at Chloe. "Are we still on? I was thinking tonight worked better than tomorrow. Is that okay with you?"

"Of course." Her cheeks stretched in a matching grin despite the headache still thumping in her skull. "Did you find everything you were looking for?"

"Not quite." She gave a sly look. "I guess we'll just have to do this again sometime between now and when the fair comes."

Chloe beamed. "Well, I guess we do have a responsibility to the public. I mean, we want only the highest quality plastic frogs and yo-yos."

"Exactly."

"Do you want something to drink?" She coughed into her hand. Her mouth tasted foul from the pill clinging to the back of her throat. She barely lasted through the sound of Nathaniel's footsteps fading before she popped the one in her pocket. "I made some sweet tea this morning."

Neve's nose wrinkled. "No thanks, I'm good." She pulled Chloe upright. "Besides, you don't need to worry about waiting on other people. You don't even need to be on your feet."

Before Chloe took offense at the snub to her tea-making skills, Neve turned her around and shoved her toward the living room. "What is it with you two and the mothering routine?"

"We care about you." They reached the couch and she pressed down on Chloe's shoulder until she sat. "Since I don't have to worry about losing make-out rights if I tick you off, unlike Nathaniel, I get to be the one who tells you like it is." Her expression gentled. "You had a rough day. It's hot. You obviously don't feel well and you have guy stress on you too. That adds up to me handling closing and you taking a break."

"You don't have to do that." Between her weak knees and the hand pinning her in place, she couldn't rise.

"Yes, I do." Neve tossed a pillow to her. "It's what friends do. We take care of each other when we're too caught up in the drama of life to take care of ourselves."

Retrieving a small fan from the kitchen, Neve plugged it in and set the dial to oscillate. Her fingers drummed the plastic top until Chloe lay down and folded her hands over her stomach.

"Good enough?"

"Stay down," Neve warned. "I'll be up to check on you in a little bit."

"Thanks." She turned onto her side. The living room was hotter than she had cared to admit to Nathaniel. She should have fought Neve about how much cooler she would be in the store than in her living room, but her eyes were already growing heavy.

In the past week, she had netted more sleep than in the last year combined. Her body must have tallied every second lost and planned to force her into repaying the tab.

Sinking into the worn cushions, she hit a comfortable spot and tossed her afghan over the back. The only lump in her road to sleep wasn't on the couch but on her conscience. Regardless of how certain Neve was that Nathaniel would forgive her, she had a hard time excusing her behavior. He'd absorbed a lot without blinking an eye, and he deserved kinder treatment than she'd given him.

Come Monday morning, she would give him an explanation of her condition and an answer to his question. His concern deserved a measure of trust in return. Without the pressure of his presence, she could reflect, and she decided she was willing to give him that small token of faith.

Her tired eyes closed. Chloe wished she had his phone number. Now that she thought about it, she had no way to contact him. No address, no phone number, nothing.

"I'm sorry." The thought lingered, then seemed to echo and fade away as sleep claimed her.

Chapter 17

Nathaniel prowled the halls of the medical wing at the Order's compound, ready to lash out at the first person foolish enough to ask what he was doing in the restricted area. His spat with Chloe had him spoiling for a good fight. Just his luck, no one met his gaze or even glanced in his direction.

He rounded a corner and spotted a door with a medical chart clipped to the front. It appeared to be the only room in use. He paused with a hand on the doorknob and skimmed the top sheet where *Bran Berwyn* was scribbled in a looping scrawl. Yeah, he'd come to the right place.

Braced for the worst, Nathaniel sucked in a sharp breath before he entered the room. When he found Bran sitting upright, he exhaled with relief. "So I hear you're going to live after all."

Bran winced when he turned his head. "That's what Hannah tells me." Blinking his eyes, he seemed to test their focus. "What the hell is that?"

Battling the fistful of balloons through the tight doorway,

Nathaniel gathered them as best he could, then presented the cluster to Bran. "A gift from a friend."

His brow furrowed. "A friend of yours or a friend of mine?"

"A friend of mine."

Bran plucked the card from his bear's paws, then lay back against the pillows, taking the baby blue envelope with him, while Nathaniel set the bear on a tray beside the bed.

He took a seat and waited, but Bran's gaze remained riveted to his card. "You're staring so hard, your eyes are crossing. Do you need help reading it?"

The card lowered as Bran glanced between it and him. "It says, 'I hope you can run home soon.' " His eyebrows rose. "There's a gift card for twenty dollars and a coupon for a free ice-cream cone in here."

Nathaniel leaned back in his chair and laughed through the absurdity of it all.

"I don't get it." Bran flipped the card over. "Is this a joke? Or am I so high on pain medication I don't get what's so funny?"

"It's no joke," Nathaniel said. "You had a handful of zeros shaved off your age."

Bran angled his head to one side as he entered a staring match with the stuffed toy, as if he couldn't decide what to make of his gift. "Is there a reason your friend thinks I'm Little League material?"

"My friend thinks I'm human. That makes you human by default."

Bran faced him with no small amount of effort. "This woman?" He checked the card. "Chloe?"

"Yes."

His expression turned thoughtful. "That's why you wanted time away from harvesting."

It looked like Saul wasn't the only one with a nose for gossip.

"She's part of the reason." Nathaniel smoothed a hand over his scalp. "It's complicated."

"It sounds serious," Bran teased.

"It is." Deadly serious. "I wanted you to know so if Saul comes around…"

"I won't let it slip by accident?" Bran stared at the ceiling. "He can't pump me for information I don't have."

It pained Nathaniel how quickly Bran jumped to his same conclusions. "I didn't want you to feel left out."

He chuckled, then flinched from the pain in his ribs. "Is this an aunt introduction, then?" He tapped the card across his palm. "She sounds like a very sweet, if misguided, lady."

"You can't imagine." Nathaniel was surprised how much he was enjoying talking to Bran about Chloe. There wasn't much information he could share without endangering Bran, but even their light banter relaxed him. "I've never met anyone quite like her."

"Well, give me the details. Tall or short? Light or dark?"

"She's short and dark," he answered automatically.

"That's the best you can do?" Bran slapped his card across Nathaniel's forehead. "You're making her sound like a latte."

With a scowl, Nathaniel elaborated. "The top of her head reaches my chest and her hair is brown, *chestnut*, and her eyes are dark, like chocolate. Satisfied?"

"Very." Bran's expression turned smug. "You proved my point for me. You have got it *bad*." He rolled his eyes. "I like how you ran with my food analogy but 'chestnut' hair and 'dark chocolate' eyes, really?"

"Who has chocolate?" Hannah, the Order's physician, strolled into the room and butted right into their conversation.

Her thumbs were hooked in the back pockets of her jeans, and the pose thrust her breasts forward in a way that strained the thin black material of her navy tank top. A stethoscope hanging around her neck was the only indication of her profession, but the quarter-sized angel wings nestled against her spine marked her as Nephilim.

All Nephilim suffered birth defects, some less obvious or more attractive than others.

"Nathaniel's girlfriend, that's who. Apparently that's what color her eyes are." Bran smirked. "Who knew he had it in him to become all poetic about a woman's looks?"

"I sure didn't." Hannah eyed the colossal mass on the bedside table. "What the hell is that?"

Bran sounded amused. "It's a gift from Chloe." He winked at Nathaniel. "If she keeps this up, she'll be my aunt in no time."

Nathaniel's cheeks burned. "I never said that. She's my *friend*. That's all. Just a friend."

"With 'chestnut' hair." Bran's mood seemed lighter, more boyish and carefree, than it had in ages. The drugs were definitely in effect, wiping away his worries. It was a good look for him. Unfortunately, he couldn't go through life hooked to a morphine drip. "I wonder where I can find one of those?"

"If you mean a woman who makes you see color in shades of L'Oréal, check any street corner in Mercerville."

Both men's attention converged on Hannah.

Bran sat a little straighter. "I would appreciate it if you kept your comments civil where Chloe is concerned."

"Sorry. It was a joke." She reached for Bran's arm where an IV pierced his skin.

"You're being cruel, Hannah, and you know it." He stared at her, waiting.

"I said I was sorry." She set her jaw. "I wish you happiness, Nate, really. You deserve it."

Bran tucked his arm at his side, then glanced at Nathaniel. "How long will you be staying?"

"I'm here until Monday or until you're up and walking."

Despite his nephew's bravado, Bran needed him, and Chloe needed time for the raw edge of her pain and embarrassment to fade. A weekend apart was a good thing, but damn if he knew how he would endure it without seeing her. He supposed if he could survive a week in Dis, then he could make it another forty-eight hours without Chloe. He hoped he lasted that long.

Bran turned back to Hannah. "Can we do the checkup later? I need to finish talking to my uncle."

She cast Nathaniel a warning glance that said visiting hours were over. "Fine."

He watched her leave. "I get the feeling I missed something there."

Bran slumped against his pillow as if the argument had sapped all of his strength. "It's nothing. She's just jealous. I could have handled the situation better, though. I know she has a thing for you, and teasing her wasn't fair."

Even drugged up, Bran remained more diplomatic than most of their kin managed on their best days. "You were pumped full of pain medication. Hannah will forgive you."

"You mean after she makes me pay for snapping at her?" He snorted, then winced. "Probably." He rubbed his face. "I can't swear to it, but it seems like Reuel swung by earlier. I'm pretty sure he was looking for Saul."

Nathaniel leaned forward. "Any idea why?"

Bran stifled a sigh. "Why does anyone ever look for him?"

"Good point." Still, it made Nathaniel curious. "If Reuel's after Saul, it's probably to do with money he's owed from the last card game. We broke up the party before anyone cashed out their chips."

Bran frowned. "I can't see Reuel needing the money."

"He doesn't." Nathaniel smirked. "He took a bet he could earn enough playing cards to live on for a year."

At the rate Reuel was mooching, Nathaniel thought he just might make it.

"Ah." Bran exhaled. "Now that sounds more like Reuel."

"He loves a good challenge." Be it women or money or damn near anything else.

"So does Saul. Good luck to Reuel." Bran sounded grim. "I doubt he'll see a dime of that money. Saul isn't big on keeping his word."

Nathaniel regretted probing an old wound but wondered if there was another reason Reuel had come here looking for Saul. "Has Saul been by?"

"Hannah told me he brought me here." Bran looked puzzled by the fact. "I'm guessing that's why Reuel stopped by."

"I'm sure it was." Nathaniel kept quiet about how he'd been surprised by the offer when Saul made it.

"I had this dream about Saul…" Bran's lips pressed together. "Never mind. It doesn't matter. It wasn't real." Bran settled lower into his bed, a sullen mask slipping over his features. "Family. Can't live with them, can't throw them into a soul pit."

Nathaniel chuckled, but it sounded strained. He wondered what Bran would have said.

"Speaking of family—Delphi got a letter from Gavriel a few days ago." Bran was trying to distract him. "I'm not sure what it said, but I got the impression the news wasn't good. For one thing, Delphi's started carrying his sword again. He's also locking himself in his library, poring over the prisoner manifests for Aeristitia." His head fell back against the pillows. "I think…someone's gone missing."

Swallowing the instant denial that sprang to his lips, Nathaniel kept his voice low. "No one leaves those cells, or the heavens, without help."

"I know." Bran stared at the ceiling. "Believe me. I think I've spent half my life in security checks waiting to get in and out of Aeristitia."

"They don't think you—"

"No." Bran flexed his foot. "I still have the lovely anklet Gavriel designed for me. After a quick check to make sure it was working, that I still can't lie, not to him at least, he interrogated me, then let me go."

"He still doesn't trust you." Ice crept into Nathaniel's tone. After a lifetime of service, acting as courier between Heaven and Hell, Bran deserved better. He deserved respect.

"Trust a Nephilim?" His lips curved. "He trusts me almost as much as Delphi does."

"Delphi doesn't trust anyone but Gavriel." A dull pang made Nathaniel rub his chest. There had been a time when he and Saul were that close. Would they ever be again? "At least Delphi didn't outfit you with new jewelry."

"Didn't he?" Bran rolled his shoulder, the one that bore Delphi's mark.

"Point taken." Most days, Nathaniel forgot the brand was

there. He hadn't thought of his in months. "I'd still rather have the brand. At least I can pass that off as a tattoo."

"Ah. It's like that." Bran's eyes closed. "So Chloe thinks tattoos are sexy, but men who wear jewelry are not?"

Heat rippled across Nathaniel's skin at the thought of her tracing his tattoo with her finger…or her tongue. "I don't know." But now that the seed had been planted, he wanted to find out.

"You're losing your touch." He chuckled. "Then again, I'm not sure you ever had one."

"Thanks." Nathaniel wished he didn't agree. "I'm going to grab some coffee. Do you need anything?"

"Nah." His eyes didn't open. "I'm good." When Nathaniel stood, Bran turned onto his side. "Be careful out there. If Delphi is combing over Aeristitia's records, who's to say he won't comb over Dis's next? He's looking for something—or someone. If he starts matching harvesters to the souls in their pits…"

Then Nathaniel would have a lot of explaining to do.

Chapter 18

Metallic clangs made Chloe push from the couch and head toward her window. She was expecting Neve to be back in a bit, but the bus stop was a block away and Mr. Johns kept to his schedule like clockwork. That meant whatever the banging noise was, it wasn't company calling.

The store had an alarm, and Chloe had armed it once Neve closed up for the day. So if someone tried to break in, she'd know about it. Nibbling her bottom lip, she considered her options. It was dark and she was home alone. Would it be so bad to write off the noise and curl back up on the couch?

Another series of clanks and bumps made her mind up for her.

If someone was out there, the last thing Chloe wanted was for Neve to stumble across them. That meant grabbing the flashlight from her nightstand and her dad's baseball bat from under the bed. Before she talked herself out of it, Chloe armed herself and then crept down the stairs.

Shadows loomed across the stairs and gave her a case of the shivers. Her imagination had always been keen, but thanks to her nightmare man's additions to her repertoire, she had no trouble imagining all kinds of things lurking in the dark corners of her store.

A flip of her thumb sent a beam of light slashing through the gloom. She tucked the flashlight under one arm while gripping the bat with her hands. Too bad Dad never got around to teaching her how to use it, but the thing was heavy enough to do damage without putting much force behind her swing, and how hard could it be to hit someone if they got close enough for her to use the bat in the first place?

Every creak of the stairs beneath her weight made her palms dampen more. By the time she stepped into the store, Chloe was having trouble keeping the bat from sliding in her hands.

She paused at the register and strained her ears.

Clink. Clank. Clink. A muffled voice, definitely male, muttered, "Damn it."

Inching to the nearest window, Chloe peeled aside the blinds and peeked into the alley behind the store. A tripod flashlight reflected off the air-conditioning units and the broad back of the man hunched over them. A man who glanced up as she was wondering whether recognizing some-one based on the fit of his jeans was the hallmark of further mental deterioration or sexual deprivation.

The culprit lifted his wrench in greeting.

The bat slid in her fingers, and this time she let it hit the floor. "Nathaniel."

He was sneaking around under the cover of darkness to…fix her air conditioner?

Crap. He must have felt guilty after the way she snapped at him earlier. The way to her heart was definitely through her store, but she couldn't let him do the work without compensation. There was nothing for it. She had to swallow her pride, make amends, and pick up the tab.

Darting behind the register, she flipped the switch on the back wall. Light burst through the blinds as the floodlights poured across the alley. This time, when she peeked through the blinds, a pair of baby blues stared back at her. She raised her voice so he heard her. "Give me a second."

Once the blinds were snapped shut, she raised them and reached for the window. The second she jiggled the lock, the alarm started chirping. She held up a finger to Nathaniel and ran back to the register, where she punched her code into the keypad. All she needed was for Piedmont PD to roll up with enough paperwork to sink her plans with Neve for the night.

Out of breath, she jogged back to the window and threw it open. "Hi."

Nathaniel was grinning. "Hi."

"Phew." Chloe fanned her face. "I think I just had my Southern belle license revoked." She plucked at her shirt. "This isn't dew. This is sweat. You scared the bejesus out of me."

His smile faded. "Are you feeling all right?" Before she could work up a good case of mad at him, he held his hands palms out. "You're the one who passed out today, remember?"

Oh. Yeah. "I'm fine." She fanned herself for effect. "Just hot." When she peered over his shoulder, he shuffled his feet. "What are you doing out there, by the way?"

"Fixing your air conditioner." He scowled at the wrench in his hand. "Or trying to."

She drummed her nails on the window frame. "I thought we agreed you wouldn't touch the AC units."

"You needed the repairs done." He shrugged. "I happen to be in the repair business."

"Well I happen to be in the book business, and it doesn't pay all that well." Try as she might, Chloe couldn't tap into the anger she ought to be feeling. She was too relieved at seeing him again. Crazy how happy the sight of him made her. "I wish you had asked me first."

"I should have…I would have, but I…"

Chloe popped her head out the window, bracing her forearms across the windowsill so they could talk without glass between them. "Do you often get the urge to home improve this late?"

"No." He leaned against the brick wall. "I wanted something to keep my hands busy."

She frowned. "Is there any particular reason why your hands had to get busy on my AC?"

Nathaniel paused. "I went to see Bran." As if that cleared up his being here.

"And?" Chloe propped her chin in her palm.

"He's sedated. He slept for most of the visit." Nathaniel rubbed his eyes and left grease smudges on his cheeks. "The longer I sat there, the louder the beeping and the dripping became until I—" He clamped his mouth shut. "I don't like seeing Bran with all those tubes and needles hanging out of him, sticking into him."

"Poor little guy." The kid was lucky to have such a doting uncle. "Was your brother there too?"

"Saul isn't really a part of Bran's life." He sounded like he'd made peace with that fact. "It's just me and Bran for the most part. His father isn't…Saul isn't well. He lost his wife, Bran's mother, and he hasn't been the same since."

"I'm so sorry." How horrible that must be for them all. In that case, tragedy must have prompted Saul's visit rather than paternal concern. How sad for poor Bran.

"It was a long time ago." He stared at his hands.

Chloe reached out, took one of his large hands in hers, and squeezed. "It still hurts, though. It's been years since my parents passed. Not a day goes by that I don't think of them. I miss them."

He let his head fall back against the bricks. They stayed like that, with her leaning out the window and him holding on to her hand. It was nice, a tad awkward, what with the brick wall between them, but he didn't seem to mind.

"I should be getting back," he said after a while.

"That's probably a good idea." Neve was on her way and Bran shouldn't wake up alone. "I'm glad you came. What I said earlier today…it had nothing to do with you. I just…I hated the fact that you had to come to my rescue. I wanted you to think I was normal."

"You could never be normal." His lips curved. "You're far too special to be ordinary."

"Ordinary would be a nice change of pace for me." She gathered her nerve to add, "If you're serious about giving us a try, then you're right, you need to know what you're getting into."

"I don't think that's exactly how I phrased it." He stared down at her, his thumb doing that rubbing thing over the top of her hand. "I am serious about you. If you ever want to tell me anything, I'm here."

"I don't want to tell you, but I think you might need to know. You said it was my decision to make if I wanted a relationship with you, but it's not. It's your choice, because if one of us walks out, it will be you and not me."

He didn't look happy. "You're not giving me much credit."

"No. I mean it." A deep breath shored up her courage and she took the plunge. "I was in a car accident about a year ago. I've always had social anxiety, but afterward, things changed. I have these nightmares…and I'm afraid of leaving my house, where I know I'm safe." She soaked up the comforting warmth of his touch in case this was the last time he allowed her so close. "So if this doesn't work out, you will be the one who leaves, because I literally can't." She glanced inside the store. *"I'm trapped here."*

"You're agoraphobic?" His voice remained level, calm.

She cringed. He'd used the A-word, but he hadn't sounded disgusted and he hadn't backpedaled to get away from her. "Yes. I don't handle crowds well, and I can't be alone in a strange place." Her throat tightened. "Pretty pathetic, huh? I guess it shouldn't surprise you to learn I also sleep with a night-light in case the bogeyman jumps out of my closet."

He remained quiet longer than she could stand the silence.

"Like I said, it's your choice." She tugged at her hand, but he wouldn't budge. "I wanted you to understand how things would be with me. It's hard to date someone who can't leave her house, and you'd get tired of being cooped up here eventually. It's probably best we both forget this whole thing happened."

"I can't do that. I won't let you do it, either." His next step brought him in front of the window. He bent down, bracing one hand against the frame while using the other to pull her until her knees hit the wall. "If you're asking me to choose, I choose you." His lips brushed over hers. "I always will."

"You'll leave when this job is over," she said. He couldn't deny the fact.

His eyes flashed dark. No longer cool and tropical waters, they were storm tossed and forceful. When his smile came, it held a sharp edge. "I'll take you with me." He nipped at her lips, forcing them open so his tongue could dip inside.

Her eyes closed to better enjoy him. Desire roared to life between them, fanned the flames low in her belly until they licked along her insides.

Leaving wasn't a possibility. When things cooled between them, he would realize she must stay. The break up would hurt, but they would both move on when his job was finished. He would return to his world while she remained here, in hers.

She groaned beneath his lips and he smiled against her mouth. God, she would miss him.

He traded his hold on the window for her. Cupped her shoulder, then smoothed down her back. Fisted the fabric of her shirt and tugged until his palm flattened against her spine, skin to glorious skin. She moaned into their kiss, leaned farther, reached for him, grabbed his belt loop, and tugged him flush against the wall, against her.

"Did you hear that?" His hand continued its downward trek, fingers teasing the waistband of her jeans and sneaking between the denim and her skin.

"I didn't hear anything." She nipped his bottom lip, slid her hand around his hip and into his back pocket. When she squeezed, his groan vibrated through their lips. Her other hand was making its way toward his other pocket when she heard it too—a familiar sharp, buzzing sound.

He broke their kiss. "You don't hear that?"

Of all the times for Neve to arrive, this was the absolute worst. "It's the doorbell."

"You're expecting someone this late?" As if remembering, he nodded. "Neve, right?"

"Right." Chloe withdrew her hand from his back pocket. She didn't even cop one last feel. It seemed kind of rude given the moment had passed. "You're welcome to stay if you'd like."

"Thanks, but I should go." He traced over the elastic band of her panties. She couldn't remember which pair she was wearing, but she sent up a quick prayer they were sexy.

The buzzing resumed and Chloe sighed. "I guess I'll see you Monday, then."

"Bright and early." He stole a final kiss and withdrew. "Enjoy your weekend."

"You too." Before he turned, Chloe added, "Think about what I said, okay?"

"I've already made up my mind." He sounded certain. "But we can finish this Monday."

For a minute, her brain hazed over. Finish this? Finish what, exactly? Their conversation or where their hands had left off before they were interrupted?

Nathaniel pointed toward the AC units. "I'll finish this up and get out of your hair."

Back to business. She should have guessed. "I'm paying for your time and your supplies."

"I'll add it to your tab." He winked as he turned, and Chloe didn't believe he would for a minute.

Muted voices outside the front door made Chloe hesitate. "Who is it?"

"It's me." Neve paused. "But I'm not alone. I brought company."

"Okay." She'd gone from home alone to party central.

Wild weekend, Chloe. "I don't mind if you—" She opened the door and glanced down. "You brought kids?" A boy and a girl flanked Neve. "Are they…?" She stopped short of asking if they belonged to Neve; the familial resemblance answered the question for her. Aware there were two sets of little ears tuned in to their conversation, Chloe shelved her questions for later.

"Can we do this inside?" Neve sighed. "Please?"

"Of course." Chloe stepped aside and let the trio enter. "Let me lock us in right quick." When Neve frowned, she gestured toward the window framing Nathaniel as he worked. "It's been a busy night around here. I don't mind surprises, but I'd rather they knocked first."

Her eyes narrowed. "What's he up to?"

"He's fixing the AC, or patching it at least." Her attention drifted back down to the two little people sticking close to Neve. "Hello there." She wiggled her fingers in greeting. "I'm Chloe."

The boy scooted behind Neve. The girl glared up at Chloe with serious blue eyes.

"I swear I used to have manners." Neve tapped the girl's nose. "Before these two ran them out of me at least." When the girl scowled up at her mother, Neve patted her cheek. "This little spitfire is Melody." Reaching behind her back, she nudged the boy front and center. "And this is Thad."

"Mama said we ought to thank you for giving her this job." Melody jutted out her chin. Her sharp tone contrasted the soft blond ringlets curling around her face. "So thank you."

Thad offered Chloe his hand. She took it, and they shook. "I'm T-Thaddeus Byrne."

"It's a pleasure to meet you, Thaddeus." Chloe smiled. "Do you go by Thaddeus or Thad?"

He rolled his shoulders and buried his face against Neve's pant leg.

The poor guy looked downright scared. Chloe reached around Neve. "Here, let me get some lights turned on in here." They all blinked as she flipped the switches and banished the darkness. When she turned back to Thad with a smile, she gasped. What she had thought was a shadow was an angry black bruise across one side of the boy's face.

"It's rude to stare." Melody stepped between Chloe and Thad.

"Melody...," Neve warned. "Chloe is an adult. We don't talk to adults that way."

Her mutinous expression said exactly what Melody thought about those rules. "It's still rude."

Before Neve opened her mouth, Chloe made an effort to keep the peace. "You know what? You're right. I was being rude, and I apologize. Thad, if I made you uncomfortable, I'm sorry."

Shooting her a look full of gratefulness, Neve tousled the boy's hair. "I know this isn't what we had planned, but I had no one to watch them tonight. I did call before we caught the bus, but you didn't answer. I figured I could order pizza and set the kids up with a movie while we talked business—if you don't mind."

"I don't mind at all." It surprised Chloe to realize that even though she had zero experience with kids, she kind of liked the idea of them puttering around. Her apartment hadn't seen so much action since...well, ever. "As a matter of fact, I was craving pizza for dinner too."

Melody stared at Chloe, her lips pursed as if keeping quiet was causing her physical pain. Chloe wondered what etiquette sin she had committed in the little girl's eyes this time but wasn't willing to risk another mother and daughter spat to find out. Thad peered up at her with longing in his dark eyes that only the words *pizza* and *movie* could inspire in a boy his age.

Thad fumbled through Neve's purse and showed Chloe his prize. "Mama said it was my turn to pick. Melody says it's a sad movie, but it has a puppy on the front, so I think I'll be okay."

"I'm sure you will be," Chloe murmured.

"Let me give you something to cover our half." Neve was already reaching for her wallet.

"No, you're my guests. That means I pick up the tab." As the words left her mouth, Chloe realized she was as bad about patronizing Neve as Nathaniel was with her. He drove her crazy by handling everything himself and not honoring her requests that she cover her own expenses. "That is to say, it's your call. I'm happy either way."

"Thanks, Chloe." Neve passed her a couple of bills. "It means a lot that you offered, but I'd rather pay my own way."

A sentiment Chloe could definitely respect.

"So." Chloe swept her hand toward the stairs. "After you guys." Melody raised one tiny brow. Chloe let her arm drop. "I meant to say, if you'll follow me, please, I'll be more than happy to escort you up to my humble abode."

Thad tugged on Neve's leg. "What's an abode, Mama?"

"It means the place where you live," Melody said, trying not to smile.

"Oh." He studied the stairs for a minute. "You live over the store?"

"I sure do." Chloe led the expedition up the stairs. "Let's get you guys settled in with your movie and your mom and I'll order that pizza."

The sound of footsteps clomping behind her made Chloe's throat close.

The noise reminded her of all the times her mom had yelled down the stairs that a herd of wild elephants made less noise than she did. The best times, though, were when Dad was with Chloe. He'd wink and pretend his arm was a trunk. Together, they'd trumpet and stomp their way upstairs into the living room. Mom would shake her head and laugh.

Dad could always make her laugh.

Clearing her throat, Chloe crossed the threshold into her apartment. "Here we are." She headed straight for the couch and the kids followed. "Do you guys know what to do?"

Melody gave her a look that said *duh* as she picked up the remote and fed the DVD player.

"Miss Chloe and I will be in the kitchen if you need anything." Neve bent down and kissed Thad's bruised cheek. "Be good now."

"I will." He plopped onto the couch and drew Chloe's afghan around his shoulders.

Melody sat next to him and hit Play, then put a pillow in her lap and patted the top. With a grin, his head hit the pillow. His sister gave him a half smile that melted into a scowl when she noticed Chloe watching them. At least she was familiar with this offense—caught staring again.

"Chloe?" Neve touched her shoulder.

Heart hurting for reasons she couldn't explain, Chloe had to look away. "Let's order that pizza."

Forty-five minutes later, they had detailed plans for the literacy booth and dinner had arrived.

The kids were absorbed by their movie, so Chloe gave them a pass to eat in the living room. That earned her a tiny smile from Melody.

Once the kids were settled on the floor with plates and drinks set on the coffee table, Chloe and Neve retreated to the kitchen for some adult time. They fixed plates, poured drinks, and dropped into their chairs with matching sighs.

Neve stared into her cup of soda. "I appreciate you not pushing me for details."

"I figure if you want me to know, you'll tell me." Chloe had enough secrets to know how painful it was to have someone dig around in them. When Neve got quiet, Chloe picked a piece of ham from her pizza and popped it into her mouth. "I'm starving. How about you?"

Not the subtlest change of topic, but she was still working on the whole conversation thing.

"Yeah." Neve picked at her toppings, rearranging rather than removing. Soon her slice had a pair of pepperoni eyes, a squiggly bell pepper mouth, and a neat row of onions for a nose.

"Are you doing okay?" Chloe noticed the tremble in Neve's hand. "Do you want to talk?"

"I'm not sure. I mean, I want to. I just…" She dropped her slice of pizza back onto her plate without taking a bite. "I'm a mess, Chloe." She dragged a hand through her hair. "I'm afraid if I confide in someone, they'll treat me like I'm some lost cause in need of repairs. You know what I mean?"

"It's pretty safe to say *yes*," Chloe said, smiling. "I understand exactly what you mean."

Neve grimaced. "Sorry, I wasn't thinking."

"It's no problem." Chloe passed her a napkin. "I'm here if you need me."

After wiping her fingers, Neve began twisting the napkin tighter and tighter as she spoke. "It's been so long since I could talk to anyone about any of this. I don't know if I can."

Chloe reached across the table. "I know what it feels like to be scared all the time. To think no one understands and that you're all alone in the world." She took Neve's hand. "That was my life." She squeezed. "Having you around, knowing you accept me warts and all, has made the fear lessen."

"I can't take all the credit." Neve's smile was lopsided and her eyes moist. "Nathaniel does a bang-up job of distracting you. He's so selfless. Always ready to shove his tongue down your throat at the first sign of fear."

Chloe couldn't help but laugh. "Nathaniel is…well, I don't know what he is." She stole Neve's napkin and started picking it apart. "You are my friend and if we have to be scared, I think we should at least be scared together."

Fat tears began to roll down Neve's cheeks. She swiped them away and took a steadying breath.

"Last week," she started, "when I said I had a reason to celebrate, I didn't tell you why."

The abrupt change in topic threw Chloe for a minute. "I assumed you were happy because you were settling in." Apparently that wasn't the case. "I should have asked."

Fresh napkin in hand, Neve twisted again. "No, I got a phone call from my lawyer."

There were only so many reasons a person would need a lawyer and only two or three Chloe could think of for a person in Neve's financial situation. "And he had good news?"

"Great news, actually." Her nervous exhale ended with a smile. "My divorce was filed."

Chloe cast about for the right response. "Congratulations are in order, I take it?"

She gave a quick jerk of her head. "It…wasn't a good marriage. My husband, he…Things went bad fast, and the kids and I had to get away faster." Her gaze drifted toward the living room. "I'm just glad it's over."

"Is that what happened to Thad?" Chloe hadn't meant to ask. She couldn't help but ask.

"It was my job to keep them safe and I didn't protect them. Not well enough. Not soon enough." Her voice wavered. "I should have realized, I should have *known*, but I didn't. And now they're paying the price for my mistakes."

Way out of her league and struggling to tread conversational waters, Chloe took Neve's hand. Sometimes touch got across the point when words, or experience, failed. "Their father did that?"

Blood rushed from Neve's cheeks. "Scott has a problem with alcohol. He doesn't drink often, but when he does…" Her chin trembled. "He came home one night, drunk. Thad was in our bed because he'd had a bad dream and couldn't sleep. I knew better than to struggle. But I did it anyway and Thad ended up paying for it."

"Neve, you don't have to—" But she didn't stop. Chloe didn't think she could stop.

"He dragged me across the floor. Thad was screaming. Scott backhanded him to shut him up. That's when Melody…" Neve swallowed. "She hit Scott in the back of the head with a vase from the hall. It didn't break or anything; it just kind of bounced off his head. That's when he let go of me and went after her. I heard her screaming at him to leave her alone. She'd locked herself in the bathroom." Neve's voice hardened. "That's when I ran to the bedroom and got Scott's gun out of the safe in the closet."

Panic fluttered in Chloe's chest, making it hard to breathe, to think, to know what to say.

"He saw the gun and he backed out the door, out of the house." Her gaze locked with Chloe's. "I think he knew." Neve's eyes were too wide, showing too much white around the rims. "I would have killed him, Chloe. If he had touched one hair on her head, after what he did to Thad, I would have killed him."

"What's your plan?" A better question. "How can I help?"

Neve squeezed her hand. "You being here helps." Grasping at napkins, she released Chloe's hand and dried her eyes, blew her nose. "The only plan I had was to escape."

More flutters, more spurts of panic Chloe struggled to control. "Will he come after you?"

"I don't know." Regret etched Neve's features. "With the lawyer, and the divorce papers being delivered, I just don't know."

"Mama."

Both women turned toward the entrance to the kitchen. Melody stood there, glancing between them.

"Thad's stomach hurts." Her chin inched up a notch. "I think we should go home now."

Neve opened her arms and Melody went stiffly into them. "This one's my guardian angel."

Pride shone in Neve's face as she hugged her daughter

close. After a minute, Melody relaxed against her and buried her face in her mother's neck. The scene before her made Chloe's chest ache for what they'd all been through to get here.

Somehow, she'd figure out a way to help them, to keep them safe.

Neve was her best friend, and Chloe wasn't going to lose her. Not after what they had each risked for better, fuller lives. Nightmares and ex-husbands be damned, she and Neve were going to thrive.

"All right, girly girl." Neve turned Melody loose. "Let me say good-bye to Miss Chloe, and we'll get your brother."

After checking the time, Chloe headed to the fridge and the list of numbers there. "It's another hour before the bus runs again. You want to take a cab home?"

"I think it's for the best." She began packing their half of the meal. "It would have been hard to carry food on the bus anyway."

As much as Chloe wanted to offer Neve the use of her van, the one she'd had delivered to replace the one she'd totaled in the accident, she doubted Neve would appreciate the gesture. So she called Piedmont's only cab company and walked her guests downstairs to wait on his arrival.

Her gaze slanted toward the window she'd left open, but Nathaniel had already left.

Once Chloe was alone, she climbed back upstairs and right into bed. She settled in with a book and a quick prayer that the rest of her weekend wouldn't be quite as eventful as tonight had been.

Chapter 19

THE WHINE OF a saw blade drew Chloe toward the window. The first day of the new week had crept in quietly, a welcome reprieve from the weekend's drama. More dreamless nights left her outlook brighter. Or perhaps she had Nathaniel's visit to thank for that.

Nathaniel was outside taking measurements of the porch, pausing to wipe sweat from his eyes every now and then. He hadn't come inside the store this morning. Instead he had set to work immediately after he parked his truck. Nathaniel had thrown himself into his work. Did that mean Bran was feeling better or worse? After their late-night chat, could he be avoiding her? Did he already regret making a commitment to her? Nope. Not going there. Not today.

"You've been staring out that window off and on for the past two hours." Neve walked over to the window and peered out. "I can see why." She whistled, taking in the scene of Nathaniel working shirtless in the hot sun. "Nice view."

Chloe faked a squint. "I think it's getting too bright outside to keep the blinds open." A twist of her wrist fixed the problem and just so happened to block Neve's view of him.

The man should be told shirts were meant for wearing, not being used as sweat rags.

Neve followed her to the front door. "Why don't you try talking to him?" She stared down Chloe's line of sight, straight to Nathaniel. Her appreciative smile returned.

Jealousy flared, white hot and razor sharp, but Chloe crushed the unwelcome emotion. She jerked the cord and shuttered the blinds covering the door too. "Blasted sun is blinding me."

"It must be getting hot out front without any shade." Neve covered her mouth with her hand, but her eyes still crinkled at the corners. "Someone should bring him a drink."

She made a step toward the mini-fridge before Chloe stopped her.

"Okay, I get it." She shoved Neve toward the register. "You want me to talk to Nathaniel."

"Hey." She spread her hands. "I just said the guy might be thirsty." She grabbed her purse. "I think I'll head out for groceries early today. If you guys happen to kiss and make up while I'm gone, that's up to you." She pushed through the side door. "Be back in a few."

Before she could change her mind, Chloe snagged a bottle of water from her office, then headed for Nathaniel.

She held the door open while staring a hole in his sleekly muscled back. An odd, raised tattoo marked his shoulder blade. Its silver shine caught her attention where three metallic ellipses interlocked. The symbol's name escaped her. Sensing her gaze, he turned and ambled over, wiping more sweat from his eyes.

"I thought you might be thirsty." She offered him the water.

He stopped an arm's length away, as if he expected her to meet him halfway.

"I thought we talked about this." Exhaling through the initial surge of panic, she gripped the sleek metal rail comprising the temporary stairs and took a step down. The way he watched, as if he were measuring the parameters of her world, nudged her into a second step that made her knees quake.

"I'm not clear about the boundaries." He came to her, rubbing his hands over her arms. "Why don't you outline them for me?"

"Boundaries—okay." Her voice trembled, so she cleared her throat. "The store is good…no, the store is *great*. The porch is…doable. These stairs…I'm not loving these stairs to be perfectly honest." She uncapped his water and took a long drink. "That's about it. Welcome to my square of the world."

Eyeing their surroundings, Nathaniel made a dismissive sound. "It's more of a rectangle really."

Another draught of water fortified her. "I haven't been outside for this long in months." Plastic crinkled in her hand. "It's nice."

"Stay awhile. I could use the company." He indicated the far side of the frame he'd built for the new porch, to a section with a sheet of plywood acting as a temporary floor.

Chloe coughed, spluttered, and flung her arms out on reflex to shove him away.

Tricky man that he was, Nathaniel stepped into her embrace, wound his arms around her, and lifted. Cold sweat blossomed across Chloe's back. Her lungs tightened and heart punched at her ribs.

She was *outside*. Not standing safe on the porch. Not in touching distance of the store. Her feet dangled over the sidewalk. Close to the road. Close to cars. Close to people in their cars.

"Take me back." Her hands turned into desperate claws as she climbed up him and wrapped her legs around his waist. "Take me back *now*." When her pleas fell on deaf ears, she buried her face in his sweet-smelling neck. "Please, Nathaniel."

"Shhh." He cupped her bottom with one hand and crossed her feet at the ankles behind his back. "There. Is that better?"

She peeked through a crack in one eye. He was picking his way through debris to reach the store. Her hand shot out. She touched brick and that contact grounded her. "Much." She trailed her fingers along the store's side as Nathaniel walked. She thumped him on the head. "Next time, ask or I'll start screaming. I might be the town crazy, but people will come running."

"I think we should talk more about boundaries so I learn not to cross yours." He turned around and sat down on the plywood ledge with his long legs swinging and her balanced on his lap.

"Let's not." Chloe sighed. "I'm tired of talking about me."

"What if I'm not tired of hearing about you?" He sounded earnest. "You fascinate me."

"Yeah." She picked at his shirt. "My life story is riveting. Everyone wants to hear about my life under glass."

"I do." He shifted her higher and his breath caught.

Chloe flushed when the juncture of her thighs brushed a particularly stiff denim ridge. "What are you doing?"

He grinned. "Nothing you'll get in trouble with the neighbors for."

She frowned with what must be relief. She couldn't be disappointed. "Why isn't that reassuring?"

He shifted her weight back so only their less interesting parts touched. "I've dealt with something similar to your situation before."

She snorted. "Yeah, because agoraphobics are so common."

"You might be surprised." His smile faded. "What happened…changed my life, my brother's and nephew's as well. The story is a bad one. I would understand if you didn't want me to tell you."

His fingers bit into her hips, but he hadn't noticed. His eyes were unfocused, far away from the here and now. Somehow she understood the cost of him reliving the memory for her. Whatever happened must be important to him. Her arms wrapped around his waist, locking them together, giving him support he probably didn't realize he needed.

"You wouldn't have offered if the story didn't matter." She rested her head against his shoulder. "You can tell me."

She felt rather than saw his nod. "Bran's mother was murdered when he was very young." Chloe jerked upright and her lips parted, but he silenced her with a look. "He saw her killed. She had hidden them so well, we spent days looking before we found him, and her body."

A shudder worked beneath his skin. "Afterward, his father fell apart, so I brought Bran to live with me while my brother grieved." He sighed with so much regret she ached for him. "Bran was so young to be so afraid. I made him promises, lied to him when I had to, but I didn't know what else to do. He wouldn't leave his room." His voice turned rough. "He would sit in his doorway and cry for his parents, for me, but he wouldn't cross that line."

"I'm so sorry. I had no idea." Chloe rested a hand over his heart. "Is he doing better now?"

He blinked a few times, separating the past from the present before nodding. "He's adjusted well. His phobia was short-lived, six months at most, but it felt like years at the time."

She could imagine. "The adjustment must have been very difficult for you both."

"It was, but we had no other choice. Bran needed me, but my job…I had to work. It was either bring him along or leave him alone." His expression turned grim. "Sometimes I wonder if he wouldn't have fared better if I'd left him home instead of teaching him my trade."

"Single parents make tough calls all the time," she said. "You can't blame yourself for doing what you had to do."

Quiet filled with old doubt-laden guilt hung between them long enough her conscience prickled from his pain. Hoping to shake him out of his mood, she rubbed his arm. "How did you help him get over it?"

"I didn't," he said. "I did what I could. I gave him a safe place, love, acceptance, but none of that mattered until he chose to overcome his fear." Turning to her, he said, "He told me later what frightened him most was learning to love someone new. So many bad things happened so fast, he believed he would lose me next. He worried every time I left the room I wouldn't come back. He was terrified of being left alone again." He met her gaze. "One day he realized I would always be there, that he could count on me, and he let go of the fear. His recovery didn't happen overnight, but once he

made up his mind, he worked toward his goal until he over-
came it."

"He sounds very mature for his age." She frowned. "How
old did you say he was again?"

"Old enough to give me gray hairs." His eyes filled with
pride. "The boy has a chip on his shoulder. I worry someday
someone is going to come along and knock it off the hard way."

"He has you, so I think he'll grow out of it one day."

Now he really did smile. "Hope springs eternal."

Before this smile crumbled, she teased, "Isn't it cheating to
borrow from the classics?"

He frowned at her.

"You know, the old *you can do anything you set your mind
to* speech?" She cupped his face. "I'm working my way off my
meds, one day at a time. It's…hard. Maybe the hardest thing
I've ever done because I've seen what can happen when you
need medication you aren't getting. My mom…" Her chest
constricted. "She stopped taking her meds after Dad died.
Her condition deteriorated. By the end, there wasn't much
left of the woman who raised me. She was a husk of her former self. I see the accident pushing me down that path, and I
can't go there. I won't go there. But for now, I've had all the
upheaval I can stand." Glancing up at the store, she smiled at
the familiar outline. "One day, I might be ready to spread my
wings, but I'm not there yet."

"Fair enough." He kissed her temple. "I should let you get
back to work. Are you ready?"

"Yeah." Her legs tightened around him as he stood and
crossed to the temporary stairs.

He unhooked her legs and let her slide down the front of
his body until her feet landed on the same step he'd plucked

her from. "I'd like to formally ask you out on a date, Ms. McCrea."

Chloe backed up a step. "What do you have in mind?"

"The new posts are set. I'll have the rest of the frame knocked out tomorrow. You'll have a new porch in a week, give or take a day." He gripped her hips to stop her backward ascent. "How about we christen the porch?"

Flames shot through her cheeks and her retort fizzled. "Um, what?"

"A date night, you and me." He tugged her down a step, closer. "We'll stay well within your comfort zone." He grasped her collar and bent her down to his mouth. "What do you say?"

"Okay." One inhale drew his scent deep in her lungs. Another and she felt resolve take root. "One week." Plenty of time to scrap up her nerve to go through with what she was about to agree to. "Mr. Berwyn, you've got yourself a date."

His answering smile made her breath catch.

"In that case"—his lips met hers, warm and soft and full of promise—"I'd better get back to work."

"Work. Yeah." That thing she did from eight to five daily. "We should get back to that."

With effort, Chloe hauled herself back up the stairs. She stepped inside the store and her stomach unknotted…mostly. Shutting the door behind her, she slumped against it.

One week ago, her life had been turned upside down when Neve walked through that door.

One week from now, Chloe would walk *out* that door and into Nathaniel's arms on her first date ever.

Funny the difference a week made.

Chapter 20

CHLOE POPPED THE cap off a permanent marker and stared at her calendar. With a squeak of satisfaction, she circled the date as one to remember. She replaced the cap and chewed on the end.

Underneath her scribbles, in bright red ink, she wrote "date with Nathaniel."

Her stomach fluttered at the idea.

The door to her office swung open. "Look what I have…"

She turned and found Neve holding a cupcake with a half-melted candle stuck from the center. After one failed attempt, Neve got the burned wick lit and held it out to her.

Chloe blew out the flame, then licked icing from the wax. "Thanks. What's the occasion?"

"As if you don't know." Her gaze touched on the calendar, then the mauled marker cap. "Sorry about the slightly used candle. It's the only one I had on hand." At Chloe's questioning glance, Neve said, "I thought a few cupcakes might lure in some business for the literacy booth."

"Good plan." She bit into chocolate so rich she barely noticed when Neve plucked the candle from her fingers. "The fair starts tomorrow, right?"

"Yep, and I have three dozen, minus one, of these iced and ready to go. The gift bags are packed, the books boxed, and our signs loaded in my car." She smiled. "It should be fun."

"Are the kids excited?"

"You know it." She wrapped the candle in a scrap of paper and put it in her pocket. "The question is, are you?"

A resurgence of nerves almost soured the cupcake in her stomach. "Should I be?" When Neve's lips clamped shut, Chloe's eyes widened. "You know what he's got planned." No wonder she looked so smug.

"It's possible he *might* have reserved my services as caterer for the festivities." She rolled her eyes. "Okay, more like I volunteered once he told me his, um, *misguided* intentions."

"So," Chloe said, sounding hopeful, "as my friend, you'll give me a hint, right?"

"No, as your friend, I plan to keep you right where you are." She grinned. "In the dark."

"I figured." She sighed. "At least tell me if we're talking after hours?"

Her face scrunched in thought. "I guess that much won't hurt. He asked me to have you ready by sundown. So we'll have time to put in a full day before you have to get dolled up."

A thrill ran through her. "He wants me to dress up?" Unbidden, the image of Nathaniel wearing dark slacks, his dress shirt rolled up over his forearms came to mind. She bit her lip.

"Your information is need-to-know." Neve made a zipping motion across her mouth. "And that is all you need to know for now." She breezed out of the office and headed for the register. "We'll discuss your outfit and accessories later."

Chloe followed her into the empty store. Neve had shelved inventory and tidied up the place earlier. Now she hunched over what looked like a list at the counter. When Chloe crept closer, Neve filed the paper neatly in the back of a notebook and then pulled out a couple of printed sheets from a tray below the register.

Abandoning the pretense of being productive today, she took a spot behind the register and mirrored Neve's pose. Elbows on the counter, jaw propped in the palm of her hand, Chloe doodled on one of the blank crossword puzzles while she spied on Nathaniel through the front door.

He held a hammer in one hand and a nail between his teeth. He was looking all kinds of repairman sexy today. No. He was looking all kinds of *her* man sexy, which made her grin widen.

"I know you hate these things," Neve said as she penned in an answer.

"I don't hate them." More like she held an acute dislike for them.

Neve drew a line through one column, then straightened. "What gives?"

"Nothing. I guess I'm just nervous," Chloe admitted, "about tonight."

"Sweetie." Neve patted her shoulder. "You're putting too much thought into this. Tonight will be fun, I promise. Besides, I'll be right upstairs if you need me. You won't be alone. And you know Nathaniel won't make you do anything you don't want to."

Heat worked into Chloe's cheeks until even her forehead burned.

Neve blinked a couple of times. "We're not talking about the actual date, are we?"

Chloe shook her head. "More like what happens afterward."

"You thank him for a nice dinner." Neve frowned. "Are you worried he'll want more?"

Her voice cracked. "More like I'm worried he *won't* want more." Swallowing hard, she met Neve's gaze and admitted, "Because I do."

"I don't follow. I mean, I've seen you guys together. The chemistry is there. If you want more, then I'm sure things will"—she waved her hand—"progress."

"What if I said things have never *progressed* for me before?"

"Then I would say...I don't even know what I would say. Give me a minute." Neve ran a hand down her face. "This is not the watercooler conversation I expected this morning."

Shoving her hands into her pockets, Chloe said, "I shouldn't have mentioned it."

"No, you're right to ask." Neve rested her chin on her palm and scratched her cheek. "Look, the best advice anyone can give you is to follow your heart. If you've waited this long to find someone special, and you think Nathaniel is the right guy, then go with your gut. If things go well, and you don't want to say good night, then don't."

"You make it sound simple."

"Just keep things nice and casual. Don't put any pressure on yourself." She offered a smile. "You'll know if the time's right."

"Nice and casual." She rolled her shoulders. "I can handle that."

The front door swung open on a sweaty Nathaniel. "What are you handling?"

With any luck, you, she thought. "We're talking shop. Literacy booth stuff."

The smile he turned on her would have made her shrivel in her shoes if it meant he knew what she was thinking. With a less-than-reassuring chuckle, he stepped inside and closed his eyes. "I think I chose the wrong profession."

"You'd get bored with nothing but books and quiet. You're too much of a hands-on kind of guy. You must be thirsty. Let me grab you a bottle of water."

She found herself grabbed instead. "Thanks, but I'm on my way out. I need to pick up some more supplies before it gets much later." He tugged her close enough for a kiss. "I'll see you tonight." He checked the wall clock hung behind the register. "How does six o'clock sound?"

It sounded like seven hours too many. "Sounds great."

"Good." He mashed the word against her mouth, then backed out the door.

After he left, Neve patted her shoulder. "That boy's got *it*, and he doesn't even know how bad." Clucking her tongue, she smiled. "They're kind of cute at that stage."

Chloe disagreed. Cute didn't apply to Nathaniel. He was too predatory, too wicked for his own good, and he had a taste for bookish clerks that defied all rules of convention or cuteness.

After tossing a bent nail into his overflowing can, Nathaniel surveyed his work and decided he liked how the porch had turned out. Seven days had passed since he asked Chloe on the closest thing to a date he could give her. Prolonging the inevitable had never been more bittersweet, but he wanted to give her a taste of normalcy before reality soured their relationship.

He picked up a sliver of wood and tossed it in with the remaining debris heaped against the building. The porch lacked trim and a coat of stain, but Neve's contribution of fairy lights cast a warm glow over the bare wood. Golden threads woven through the cloth covering his plywood table sparkled. Light gleamed off the silver handles of the over-turned supply buckets he meant them to use as seats. A few feet away, a battered chair held a borrowed radio. Its extension cord snaked through the banister and out of sight.

He rubbed his chin and wondered if he should have ap-proached this in a different way. Days after his talk with Chloe about the harsher side of Bran's upbringing, he still couldn't believe he'd told her. He hadn't spoken to anyone about how Mairi's passing had affected all three Berwyn men since approaching Delphi all those years ago. He wouldn't have said a word then if he hadn't been forced to secure his nephew a place in their world.

If only he could find one for her so easily.

With a grimace, he reminded himself that no such place existed. She no more belonged among the living than she deserved her sentence among the damned. He couldn't save her life, but her soul was well on its way to salvation. All he needed was more time.

The hairs at his nape prickled. His brother had arrived, roosting in the church's bell tower in shadows too deep for Nathaniel to distinguish his outline. From across the street, Saul had a clear view of the porch, of the store, and soon, of Chloe. A second of doubt rippled through Nathaniel, but he dismissed his unease. She would only go so far, and if Saul wanted to watch, he would find a way no matter the location.

"Is everything ready?" Neve regarded him from the doorway.

He nodded. "Is Chloe?"

With a coy smile, Neve said, "You'll have to wait and see, won't you?"

He straightened. "That's not fair."

She placed her hands on her hips. "Some things are worth the wait."

No argument there. Chloe was worth the lifetime Nathaniel had spent looking for her.

He now understood a fraction of the pain Saul had endured when he lost Mairi. The thought of losing Chloe crippled Nathaniel worse than the loss of his wings ever had.

"A girl gets all these romantic notions in her head when a guy like you pays her so much attention. Chloe has that glow about her, and I don't want to see her hurt. Even if you don't mean to do it, you're setting her expectations high." Neve paused. "Don't let her down, okay?"

Neve's show of affection for Chloe knotted his gut. While her admission made several more pieces of his plan click into place, her words were the last thing he wanted to hear. They meant his time with Chloe was running out, and he was nowhere near being ready to let her go.

"I'm serious about her," he admitted. "More serious than I've ever been about any woman."

"Good." Her smile turned radiant. "I think you guys are good together." The click of heels on hardwood spun her around and caught his attention. "You were supposed to wait upstairs," she said to Chloe while blocking his view of the interior.

Nathaniel heard muffled conversation ending with a resigned sigh on Neve's end. She glanced over her shoulder with a plea in her eyes. He nodded his promise that Chloe was safe in his hands, for now at least.

"Mr. Berwyn, I believe your date has arrived." Neve's eyes narrowed as they swung back toward the interior of the store. "Ahead of schedule." She pushed open the door and Chloe took a halting step over the threshold.

Her fingers trailed along the exterior of the building until her hand closed over the new railing. Her approach wound his chest tighter with every step. Air left his lungs. He couldn't breathe, couldn't move. Locked in place, he waited. When she flashed a shy smile, the stars above paled in comparison. Her hair curled around her shoulders, giving her a dark halo. The delectable shade of red on her lips invited all kinds of unholy thoughts as her smoky stare met his. The crimson dress she wore fluttered around her knees. Its dainty straps made his fingers itch to pluck them free of her shoulders.

Forever passed in uneven heartbeats as she followed the path down to where he stood, releasing her grip long enough to seek his hand. When their skin touched, their bond crackled and they both sighed with relief. His heart clenched and he wished the moment were private, the sight of her his alone to savor.

"You look beautiful tonight, Ms. McCrea, but then"—he cleared his throat—"you always do."

"Thank you." Her cheeks turned a complimentary shade of red. "I didn't want to overdress, but Neve said…" She released his hand and straightened his tie. Something so familiar in the gesture told him she'd done it often. "Sorry, my dad had the same trouble with his knots." She smiled up at him. "You look very handsome."

Before he replied, Neve pushed through the door. "Are we ready out here?" Long-stemmed glasses hung between her fingers and a bottle of wine was tucked under her arm. Her other hand held a bowl of mixed salad greens balanced on top of a pair of small plates.

"We are." He offered Chloe his arm while Neve set up their table, then disappeared inside the store. "Would you care to join me for dinner?"

Her small hand fit in the crook of his elbow as he led her to the makeshift table and pulled a bucket out, topping it with a pillow she probably recognized as coming from her couch.

"Thank you." She took her seat and laughed while he pushed in her chair with his foot.

He sat across from her and had to agree Neve was right. She glowed as bright as any star in the heavens. "You're welcome."

Her shoe bumped his, and even that small contact made her shoulders relax.

"Be careful because this stuff is hot, hot, hot." The table wobbled when Neve dropped their plates, then blew on her hands. "My warming tray at home isn't quite as effective as Chloe's."

"Are you okay?" Chloe started to rise, but Neve pushed her down.

"I'm fine. Ignore me. Pretend I'm invisible." She glanced his way. "You have the store's number, right?" He nodded. "Good. I'll head upstairs and get back to work. Call when you're ready for dessert."

Once the door closed behind Neve, Chloe let out a laugh. "Part of me says she's being a good friend by helping you out, but the other part feels as if we're being conveniently chaperoned."

She glanced up, checking the windows for signs of Neve, which was not where he wanted her attention focused.

He poured them each a glass of wine and raised his in a toast. "To first dates."

Her gaze strayed over his shoulder as she did the same. "We're barely six feet from the door."

"Are we?" He begged her with his gaze to play along. "I didn't notice."

"My mistake. I must have gotten some of that moonlit sky stuck in my eye." She tossed the salad and plated a portion for each of them. "I hope you don't mind if I skimp on the lettuce, but the smell of our main course has been driving me nuts for the past hour."

Since his palate rarely stretched beyond what could be delivered, his stomach growled in appreciation. He'd been too nervous to eat earlier. Afraid he wouldn't finish getting ready in time or wouldn't clean up to her standards.

"I don't mind." His tone must have implied his question for him. "It smells great."

"It's fusilli with summer tomato sauce, or so says the chef." She picked up her fork and dug in. Three bites later, they had finished off the handful of leaves she'd given each of them. She plated the pasta with much more vigor and a low hum of anticipation.

"Delicious." Her first bite left a smudge on her lips, one her tongue didn't let go to waste.

He traced its path in envy. Turning to his food, he tried to savor the dish. But Chloe looked much more interesting. She alternated nibbling on a garlic roll and picking her way through the corkscrew pastas on her plate.

Caught staring, he smiled when she dabbed her mouth with a napkin. "Did I miss some sauce or something?"

"No." Her quick little tongue made certain of that.

She placed her napkin on the table and took a sip of wine. When she set her fork on her napkin, he understood he'd made her uncomfortable. "I'm sorry. I shouldn't have stared."

"You're fine." She reached for his hand. "I should save room for dessert anyway. It's not every day someone bakes chocolate soufflé. I hope it rises. My oven isn't a believer in consistent temperature."

Almost on cue, the phone in Nathaniel's pocket rang. A fire alarm blared and choking coughs pierced his ears. A woman's strangled voice cut through the noise. He knocked his bucket over when he stood. "Neve?"

Chapter 21

Fᴇᴀʀ sʟᴀsʜᴇᴅ ʜᴀʀsʜ lines through Nathaniel's usually placid exterior. His bucket rolled from beneath him and thumped against the railing. When he paced into the darker half of the porch, Chloe closed her eyes and clenched her fists in the tablecloth.

"Remember to breathe," she said to herself. "He's right there. I could take four steps and touch him if I had to."

Walking onto the porch was one thing. Being left alone on it in the dark? Not happening.

His head jerked up and he strode to her side in less time than it would have taken to call his name. "Sorry," he muttered, then turned his attention back to his caller. "Neve? You did what? Hold on and I'll ask her." He glanced down. "Neve wanted me to ask if your fire alarm is hardwired into the building." She told him no and got to her feet, half expecting flames to lick up the side of her store.

"Chloe said no, so you need to pry the cover off and pull the batteries out. Are you sure you don't want me to—" He frowned. "No, the fire department can't monitor—" Pinching the bridge of his nose, he said, "Fine. I'll tell her. Open a window and turn the exhaust fan on. If you need help, call. I'll keep the phone in my pocket." His eyes met Chloe's. "I'll keep her occupied while you clean up." His smile made her tremble. "It would be my pleasure."

He closed the phone and slipped it into his shirt pocket. "Dessert has been postponed indefinitely."

"So I figured." Above them, the slide of windows opening drew her attention. "Nothing is on fire, right?" The scent of char and burned chocolate reached her nose. "I'm going up there."

"No." He caught her arm. "You're staying right here. With me."

"But I should—"

"Enjoy the rest of our date? Yes, you should." His gaze drifted up as coughs and sneezes broke the quiet night. "She'll call if she needs us."

"I don't know..."

A tug on her wrist reeled her in close. He pressed warm lips to hers, and the taste of wine and man filled her mouth.

"You don't play fair." She sighed into his kiss.

"I don't play with you." His eyes sparkled beneath the tiny Christmas lights. "Everything about you, I take very seriously." Threading his fingers through her hair, he brought a handful of curls to his nose. "From the way you smell." His lips closed over hers a second time. "To the way you taste." His calloused hands rubbed her bare shoulders. "To the way you feel. All of it, all of you, means too much for me to play games."

Unable to form a complete sentence, she hoped her blush wasn't too telling.

Guiding her toward the railing, he flipped on the radio and pushed the Play button. As a slow song drifted from the speakers, he held out his hand. "May I have this dance?"

"I never learned how." She stepped back, but he followed.

"I'll tell you a secret." He leaned down so his breath blew warm across her throat. "I didn't either."

"Then why offer?" She laughed.

"I have another confession to make. I haven't dated much, and not in a very long time." When he kissed her pulse point, she shivered. "I asked Neve for suggestions. She gave me some pointers and promised if the music was slow enough, we could fake it."

"Ah. I wondered what kept her grinning all week." She shook her head. "I should have known she was up to no good."

Cool air nipped at her neck when he pulled back. "You're not enjoying yourself?" He grimaced. "This was a foolish idea."

"No, this is great, better than anything I imagined. I am definitely enjoying myself." She led him to the center of their private dance floor. "Let's hope Neve's right about the music."

He cupped her hips and her fingers linked behind his neck. With her cheek resting against his chest, she let the slow ballad guide her feet as she gazed down the quiet street.

She recalled a time when the roar of car engines and laughter had filled her with such longing. No boy she envisioned back then measured up to the reality of Nathaniel. This man was more than worth the wait. She buried her face in his shirt and left the past where it belonged.

Much too soon the final notes faded, but she didn't mind. Everything was right with her world. Upstairs, her friend rattled around. Soft curses mingled with coughing fits. Smoke faded and the scent of honeysuckle and dew filled the warm night air. In her arms stood the closest thing this girl imagined to the man of her dreams.

His kindness humbled her and patience boosted her confidence. Small gestures and the constancy of his affection won her over more with every passing day.

She didn't want the night to end, didn't want him to leave when their last danced ended, or her to wake up alone and count the hours until she saw him again.

What she wanted was to find out if the skin of his abdomen tasted salty from the humid air or if he would shiver as she kissed her way down his stomach, where she suspected he might be ticklish. Hours could be spent working her way over his body, paying special attention to his back and shoulders, where his silver marking made her consider the difference in his taste.

"I'm sorry about the chocolate," he said after a while. "And the smoke."

Jarred by the sound of his voice, she startled. "It's all right. Like I said, the stove's old. The oven rack tilts to one side. All it takes is for something to bake up and ooze over the edge. Instant smoke bomb…not that I have personal experience, mind you."

He chuckled. "I'm sure it's pure speculation on your part."

High overhead, windows kissed their frames and sealed their lips for the night.

"I guess Neve's ready to head home."

His grip tightened. "I guess so."

Chloe suddenly wished she'd drunk something harder than wine. Her courage stood on wobbly legs and threatened to collapse under his gaze. Uncertain where her boldness came from, she asked the question they had danced around all evening. "Is this the part where I invite you upstairs?"

Emotions darkened his expression, shifting too quick for her to peg a single one. Hunger was there, acceptance, but so were regret and the same edge of sadness he always carried.

"I guess that was your move to make," she said. "I didn't mean to step on your toes." Nerves made her babble when she should have kept quiet. "I've never done this before. I didn't mean to put you on the spot."

His expression finally settled—on surprise. Not the response she wanted.

Behind her, the front door opened. "Don't let me interrupt." Neve pantomimed an exaggerated exit, stage left.

Nathaniel hadn't managed an answer of any kind, so Chloe called to Neve before she reached the shadows. "Did you have any more trouble?"

Neve paused, as if deciding whether to slink off or respond. "I got the mess cleaned up. The batter spilled, that's all. The kitchen is going to stink for a while, but it's safe for the next time you need the oven." She paused. "Sorry about that."

"I should have warned you." Forcing her legs to step away from Nathaniel, Chloe moved toward the door. "Besides, dinner was delicious. And it looks as if you were right. We managed a slow dance with minimal style."

"Glad to hear it." Neve stepped onto the sidewalk and covered a yawn. "I'm beat. I'll catch you two later. Enjoy the rest of your night."

Alone with a wary Nathaniel, Chloe faked a yawn of her own. "All that wine made me sleepy. I think I'm ready to call it a night."

He closed the gap between them, cutting off all handy escape routes. "What you're offering, it's a gift." He traced the neckline of her dress with his finger. "Are you sure you want to give it to me?"

Her breasts tingled from his slight touch. "I...yes, I am."

He considered her for a long moment while heat tingled through her chest and the back of her neck. "I don't think I should walk you up tonight." His lips curved in a gentle smile. "Or I might take you up on your offer."

"That was the general idea."

"Think about it." He pressed a lingering kiss to her forehead. "I don't want you to regret me, Chloe."

"The only thing I would regret," she said as she hooked a finger through his belt loop, "is not being with you when I had the chance." Before he protested, she led him through the store and up the stairs into her apartment. When she turned, she smiled up at him. "I should have planned this better. Dimmed lights, poured more wine, done something to seduce you."

"Your every breath seduces me." He cradled her face in his hands, leaned in close enough her tongue could have traced his lips. Near enough she smelled caramel on his breath and decided he had a thing for hard candy. "Forget your plans. I've forgotten mine."

His mouth covered hers and she had no trouble forgetting everything but his taste. His kiss migrated down her chin and throat as he sank to his knees. When his tongue dipped inside the neckline of her shirt, she jumped.

He stared up at her from beneath dark lashes, his vibrant eyes amused. "You okay?"

Chloe's pulse jolted. "I wasn't expecting your tongue there."

His dark chuckle made her nipples harden, ache for more of what she'd interrupted.

Fascinated by the play of his large hands over her hips, she watched as he lowered the side zipper of her dress, then slid the delicate material down her arms. His fingers pressed into the skin of her back and her bra straps slipped from her shoulders. She caught the bra and cupped it to her breasts on reflex, but he plucked away her fingers one by one.

The scrap of fabric fell to the floor, leaving her exposed. Her hands balled at her sides to keep from covering herself. He took her hands in his, linked their fingers, and lowered his head.

His breath was hot, his mouth damp as he covered the tip of her breast. Her arms were chained at her sides. Her nails dug into his hands, unable to touch him otherwise. She urged him on with soft whimpers as pleasure glutted her senses.

Her imagination hadn't done the reality of Nathaniel justice. His every touch aroused. Each dark look enticed. His delicious intent made her weak with desire for more.

When his teeth closed lightly over her pearled nipple, she swayed on her feet, forcing him to release her hands and hold her upright. The spike of heat subsided, but his lips were on the move, trailing openmouthed kisses across her ribs down to her navel.

He hooked his thumbs through the sides of her panties, lips following their downward progress, teeth nipping at her bare hip, and her throat tightened. As he nuzzled his way across her stomach, he held her steady with his hands on her hips. Her eager body wavered on the edge of orgasm as she imagined where his hands and...*she swallowed*...mouth were headed.

She had brought them here, ready or not. "What if you do all this…and I can't…What if I can't return the favor?"

"Sex is about reciprocation." His breath came out in a rush of warm air below her navel. "This is not sex." His lips whispered over her skin. "This is me, making love to you."

"Oh." Such similar acts, but her heart registered the difference just fine.

His laughter vibrated through her hip bone. "Or I could be."

"Sorry." She tried not to fidget. "I'm nervous." When his eyes filled with a question, she covered his mouth and he held perfectly still. "I'm nervous, not afraid." She dropped her hand. "I want you, and you're not going to talk me out of it."

"I told you, *meira*, I gave up my plans." His smile was bittersweet. "There's nothing I want more than you and no price I'm unwilling to pay to have you."

His palm curved her spine until she had to brace on his shoulders or topple over. Her bare sex met his lips and her hands fisted in his shirt. She gasped again, definitely not expecting his tongue there, either.

She shivered as he parted her folds, pressed kisses over her sensitized skin. His mouth closed over her clit while his tongue flicked at her with lazy movements. He was the perfect Southern gentleman with nothing but time on his hands and pleasure on his mind.

Pressure built low, tingled in her stomach. Breathing heavy, she dug her nails into his shoulders as the rush of sensation made her dizzy. Desperate for release, she moaned when he caressed her achingly empty flesh and then slipped a thick finger inside.

Her eyes closed and muscles clenched around him while

the sharp ache of penetration made her whimper. He massaged the delicate tissue, stretched it gently as he pressed foreign words, beautiful words against her breast.

Coaxed by his gentle ministrations, she accepted more of him in slow increments as arousal loosened her muscles, lessened the pain. His thumb found her clit with sure strokes while his pointer curled deep inside her. The delicious pressure from earlier resurged, redoubled, and rocked her up on her tiptoes from the force of her orgasm.

Her world became soft edged with blind contentment as fading tremors rippled through her tender flesh. Boneless and sated, it took a full minute to pinpoint the sound of a zipper's rasp and realize what it was.

Breath whooshed from her lungs when she looked down and saw Nathaniel's shirt crumpled a few feet away, slacks past his hips, and nothing but bare skin beneath them. Shucking them off and tossing them aside, he stared up at her, very naked and very aroused.

Carpet met her knees as she sank to the floor before him. The flushed crest of his thick erection held her stare. Her arm outstretched, she closed her fingers around him long before she thought to ask permission. "Is this okay?" She pumped her fist, reveling in the glide of smooth skin under her palm.

Nathaniel groaned and thrust into her hand. More strange and hungry words fell from his lips. They sounded like a prayer and Chloe hoped she was their answer.

He let her stroke him once, twice, before he clamped down on her wrist. "Come here." Strong hands grabbed her hips and set her on her feet. Forcing her legs wide enough to straddle his thighs where he knelt, he leaned back on his palms and gave her room. "This way you're in charge. You set the pace." Deep breaths flared his nostrils, cut his words short. "Stop when you need to."

On his knees, head tilting back and sweat gleaming, he was beautiful. And he was hers, at least for now.

Bent on unsteady knees, she reclaimed her hold on his erection, held it upright, and lowered herself slowly. The smooth head drew a wince from her as it nudged her core and slid inside.

Untried muscles tightened, fought against his invasion, but she braced on his shoulders and used her weight to increase the pressure, the pleasure this position allowed. She grinned when his teeth bared and he hissed. Sinking slow and steady, she gave her body time to adjust. But when her hands slipped on his sweaty skin and she came down harder, faster than she'd meant to, it hurt.

"Shhh." He tucked her to his chest and rocked her as best he could with their bodies joined. Tears burned her eyes, but she wouldn't let them fall, refused to let him see them. Once the sting subsided, the rhythmic shift of his hips beneath hers rekindled her desire. She shuddered through a hard breath and knew she had to have more.

"I'm ready," she said, already moving against him.

"Thank God." He covered her mouth with his as he thrust upward and swallowed her short, startled cry. Hard and thick, he overfilled her as his long strokes turned to shorter, urgent thrusts.

Each powerful flex of his hips pushed her closer to the edge. For the second time tonight, her inner muscles tightened. Clenched over Nathaniel's erection, her sensitized flesh registered his every retreat, every return to her.

Stomach tensed, her body quivered as white light exploded behind her eyes and blanked her vision. Nathaniel growled his release against her neck. Clutching her to his chest, he shuddered, holding her so tight her sight swam as it tried to return.

Even after their heartbeats slowed, his large body still cradled hers. His warmth seeped into her bones and made the thought of moving impossible. Pins and needles stung her right foot, and she would have bet money his legs were numb too.

"Thank you." Chills spread across her skin as his lips feathered the words over her throat.

She tucked her face against his neck. It was a silly thing to do because he must have seen her blush a hundred times by now. "You're welcome." Her nails scratched his back in light strokes, earning her another kiss, this one pressed to her shoulder.

"Are you tired?" he asked.

All that held her upright was his arms around her waist. Otherwise, she would have melted into a puddle on the floor at his feet. "Maybe a little."

He slipped from her body, then locked her ankles around his hips and stood. She didn't mind. Her forehead braced on his chest and her eyes drifted closed a few times on the short trip from the living room to the bedroom.

Springs squeaked as he laid her on her bed. Right before he pulled away, she trapped his face between her palms and poured her thanks into the soft press of her lips over the seam of his mouth.

He wandered into the bathroom with a lopsided grin plastered on his face. He returned with a damp cloth. Careful of her tender spots, he cleaned her thighs and between her legs, then cleaned himself.

His gaze traveled between her face and the spot next to her. His decision to stay or go was a tangible weight pressing on her chest. When his expression turned dubious, she realized she'd missed her cue and patted the mattress beside her. She wished her sheets were sexy instead of covered in cartoon dolphins, but she hadn't thought to change them. "Would you like to stay?"

His answer was to fall into bed with her, scoop her back to his front, and curl his much larger body around hers. One arm bent so he could prop his head in his hand and look down at her while the other tucked her against him. "You should get some sleep."

Stifling a yawn, she asked, "Aren't you tired?"

"Exhausted." His voice softened. "I just want to hold you while I can."

He really did say the sweetest things. "Mmkay." As far as she was concerned, Nathaniel could hold her as long as he wanted.

Chapter 22

Tingles worked through Nathaniel's hand where it had fallen asleep sandwiched between Chloe's thighs. A strand of hair clung to her forehead and curled under his nose. He brushed the strand aside with gentle fingers as her soft sigh blew heated air across his chest. Their connection filled his ears with a steady hum, almost a purr of contentment from his soul as it sought out hers and reveled in her nearness.

Sex had changed things, awakened the side of him tired of masquerading as a human. His true form peaked through the veil cast by his pendant, eager to share all he was with her and know exhilarating acceptance for once in his staid life. His soul thought it had found its mate.

Focused heat on his cheek turned his head toward an uncovered window. Acceptance, he reminded himself, was a dream made of mists and easily evaporated by morning light.

A sleepy sound brought his attention back to Chloe. Or maybe the disturbance hadn't been a sound but a sliver of awareness drifting tentatively in his direction.

He traced the curve of her cheek and his skin tightened with the perfect memory of last night. If he had a lifetime, or if she had eternity, he suspected he would never tire of waking in her arms.

Yawning, she opened one dark eye. "You're staring."

"You're beautiful." He kissed the tip of her nose, the only part of her within easy reach. "So you have only yourself to blame.

A lion's share of doubt filled that one eye. "So you say." Another yawn, this one covered, and she rolled to her side of the bed. Back arched, her knuckles brushed the headboard, and toes peeked from beneath the covers.

Beneath the thin sheet, her nipples hardened and strained as she stretched. Failure to resist temptation led him to cup one of the soft mounds in his hand. Her low moan strangled after she blinked a few times. "It's bright in here." She bolted upright. "What time is it?"

Time had gone the way of his plans, right out the window. "I'm not sure."

Shoving him back against his pillow, she crawled over him and knocked something from her nightstand. "The store opened hours ago." He grunted when she swung her leg over him and wiggled until her foot touched the floor. She glanced back. "Sorry about that." She walked gingerly to her closet; then he heard hangers scratch across metal. "I'm used to rolling right out of bed in the morning." She made a pit stop at her dresser. "This is the first time I've had to roll over somebody to do it."

"I'm fine." Or he would be after a long, cold shower.

With a towel hung over her shoulder and an armful of clothes, she took one step toward the bathroom, then one step back. "Do you need to grab a shower?"

Her invitation was clear, but her steps were careful this morning. She was sore. So the last place Nathaniel should be was naked in a shower with her. His hands, yeah, they had minds of their own where she was concerned.

"You go ahead." He stood and let the sheet fall. Her focus homed in below his navel and did nothing for his resolve. "I should swing by and check on Bran." He needed to know if there had been any other Saul sightings. "I think I'll grab a shower and a change of clothes while I'm there." Her lips turned down at the corners and his resolve took a hit. "Since we're already late for work, what if I pick up some bagels and coffee on my way back? Neve can handle the store, and I can give you a proper good morning."

Another measured glance at the clock said the idea of calling in late was foreign to her.

"You know, even bosses get the occasional day off here and there." He found himself talking his way into a day with her. "I could tell Neve you'll be out sick today."

She tried to frown, but her lips curved in the wrong direction. "You're a bad influence on me." She stared down her nose at him. "Besides, I would never lie to Neve."

"You wouldn't have to." He bent to retrieve his pants. "I'd do it for you."

"Shoo." A wad of terry cloth bounced off his shoulder where she'd thrown her balled up washcloth. "The sooner you leave, the sooner you'll get back."

He glanced between her and the mattress, imagining a day spent under the covers with her in his arms. "I expect to find you right here waiting for me."

"Dream on," she snorted. "You mentioned food and now

you have to deliver." She spun on her heel with a laugh and left him to appreciate the sway of her hips as she disappeared inside the bathroom.

The fabric clutched in his hand was a poor substitute for the soft woman whistling as knobs squeaked and she adjusted water for her shower. He yanked his slacks on with a frustrated growl.

The rock-hard lump in his pants promised he could watch her bathe without joining in, but his hard-as-a-rock head knew a good lie when he heard one. He smoothed a hand down his face. *I need some air,* he thought. Arousal flushed his face, made his skin dampen. *It's stifling in here.*

The knob rattled and Chloe's head popped around the door, locating him right where she'd left him. "Are you hot?" Her cheek rested against the doorjamb. "The thermostat is down the hall, across from the spare bedroom."

"I— Thanks." He watched her for a minute. Long enough that she gave him a strange look. He almost thought...but it was impossible. *She* couldn't have read *his* mind. She had no angel blood. "I'll dial it down before I leave."

"It's not too late to change your mind." The door opened a fraction more, enough for him to see the shower's steam had made her skin rosy with its heat. "About leaving, I mean."

His fingers brushed the button of his pants before his resolve caught up to him. Instead, he tucked his hand into his pocket. "I'm already dressed." Despite her invitation, she must be sore. He knew better than to think if he stayed he could keep his hands to himself. "You're hungry. I should go."

"All right," she said on a sigh. "Hurry back and be careful."

His lips parted and his heart skipped a beat. "I will be."

Long after she closed the door, he walked over and pressed

his palm flat against the raised panel. Soft words were muffled by the splatter of water and density of wood, but if he focused, he could hear her song in his head.

Throughout his existence, whether armed with a holy sword or his shears, no one ever questioned his ability to get his job done. No one ever doubted he would return unharmed, and never had anyone asked him to be careful. Until Chloe.

He thumped his forehead against the hard wood as the apple scent of her shampoo filled his next breath. Cheerful notes sang through lips he lived to kiss, made him smile despite himself.

His *meira* had sliced a rift through his heart and walked right through it.

Heaven help him. He loved her. More than anything or anyone, she was his.

Chapter 23

Aᴛᴛᴇʀ ᴅᴇsᴄᴇɴᴅɪɴɢ ᴛʜᴇ stairs from Chloe's apartment, Nathaniel spotted Neve and cut behind the counter. He kept as close to the wall and as far from customers and her as he could. Still, she caught his eye and gave him a look that promised they would talk, and his honorable intentions would be discussed.

Lucky for him, she had her hands full at the moment and he was able to slip outside without comment.

"You look well rested," a familiar voice mocked.

Nathaniel froze. Cold sweat trickled down his spine as he turned. A flicker of movement to Nathaniel's right drew him around the side of the building to where Saul sat at the picnic table. His arms were folded and legs crossed as if he had waited a while rather than arrived as Nathaniel exited the store.

"What? No comment?" Dusting his pants, Saul stood. "Your truck hasn't moved since last night. It's still parked at the curb where you left it."

Nathaniel's steps slowed. "How would you know?"

"I had a collection to make near here last night." He swiped his thumb down by his nose. "I figured I would swing by and check on things. Make sure your woman was locked up nice and tight." He shrugged. "I noticed the truck on my way past."

Swallowing something too deadly to be anger, Nathaniel leveled his tone. "I would appreciate it if you left Chloe's safety to me." His hand went to his hip out of habit but touched air. Saul noticed the move with a twist of his lips.

"You seem nervous." Saul gazed at Nathaniel's side. "I wonder why that is?"

"I would think it was obvious." Harvesters were territorial and he was no different.

"You're not carrying your shears." Saul clicked his tongue. "Dangerous to allow yourself to be caught unarmed."

"The shears are tainted." So many had died by their jaws, he couldn't bear having them near Chloe.

"Your human is too precious to be exposed to our world, is she? Can't let her know what she's really lying next to at night, can we?"

"No good can come of telling a mortal anything about us," he said. "Bringing them into our world only invites pain."

"I agree." Saul stalked a slow circle around him. "Still, she must mean something to you if you're courting her." He spoke conversationally. "She'll die, of course. They all do." His voice dripped with ice. "If she's a good girl, she'll flitter off to Aeristitia. If she's a naughty pet, she'll burn."

"Play your games with someone else," Nathaniel said. "I'm tired of them."

"Fair enough." He paused. "Humans have such warped perceptions of time. They think their love will last forever, but they haven't a clue how long eternity is." He sounded thoughtful. "Does she know you'll leave her? Maybe not for several years, but you will eventually. You'll have to once she reaches a certain age."

"You're still baiting me." He sighed. "Or have you forgotten how to have a civil conversation?"

"You take yourself too damn seriously."

"One of us has to."

"Oh yes, here comes the lecture." Saul threw out his arms. "Take your best shot. What's today's topic? Parenthood? Again? Bran is a grown man and it's time you cut the apron strings," he scoffed. "What else have you got? How about a speech on the follies of loving a mortal woman? I might actually pay attention now that you've had a practical learning experience."

"You fell in love easy enough," Nathaniel reminded him.

"Nothing about loving Mairi was easy." Saul set his jaw. "Nothing worth having ever is."

"I agree." Nothing about being with Chloe was easy, but she was worth it all.

"The love of a good woman will shatter you." Saul spun his wedding band. "She'll pick those pieces up and fit you back together in ways you never imagined. She will remake you." His breath escaped on a sigh. "And when you lose her"—his tormented gaze lifted—"she will unmake you. All those shattered bits will fall apart, burrow under your skin, slice out your heart."

Nathaniel pressed him. "Then you'll respect my wish to experience that for myself."

"You ask me to stand back and watch you suffer." Stark pain darkened Saul's eyes.

"I'm asking you to understand that Chloe is to me what Mairi was to you."

In a blink, that second of empathy vanished. Saul's gaze cleared, his eyes sparkling cold and cruel. His tongue ran along the edge of his exposed teeth. "See, that's where you're wrong."

The brittle edge to Saul's voice told Nathaniel he'd gone one step too far comparing Chloe to Mairi when there was no comparison between the two where his brother was concerned.

"You've known your human a matter of weeks. You think you're protective now? Give it a few years. Let her get frail. Watch her grow old. She will. You know she will." Saul seemed to relish reminding Nathaniel. "Loving her now will damn you later."

"I don't have time for this." What time Nathaniel had left with Chloe he wanted spent with her. He had eternity for these petty arguments with his brother.

"You'll want to make time for this." His smile turned grim. "I came here because Delphi expects me to report for an inquiry, and I'm not going empty-handed." He shook his head. "I've given you more time with your mortal than you deserve. Now my clock's run out, which means you're going to make time for me. Right now."

"What do you want?" Nathaniel asked with calm he didn't feel.

"There's still the small matter of a missing soul." Saul stepped forward. "You remember it, don't you? One night, a couple of weeks ago, you took an assignment and only half-ass completed it." He closed the gap between them and fisted Nathaniel's shirt in his hand. "Delphi does. He's been riding me around like a fucking pony because he thinks *I* failed to turn it in."

Nathaniel's confusion must have been evident as he shoved Saul back.

"Don't look so surprised," he sneered. "Late-night game of cards. Too much alcohol. None of the harvesters seem to remember who took that first job, but oddly enough, they all seem to remember who took the last one." He growled. "And better yet, while I thought I was leaving my *son* and my *brother* to find a replacement for me, or at the very least see my pit was credited with the collection, it turns out they did neither."

"I had no idea you were being blamed." Nathaniel ran a hand over his head. "I didn't ask them to cover for me."

"You didn't have to. The fools lined up three deep to jump on the funeral pyre in your place all by themselves." He scowled. "Even *my* son, the only other person who could vouch for me, has been conveniently out of contact since his run-in with the seraphs. Not that he would ever admit what he knew one way or the other. The runt would cut out his heart before betraying you." Then his expression turned speculative, as if he'd only realized something. "I wonder what Delphi would think if he learned about his gofer's defection?"

Nathaniel's jaw clenched. "Leave Bran out of this."

"Or you'll what? Go to Delphi in his place?" Saul's silky laughter left him cold. "Then your human would be left alone, unguarded, and I think we both know what happens when mortal lovers are left behind while we grovel at the master seraph's feet."

A twinge in Nathaniel's chest spiked fresh foreboding in his heart. He did know.

He had trouble understanding how his brother stomached making such a warning after what happened to Mairi. Though Saul's delivery promised the threat hadn't been idly made. Nathaniel forced himself to look at Saul, to really see the man he had become. Too late, Nathaniel realized the danger this man posed to those he held dear.

The brother he'd given up his sword and station in Heaven to protect was no longer present in any part of Saul. His goodness, his joy, met a hard death long ago. Only now did Nathaniel realize his integrity had also withered and died. "What do you want from me?"

"The soul you owe for starters. Where is it?"

"I can't say." Admitting it was Chloe was tantamount to signing her death warrant.

"Oh, I think you can." Saul scanned the brick building beside them. "And I think you will."

Fear tightened Nathaniel's chest, and he cursed his foolishness at ever leaving his shears.

Saul already had what he wanted. He just didn't know it yet.

Chapter 24

Walking a slow circuit of her apartment, Chloe couldn't put a finger on her problem. After chewing her remaining fingernails to the quick, she moved on to her lips. Her palms dampened and her chest tightened. For the first time in days, she had resorted to popping a pill right off the bat this morning. Still the feeling wouldn't shake loose.

Something was wrong.

Turning a slow circle, she took stock of her apartment and found small comfort in the familiar routine. Everything was as it should be. Nothing was out of place. She wasn't alone. Neve was downstairs and Nathaniel…

With a groan, she hoped last night hadn't turned her into one of those clingy girlfriends men would chew off their own arm to escape. It's not as if she had a ring chart out ready to size Nathaniel when he walked through the door. And she hadn't allowed her heart to clog her throat when he clarified they were making love, though she'd almost choked on the implications. Every word had proved he cherished her; every touch showed he desired her. Her sigh blew still-damp hair from her face.

Looking for any distraction, she went to the window and glanced down the street. A flash of dark caught the corner of her eye and brought the taste of her pill back up her throat. Stumbling back, her gaze bounced between her bathroom, where she stored her sanity in amber vials, and the staircase, where an odd sense of urgency beckoned her downward.

Her feet chose the steps for her. Long before her brain protested their decision, she stepped into the store and ran smack dab into Neve.

"Good morning, sunshine." She caught Chloe by the arm and steadied her as her probing stare raked her, seeming to hunt for boo-boos of the emotional or physical kind.

"Hey." Chloe made herself stop and talk. "I'm really sorry about sleeping in."

"It's no problem at all." A frown tugged at her mouth. "You okay? You seem wired."

She felt wired. Strung tight and ready to snap. "Have you seen Nathaniel?"

"Um, I saw him an hour or so ago when he passed through on his way out." Neve held out a book and someone, a customer Chloe hadn't even noticed, took it from her hand. "He didn't say where he was going. Why? Is everything okay with you two?"

"We're good." Her stomach cramped with dread so hard she rubbed the sick knot. "He went to pick up breakfast. I thought he would be back by now, that's all."

"Chloe?" Neve pulled her hand away and they both watched it tremble. "What's wrong?"

She snatched her arm back. "Nothing is—"

"Don't even try to sell me that load of bull." Neve grabbed her by the shoulders. "You're pale and you're shaking like a leaf. Something is wrong and you're not leaving my sight until you tell me what's going on."

"I…I forgot to take my pills before bed." The lie sounded good enough Chloe expanded on it. "My head is all over the place right now. I'll be fine in a few minutes."

"Do you need to sit down?" With Chloe tucked under her arm, Neve turned her toward her office before she argued or did something crazy, like knock her aside and bolt for the door.

"Excuse me, miss?" A round gentleman with circular wire–framed glasses tapped Neve on the shoulder. "I don't mean to interrupt, but I wonder if you could help me find a book I'm searching for? It's somewhat rare and I can't find it on the shelf."

Chloe recognized the stout man as a dealer, one of her regulars. "Go help him."

"Give me one minute, sir, and I'll be right with you." Neve turned her full attention back on Chloe. "I don't think I should leave you alone like this. Why don't you go back upstairs? As soon as Nathaniel gets back, I'll send him up to you."

"No, I'll head to my office and grab a chair and a bottle of water." She smiled until her cheeks hurt. "I took a pill before I headed down, so relief should kick in soon. I need somewhere cool and quiet until then." She grasped Neve's elbow and steered her toward Mr. Owlish Impatience.

"If Nathaniel takes much longer," Neve promised, "I'll come check in on you."

"Fine. Great." Chloe gave her a shove. "I'll be waiting."

The pull to find Nathaniel made her legs shake with the effort of standing still. Wrapping her arms around her middle, she inhaled sharp enough she got a stitch in her side.

Outside wasn't an option, not alone. She wasn't ready. She couldn't do it without him.

"Nathaniel, where are you?" She could make it a little longer. He would come back. They would eat breakfast and laugh about how silly she had acted.

Then she heard Nathaniel…inside her head. *"Don't leave the store."*

Chloe tripped over her feet. *No, no, no.* That was not his voice. Not in her head. He had to be close. She must have overheard him. That's all. Nothing crazy. Perfectly normal. He was probably standing on the porch or something. Feeling a smidgen calmer, Chloe smoothed shaking hands down her shirt.

"Go to your room. Wait for me there. Please, Chloe." Nathaniel's voice sent pain drilling through Chloe's skull until her brain wanted to leak out of her ears. *"Listen to me. I'll explain everything later."*

Her jaw dropped. This couldn't be real. People couldn't talk mind to mind. It was impossible. A quick glance proved no one else's head had lifted or eyes turned in her direction. He'd all but yelled at her somehow, yet no one had moved a muscle. *They hadn't heard him.*

But she had. She knew his voice. Recalling all the times he had pulled the words from her mouth, she accepted something greater than her understanding was at work here. She could figure it out later. Right now, he needed her. How she knew mattered less than what she was going to do about it.

Focused on Nathaniel, picturing his face in her mind, she cleared all thought and pushed outward, *"Please, tell me where you are and I'll come to you."*

"No." His reply was a hard slap of pain between her ears.

"Stay with Neve. Don't—" The words ended on a grunt of pain.

Her frantic eyes spotted Neve. Still with the customer, her back turned. A path through the handful of meandering customers parted as if by divine providence.

Nathaniel was outside; she knew it. He was hurt; she felt it.

Whatever lurked beyond that door made the hairs on the base of her neck stand at attention. Raw energy danced over her skin. The pull of something *other* kept her walking past the point of no return. Her hand closed over the knob and the door opened on her worst nightmare come to life.

Saul rested a hand at his hip, taunting Nathaniel with the copper dagger sheathed there. "It's not a difficult question." He stroked the handle. "Where is the soul?"

"It's my responsibility," Nathaniel said. "I'll handle the situation."

"Like you have so far?" Saul scanned the windows overhead. "I don't think so. Besides, I'm here now. It seems rude to leave without at least saying hello to your mortal."

"You have every right to be upset with me"—his jaw clenched—"but you will leave her out of this."

"That's rich coming from you," Saul said. "Don't worry. I'll give your lover the same consideration you gave mine." He resumed tapping the hilt of his dagger. "What I don't get is why the risk? Why put off a collection you've done countless times before this one? Was the soul special?" He chuckled mirthlessly. "Did you get a little misty-eyed thinking of it while drafting the other damned souls to weave the soul cloth?"

"It wasn't like that."

Saul wheeled on him. "Then tell me what it was like. What is worth my neck and yours? Why shouldn't I walk right up to Delphi and turn your ass in?" He shoved Nathaniel. "Like when you turned me in to Gavriel."

"I didn't—"

Laughter from a couple walking down the street bounced through the alley to where they stood. Nathaniel waited for the mortals to pass. "We can't do this here. It's too public." And he wanted their fight taken away from Chloe.

"Oh, I can fix that." Saul caught Nathaniel by the neck with one hand while the other fished out his pendant and broke the chain.

Shivers danced across Nathaniel's skin as his spiritual form shed its human shell. He ripped the pendant from his brother's grasp before he faded to immateriality and tucked the chain carefully away.

Saul yanked his own pendant over his head, then flattened his wings against his back. "There. Now we have a private room for two." He faded to a solidified mass of black matter. "You always were a self-righteous bastard. Always thought you were better than me. First as Gavriel's favored archangel, then as Delphi's precious Weaver."

"I *lied* for you," Nathaniel snarled. "Gavriel asked me where you were and I lied to his face because I loved you and wanted your happiness above my own."

"You were a Goody-fucking-Two-shoes who couldn't keep his nose in his own business." Saul's eyes glittered. "Your bleeding heart practically led Gavriel to Mairi."

"She sought me out," he said, "not the other way around."

"She didn't know any better," Saul growled. "You did." He pointed his finger. "Gavriel couldn't sneeze without you handing him a tissue. So of course he noticed when you came to Earth, to her door, without his sanction."

"I had no choice," Nathaniel said. "Bran was dying." He rubbed a hand down his face. "She begged me to find someone who could help, and I did. He is my nephew. How could I say no?"

"You should have said no the same way I did when she asked me," he thundered. "Bran was born sick. He was always sick. We had no reason to think he would live past his first year. If she had waited, we could have had more children." He threw up his hands. "I thought since you've taken a human lover you might...but you don't understand." His voice broke. "She was my life. Not Heaven. Not Bran. *Her.* And because of you, Gavriel took her from me."

"No one could have known her village would be raided during our sentencing," he said softly. The two of them had invited punishment by breaking Gavriel's law, and justice had swooped down upon them at the worst possible time. Nathaniel ached for his brother, for a past neither could change. "It was one night—"

"—that changed everything." His vacant eyes were locked somewhere in their far distant past. "I still smell the smoke. At night, when I close my eyes, I still see her burned body." He shuddered. "If she had left Bran, they never would have found her hiding place."

Instead, a sickly child's cries had led them right to her. She had been brutalized and burned. Bran had escaped unscathed. Mairi had done that, Nathaniel knew, protected her son at all costs because she had loved him, and loved Saul, beyond reason.

There was nothing left to say that hadn't been said a thousand times before, and though he meant the words, Nathaniel knew they rang hollow. "I understand your pain." And he wondered if hatred wouldn't eat a hole in his gut over time as well when he lost Chloe.

"Not yet you don't." Saul's focus snapped into place. "But you will."

Saul's first punch caught Nathaniel by surprise.

He rocked back on his heels, reeling from the unexpected assault.

Nathaniel dodged Saul's next blow. He ducked low, then slammed his fist under his brother's jaw. Saul snarled from the pain and staggered backward while Nathaniel regrouped. When Saul charged, he was ready.

"I'm coming to you." The clarion sound of Chloe's thought sliced through Nathaniel and the distraction cost him. He grunted with pain as Saul sank his shoulder into his chest and sent them sprawling across the ground.

"No." He panted as he shoved Saul aside. *"Stay inside where it's safe."*

But it was too late. His ears rang when a metal door cracked against brick.

He saw Chloe's knees give out in a slow slide down to the concrete steps.

A static *click* and Nathaniel felt the deep resonation of Saul's harvester bond snap into place. The connection was instinctual, automatic, and now he, Saul, and Chloe were snared in the same telepathic bond. Nathaniel reeled from the sensory overload.

Never had he linked with another harvester. Their bonds were one-sided, meant to trap prey, not be ensnared by one another.

Chloe's fear amplified the chaotic chatter in Nathaniel's head, fed him images ripped from Saul's mind. Her bond with Nathaniel had made her a conductor for Saul, and now Nathaniel staggered as his brother's suffocating rage boiled under his skin.

Saul hissed in shock and leaped to his feet. "She's the mark."

Chloe flinched at his voice, and hot, sick fear radiated through their bond in waves.

Saul watched with a vicious, mocking smile. "Why, pet, if I didn't know better, I'd think you could hear us." He wiggled his pinky in his ear. "What's that? I didn't catch your answer."

Her terror-filled gaze swung between Nathaniel and Saul.

"You can see us as well?" With a sharp flap of his wings, Saul took to the air, sailing over Nathaniel's head to land beside Chloe. From her seat on the steps, she pressed her back to the brick wall and inched away from him.

"Come here, Chloe. Give me your hand." Nathaniel reached for her. "I won't hurt you."

Doubt creased her brow. She hesitated, and Saul took advantage.

He stroked her hair, her cheek. "Ah. I thought so." Marvel lit his face when his hand touched skin rather than air. His head shot up, finally concerned they might be interrupted. "Let's find a better place to get acquainted."

"Saul—" Nathaniel lunged for his brother.

"I wouldn't do that if I were you." Saul crushed her to his chest, squeezing until her scream stopped in her throat. "You know how easily mortal toys are broken." To Chloe, he said, "Come on, pet, let's go play."

His wings spread as he glided the several yards between

the door and the rear of the building. With a bloody smile cast over his shoulder, Saul taunted Nathaniel, daring him to follow with the look.

Nathaniel ran, skidded around the corner, and found Chloe pressed against the rear wall. Wide-eyed, she gasped for breath through the hold Saul had on her throat.

Saul glanced over. "I knew you were hiding something, but I never imagined your secret was anything so interesting."

"Release her, Saul." Nathaniel crept closer. "Your quarrel is with me."

"Is that what you want?" Saul's voice dripped with pity. "You want to go to Nathaniel?"

Chloe vibrated with alarm and flooded Nathaniel with her anxiety through their bond. Her wild eyes latched on his golden form. *"Nathaniel?"* Her tone pleaded with him not to answer.

"I am so sorry, meira.*"*

Her eyes squeezed closed. *"This isn't real. This is one of my dreams."* She shivered visibly. *"Nathaniel isn't…he can't be…"*

Saul pretended compassion. "You have no idea."

"Enough." Nathaniel locked gazes with Saul, but he stood his ground. "Release her."

"Don't make me do something we'll both regret. Stand back." Saul clamped his hand over Chloe's jaw and jerked her head backward until her spine bent; then he tapped the end of her nose. "Good girl. No screams. No struggles. If anyone comes back here on your account, I will kill them. Understand?"

She couldn't speak through the hold he had on her. Her answer flowed through their connection, pinging from Saul to Nathaniel and making Nathaniel's head ache. *"I understand."*

"Good." Saul shot her a patronizing grin. "Now keep quiet or I'll find something to occupy that pretty mouth of yours."

Nathaniel gritted his teeth. Another step closer, one more step and he could…

Saul grinned. "I see now I wasn't the only one who believed Reuel, though I admit your attempt appears more stable than mine." His attention turned from Nathaniel to Chloe, eyes gleaming. "How does she work, I wonder…?" He cupped her mouth and positioned his hand over her heart. The tips of his fingers pressed through skin and her mental scream stunned Saul.

With a mindless roar, Nathaniel charged. His shoulder sank into Saul's ribs and sent him scrabbling across the ground.

"Touch her again, and I will stuff your soul into a pit myself." Nathaniel knotted his pendant's broken chain and settled it over his head. The second he had substance, he ushered Chloe behind his back, standing between her and Saul.

Saul rolled to his knees, flapping his wings to gain his feet. "You've bound her soul to yours." Saul managed a single, winded laugh. "I'd almost given up hope, but she's proof that stable resurrection is possible." Hovering several feet aboveground, he whooped with triumph. "You've really done it." His smile was fierce with relief. "Bring her and the shears. We'll meet at your cabin and—"

"The only place you're going," a familiar voice called, "is Dis."

Bran's limping gate was broken by the use of a silver cane. "Delphi is expecting you." He stopped a few feet away and planted his feet wide. "Now."

Nathaniel breathed a sigh of relief even as Saul's gaze met his in a clear warning.

"Do you know what the problem is with eavesdropping?" Saul settled to the ground close enough his wings eclipsed Bran. "You miss important parts of a conversation."

"Then why don't you fill me in?" Bran waited. "What? Nothing to say? Things looked tense when I arrived, so I doubt you two were discussing the weather."

Saul shot Nathaniel a look. "Not that it's any of your business, but we were making plans for tomorrow—*after* the inquiry." His expression turned apologetic when he glanced back at Bran. "Sorry, I would have invited you, but it's for adults only."

Ignoring the insult, Bran turned to Nathaniel. "Is he telling the truth?"

"Of course I am." Saul didn't give him a chance to answer. "I wanted to learn about the woman who's captured Nathaniel's interest. So he invited me for lunch at his cabin."

"Nathaniel?" Bran sounded doubtful.

"I can't keep Delphi waiting." Saul tapped the hilt of his dagger and Nathaniel got the message. Pay now or pay later. "So am I meeting you for lunch...or should I plan on seeing you in Dis?"

"I'll meet you." He had no other choice.

"Good." Saul chuckled. "Until then, I can see you two lovebirds need some time alone." He pointed farther down the wall where Chloe had crept several feet from behind Nathaniel. "Let me give you some brotherly advice. Women aren't keen on being lied to, no matter the reason."

He leaped skyward and vanished through a portal sliced by his blade.

Nathaniel watched until the rift healed itself, then faced Bran. "I'll meet you out front."

Though he didn't look happy, he nodded and made his way toward the sidewalk.

When they had some privacy, Nathaniel approached Chloe.

She shrank back against the bricks. "Don't touch me." Imprints from Saul's fingers dotted her throat and deepened her voice. Tears spilled over her cheeks, but her palms were too busy feeling their way along the wall to reach up and wipe them away.

The fear in her dark eyes cut him to the bone. "You lied to me."

"I didn't have a choice." Not if he wanted to save her soul. "I still don't have a choice."

"If you think I'm going anywhere with you or that thing, you can forget it." Her chest rose and fell with frantic breaths. "I know what you are. I've seen it." More tears fell. "I've *felt* it."

"I didn't know you were being hurt." The need to touch her, hold her safe in his arms, brought him closer. Her sharp cry made him take a step back. "You have to believe me."

"I don't have to believe a word you say," she said. "You're not who I thought you were. You're not even human. For all I know, you're not even real." She swallowed past her bruised throat. "I'm going upstairs, I'm taking my pills, and you're going back to whatever hole in my psyche you crawled out of." Shoving past him, she broke and ran for the door.

From the mouth of the alley, Bran's worried gaze lit on him and Nathaniel knew he had to let her go, for now. There were precious few hours left and he needed a plan.

Chapter 25

SAUL'S MIND SPUN with possibilities until he was drunk on them. His brother had done what he failed to do. Instead of the usual sting those revelations brought, Saul felt only renewed hope.

Nathaniel had done it.

How had he done it?

The woman, Chloe, was a marked soul. The harvester bond had linked them. Damn it. He'd been inside her head, but her images were garbled and useless. She'd committed no crimes. She was clean, a blank slate, almost as if something had shielded her thoughts, memories, from him.

Nathaniel, on the other hand…Saul's wings lifted him higher and higher into the sky. Oh, his brother had been a very, very naughty harvester. Saul would have never thought his brother had it in him to defy Delphi, let alone over a woman, and not after the way Saul had lost Mairi.

Yet he had. Oh yes, he had. The scandal was delicious, and Saul took a moment to savor it.

"Nice. Real nice," Reuel drawled. "Is that your handiwork?"

Saul blinked, confused for a moment. In his excitement, he'd sliced a rift that spat him out at Mairi's gravesite. He applied a somber expression before turning toward Reuel. "Of course not."

"I figured that's how you'd want to play it." Reuel tapped his wrist. "Time's up. I'm here for the soul. I trust you have it for me?"

"I was just on my way to collect." Saul took a step back, palmed his dagger.

"Do you really want to play this game?" Reuel loosed a shrill whistle.

Air stirred and dust blew into Saul's eyes. His mouth parched when he heard it. Feathers rustled, twelve sets of wings thrust. It was the sound of his end approaching if he didn't act fast.

Trates hit the ground first. His head fell back and his lungs filled with fresh air. "I remember this."

"It's too bright." Arestes squinted. "I don't like it. Let's be done with this and return home."

The seraphs were panting, but not from the flight. They wove on their feet, blinking rapidly.

Saul suppressed his glee. Poor little seraphs weren't used to this altitude compared to Dis.

Pity their handler had forgotten how long it'd been since these seraphs last saw Earth.

"Wait a minute." Reuel stepped between Saul and the seraphs. His expression was grave. "I warned you this day was coming. If I don't turn in either you or that soul, then Delphi will skin me alive, and that's not really how I see myself going. Tell me where the missing soul is and we'll collect it, together. "

Turn in Chloe? Never. Saul wanted to crawl inside her and

figure out how she worked. Take her apart, piece by piece until he understood how Nathaniel had succeeded where he had failed.

If his brother knew the secret Azrael had withheld, then Saul would be freed of that burden as well. No more bowing and scraping to the warped angel. No more Zared. No more Hell and no more creatures to feed and coddle when he'd just as soon slaughter them all and be done with it.

He was tired of all the hiding, secrets, and lies. He wanted peace. Was that so much to ask?

Saul braced himself. "I'm afraid I can't do that."

"Glad to hear it." In a blink, Trates stood before Saul. "I've waited a long time for this."

Arestes appeared a heartbeat later. "I anticipated a hunt." He sighed. "Ah well."

"Grab him, boys." Reuel had his knife in hand. "Let's get him to Dis before he gets ideas."

"Delphi said to bring Saul to his office." Trates grasped Saul's upper arm. "He didn't say we couldn't interrogate him first." The seraph grinned. "I'm sure our master would appreciate any information you could give us before your punishment commences."

Saul kept calm. He waited until Reuel sliced his portal and it shut on his heels, waited until Arestes grabbed for his free arm, then Saul struck. He sank his knife into the column of Arestes's throat. Blood spurted. Trates howled. With a quick twist, Saul freed the blade from Arestes and sank it into Trates's gut. The seraph staggered. Surprise lit their eyes as they bared their teeth.

"It's been a long time since you two came topside." Saul staggered out of reach while Trates helped Arestes to the ground. "How are you feeling? A little dizzy? Headache? Stomachache?"

Arestes gurgled. Trates hissed but had removed his shirt to cover his brother's wound. They were trapped and they knew it. If one twin died, the other did too. Trates wouldn't risk that loss.

"You've signed your death warrant." Trates's wings ruffled. "We are Master's favorites. He will come for you."

Saul shrugged off the threat. "He'll have to take a number."

With that, Saul sliced a rift straight into Nathaniel's bedroom. He had to know if his brother was armed. No. He spotted the shears in the same place they had been. Drawn to them, he had to touch them, had to try one last time. He picked them up. "Work, damn you." He squeezed them, but no energy pulsed, no soft glow emanated from them. "Work. *Work.*" His pleas went unanswered.

Furious, he flung them across the room. They clattered on impact. The empty sound mocked him. He forced himself to walk to them, pick them up again, and arrange them exactly as they had been. It wouldn't do for Nathaniel to become suspicious. He must be tending his mortal. Once he had her calmed, he would return for his shears. Saul had no doubt of that. Once they were in his brother's hands, then Saul could bargain. Finally he had leverage. Finally Nathaniel had been the one to screw up beyond salvation. Now he had a choice to make. Either he transferred the shears to Saul or Saul gave Chloe to Delphi. Nathaniel would never allow Delphi to snuff out her life.

Of course, what Nathaniel might not know was that Saul wouldn't either. He would protect her to his death, anything to discover the secret of her creation. The time for revolution was now. All the careful centuries of experimentation were over. Armed with the shears, Heaven would be forced to kneel at his feet. Tempted as he was to cut Azrael from this moment of glory, Saul had to have the angel's backing. His throat burned and he tasted bile. If he fell, he expected Azrael to make good on his promise. Damn the consequences. Saul was taking the shears and the woman.

With a trembling hand, he sliced a rift into Hell and went to rally his soldiers.

Chapter 26

CHLOE SLAMMED THE door to the store shut behind her. Customers glanced up. Neve called her name. She saw them, heard Neve, and she tried to speak, but her feet were running on autopilot and her legs wouldn't stop pumping. She ran past Neve, shouldered past her customers, and hit the stairs leading to her apartment.

Seconds later, footsteps thumped behind her as the old staircase protested such rough use. Somewhere below, a patron asked if anything was the matter. Neve paused to tell him everything was fine.

By the time Chloe heard Neve jog over the threshold, she was sliding across her bathroom's tile floor. She opened her medicine cabinet with a shaky hand and her fumbling fingers knocked amber vials into the sink and floor, as well as into the trash and toilet.

Neve skittered to a stop seconds behind her. "You went out," she panted, "alone."

Chloe ignored the implied question and shouldered past Neve to reach the kitchen and her cupboard. There was nothing to tell. Nothing had happened. None of it was real. *Everything was fine.*

"God, Chloe, your throat." Neve grabbed her shoulders and spun her around. "Are those *fingerprints*?"

Chloe blinked. Could two people share the same delusion?

"Who did this to you?" Yanking aside the collar of Chloe's shirt, Neve fanned her fingers as if testing the distance between dots. "Whoever it was had a mighty large hand." Her eyes narrowed. "I don't suppose he has a hammer and knows how to use it?"

"No." Chloe blurted her denial. "Nathaniel wouldn't… He would never hurt me."

God, she was an idiot. He was some kind of supernatural killer. Of course he would hurt her.

"You don't sound convinced." Neve grabbed Chloe by the hand and dragged her to the table, shoving her down in a chair long enough to pour her a glass of water and pry the pill bottle from her hand. "Half or whole?" she asked.

"Whole." She definitely needed the whole thing, because if Neve saw those fingerprints, then Chloe wasn't crazy. On impulse, she unbuttoned her shirt and pulled the halves apart. Four purple-black splotches dotted across the puckered scar on her chest. She couldn't deny the truth. The proof was written in her skin. Whatever those things were, they were real.

"What in the world are those? More bruises?" Neve yanked her shirt open before she could fasten it. "Chloe"—her voice shook with emotion—"I understand if you think you need to protect Nathaniel. Really, I do. But you can't let him hurt you." She sank into a chair opposite Chloe. "He seems like a nice guy, I liked him too, but my ex was the same way. He always had a smile for everyone but me. Always had big plans and other people to carry them off for him. When we were alone, though…" She shivered. "A nice guy wouldn't treat you this way."

That was the problem. Since meeting Nathaniel in the flesh, he had been a perfect gentleman. Her graphic dreams had stopped, and being freed from that nightly fear had been euphoric all on its own. The nightmare she remembered was cruel and merciless, but the man was thoughtful and kind. They were polar opposites. So which was the real Nathaniel?

She jumped when Neve touched her arm. "I don't want you to take this the wrong way, but maybe he picked you for a reason. A woman with your condition, living alone, he might have seen you as an easy target."

He had targeted her, months ago, though Chloe couldn't begin to guess why.

"Are you listening to me?" Neve shook her arm, jarred her from her thoughts.

"I am." Chloe pulled back. "It's…complicated."

"From the inside, it always seems that way." She folded her arms across her chest. "Mark my words, with distance comes clarity."

Distance was a luxury Chloe couldn't afford. She was stuck in here, and he was…"Can you do me a favor?"

"Name it," Neve said without hesitation.

"Check the front window and see if Nathaniel is still out there."

With a frown, she checked and then returned with her report. "He's talking with another man. It's not the same one as before. This one has a cane."

It must be the third man from the alley, the one who

sent Saul away. Could that monster really be Nathaniel's brother?

Dropping her elbows to the table and her head in her hands, she groaned through a budding headache. Nothing added up. Not the dreams. Not Nathaniel. Not the man with a cane or the demon with an attitude.

Each question fed into another question. Why her? Why now? What exactly had Nathaniel done to her to make Saul want her so badly? He'd mentioned binding their souls. That wasn't possible, was it? And why were they keeping the third man in the dark about it all? He seemed to have some status since he ordered Saul away, so why did he allow the others to shut him out?

"Is he part of the problem?" Neve's lips set in a hard line. "I can call the cops and get them shooed away from the store if you want."

Chloe doubted the cops could do much with either of them. Saul had vanished before her eyes, and she knew from her dreams Nathaniel could manage the same trick. The same held true for the third man. He was in good company if he needed to pull a disappearing act.

"No, I've never seen him before today," she said. "I don't know who he is."

"You know," Neve said, "you could always pay what you owe on that porch and tell Nathaniel you never want to see him again."

Chloe's laughter rang sharp. "I doubt that would work."

Nathaniel had given his word to Saul that he would bring her to his cabin, and she got the feeling the terms were non-negotiable. As far as they were concerned, she was going to that cabin one way or the other. All that remained was whether she put up a fight or caved like the coward she feared becoming.

"I know it's a stretch for you—but is there any place I could take you? Somewhere Nath—that no one knows about? How about my place? It's not much, and you'd be dodging the kids, but…" Neve searched her face. "You could take some time to think, get yourself together before you deal with him."

Risk dragging Neve into her private hell? No way would Chloe do that to Neve or her kids. Chloe was tired of running from her fear. She was going to make her stand, here, in her home, on her terms.

"Chloe." Nathaniel's voice rolled through her mind as comforting warmth embraced her.

Her traitorous heart accelerated at the sound, and something unfurled inside her, reaching for him through some undefined channel. Her sigh was one of relief when they connected. What that said for her questionable sanity and her sense of self-preservation, she didn't want to know. Forget a ring on her finger; she'd settle for a soundproof box for her brain.

"I'm not listening to you." She thought hard in his direction. *"Stay out of my head."*

"And I've lost you again." Neve sighed. "Well, it didn't hurt to toss the idea out there." She tucked a hair behind Chloe's ear. "You're strung out and hurting, sweetie. You need to rest. I'll lock up early so you don't have to listen to all the bumping around downstairs."

Noise was part of life over the store. Chloe barely heard it anymore. Still, if a few locked doors between her and Nathaniel would make Neve feel better, she wouldn't complain.

"Thanks." Chloe smiled up at her. "I mean it. I think I'll

go lie down and try to read for a while. Get my head back on straight."

"Do you want some company?" Neve took Chloe's elbow and helped her stand. "My sitter gets off at six, but I could catch the bus home, grab the little monsters, and be back before it gets dark out."

"I'm fine. Some quiet time will be good for me." Chloe wanted Neve gone long before Nathaniel returned for her.

Neve worried her lip. "If you're sure…"

"I'm sure." Chloe shooed her. "Go on."

"Okay, okay." Neve gave her a quick one-armed hug. "Call if you need me."

Chloe nodded, but she didn't make it to the bedroom. Her couch beckoned and she crawled under her favorite ratty afghan and tried to ward the chill from her bones. She had so many questions, and unfortunately, Nathaniel was the only one who had any of the answers.

The confrontation with Saul drained Nathaniel, but he still had Bran to face and amends to make. More questions to dodge, fewer answers to give, and one last favor to ask.

"Do I even want to know what I interrupted?" Bran leaned more heavily on his cane now, and each shuffling step caused his face to crease with pain. His show of strength had been put on for Saul's benefit. Wise move on his part since predators lived to find signs of weakness.

"It was more of the same." Nathaniel cupped Bran's elbow and guided him around the mess of construction. "Nothing much changes between my brother and me."

"I know exactly what you mean." Bran glanced toward the store. "I assume the woman hiding behind your back was

Chloe since she didn't run screaming at all Saul's huffing and puffing." He grunted as Nathaniel helped him sit on the tailgate. "She did look shaken up, though. Are you sure you don't want to go up and check on her first?"

"No." She made her wishes clear and wouldn't welcome his intrusion. "She has a friend inside. Neve will take care of her for me. The talk Chloe and I have coming…won't be pleasant."

Casting Bran a second glance, Nathaniel frowned at how the sick pallor still clung to his skin. With Saul already in Dis and under Delphi's watchful eye, he saw no point in dragging Bran into whatever plans his father had for him and Chloe. Bran didn't have the strength to help, and Nathaniel couldn't risk another liability. So he changed the topic.

"You weren't supposed to leave the compound for another week at least."

"Delphi calls, and I answer." Bran's shoulders lifted in what should have been a shrug. "He gave me more time than I thought he would. I can manage."

"You can barely walk. He had no business sending you into a confrontation in your condition." The heel of Nathaniel's palm slapped the tailgate and rattled the metal beneath them. "He shouldn't expect you to work until you've healed."

"He was right to call me. My father isn't my business, but a soul gone missing is." He smoothed a shaky hand down the fender of the truck. "I didn't realize they were blaming the missing soul on Saul until today, when Delphi summoned me to ask about it."

Bran tapped his skull and the neat row of stitches hooked behind his ear.

"Too bad he didn't catch me a couple of weeks ago. Neurological injuries are funny things. My memories of certain events are crystal clear." His smile was unintentionally slanted. "While memories of certain other events were wiped completely clean."

"What if he asks Gavriel to question you?" Delphi was no fool; it would occur to him.

"Then we'll have a situation on our hands." Bran opened his palm and smoke rose. He couldn't manifest even a simple flame. "I can't fly. I don't have the strength. That means daytrips to Aeristitia are out. Until I can ignite my wings, you've got some time to make this right."

Nathaniel closed his eyes and thanked Heaven for even a second longer with Chloe.

"You are working to make this right, aren't you?" Bran pegged him with a hard stare.

"I am." Just not how Bran imagined.

"Good." He glanced at his wrist. "Time's up. I have to get going."

Grateful for the lighter topic, Nathaniel admitted, "I'm surprised you escaped the compound, even on Delphi's orders."

"Escape?" Bran pointed at a beige sedan parked across the street. "Not hardly."

"Hannah?" The driver's scowl should have tipped him off.

"Who else?" he scoffed. "She thinks she's my guardian angel."

"She does have those cute little wings."

"Funny." Bran scratched his chin. "I didn't hear you mention the cuteness of her wings to her face."

"I'm not crazy. You don't tell someone like her something

like that when there are scalpels within her reach. She would slice off my head and spit down my neck."

"You're right." Bran laughed hard enough he braced his hands on his ribs to ease the pain of it. "She would."

A horn honked behind them. Hannah wouldn't wait much longer.

"Could you do a favor for me?" Nathaniel hated to ask, to drag Bran in again.

Bran lifted a hand, signaling to Hannah that he needed another minute. "Do you even have to ask?"

"In this case, yes, I do." He paused. "I want you to pass along a message to Delphi. Ask him to meet me at my cabin tomorrow, around noon. Tell him it's about the missing soul."

"I'll pass along your request, but you know how Delphi feels about leaving Dis." Bran grunted as he shifted toward the tailgate's edge, then grunted when he went to his feet. "If things take a bad turn with him"—he peered up at the bookstore—"or anything else goes wrong, you know my door is always open. You have sanctuary at the Order's compound whenever you need it."

Nathaniel nodded, grateful for the offer. "Thank you." But the coming battle for Chloe's soul was between Nathaniel and Delphi, and he didn't want Bran to get caught in the middle.

Not to mention that the Order housed too many women and children for him to accept the offer of shelter. He couldn't endanger them because Delphi would place no value on their lives if they stood between him and what he wanted.

Order restored. A life taken. Balance returned.

"Whatever happens, don't blame Delphi for the choices I made." Nathaniel silenced Bran's rebuke before he started by pulling him in for a tight hug. Bran hissed from the pain but didn't complain. Perhaps, he too sensed an end coming. Pulling away, he said, "I wouldn't change a thing even if I could."

Bran jerked back. "What is that supposed to mean?"

An irritated feminine voice intruded. "It means you've been out in the sun long enough." Hannah grabbed Bran by the elbow and her tone brooked no argument. "It's time to get you home and back in bed."

His lips tightened, but he appeared too weary to argue. He gave a stiff nod of his head. "We'll finish this conversation later."

Nathaniel hoped so. "Remember to give Delphi the message."

Hannah pulled Bran along at a tottering pace and put him inside her car before vanishing with an impatient squeal of her tires.

His departure was for the best. Nathaniel needed time to think and to prepare.

He sensed Chloe's gaze locked on him from the upstairs window. These next few hours would bring the end. Hers, his, or perhaps both, and he planned to meet it by her side whether she wanted him there or not.

But first, he had to leave. Time was short and he needed every advantage when Saul returned. Right now, his best weapon lay on the nightstand by his empty bed.

Chapter 27

CURIOSITY DREW CHLOE toward the window. She sneaked a glance over her shoulder, then strained her ears. Below, murmured voices meshed with the clicks and scraps of footsteps on hardwood. The slap of books as they opened and shut played a soothing melody. Neve's distinctive laughter rang out, the sound she had waited for to prove she was alone in the apartment.

By the time Chloe worked up the nerve to peer through the window, Nathaniel's blue eyes already stared up at her. She dismissed the idea he had waited, hoping she would appear.

His startled relief crushed her hypothesis. Genuine surprise softened his expression. He half rose as if she had called him. When he sank back to the porch steps, her heart gave a twist.

Bracing her forearm against the window frame, she leaned her cheek against her wrist. With ease that frightened her, she followed the source of comfort radiating through her chest, down a thin line she imagined tethered her to Nathaniel.

Embracing her earlier determination to stand her ground, she tapped into their connection. *"You and I need to talk."*

His response was immediate. *"Should I come to you? Or would you rather meet me down here?"*

"Seeing as how you can come and go as you please regardless…" Her mental chuckle must have sounded strained because he frowned. *"Come on up. At least here we'll have privacy."*

In a blink, he was gone. He rounded the corner, and she thought he meant to use the side entrance. She was turning to let him in when Nathaniel stepped into her living room from thin air. A pair of burnished copper scissors fit in his hand. Their jaws gleamed with unnatural light. The snip as their teeth snapped together raced chills down her spine.

Her back hit the wall before she realized she'd taken a step.

Even relaxed in his hand, the scissors exuded menace.

"Can you put those away?" Her voice cracked. "Please?"

Once he secured them in a battered leather case at his hip and the snaps closed, her dread lessened. When his hand broke contact with them, she could breathe again. At least until she got a good look at Nathaniel's face.

Gone was the teasing man from the past weeks. What stood before her now was danger wrapped in a thin skin of humanity.

"So." Chloe steadied her legs under her. "What exactly are you and how afraid should I be that you've camped out on my doorstep?"

He took his time answering, as if deciding on the best approach.

"I was an archangel once, before I fell from Heaven."

Her mouth ran dry. He was an archangel? Heaven was

real? She'd always hoped, especially after her parents died, but to have it confirmed, to see the proof right in front of her…Her parched throat constricted. If Heaven existed, Hell must be equally real.

When he grew silent again, she shoved down her shock and prompted him. "And now?"

"I'm called the Weaver of Souls, and I'm in service to the master seraph governing Hell." She sensed his hesitancy and wondered at the cause. "I, and others like me, collect marked souls and confine them. So, no, you don't want to find me or my kin at your door."

She considered his answers. Oddly enough, if she tried, she could picture Nathaniel as an avenging angel. She'd seen him mete out punishment often enough in her dreams to know he was merciless in his pursuit of justice. Her understanding failed when she tried reconciling his fervor to a fallen angel. Weren't they by definition the bad guys?

"So the job is a punishment because you fell from Heaven. How did that happen?"

His silence gave her the impression he'd rather not answer. "I was cast down for a lie."

The irony of their situation wasn't lost on her. "I see you didn't learn your lesson." She choked up a laugh. "What did you lie about?"

Nathaniel ran a hand over his scalp. "My brother fell in love with a human woman named Mairi, but relationships between angels and mortals are forbidden." He paused. "I learned of their affair when Mairi approached me during a visit I made to Saul. She beseeched me on her son's behalf. Bran was dying and she was desperate to save him. I agreed to help."

He chuckled now, the sound harsh and self-directed. "When the master seraph, Gavriel, asked me if I knew about Saul and Mairi, I covered for them. Of course, Gavriel already knew about their relationship. He had wanted to test me, see if Saul's corruption had spread, and I failed. We were taken to the city of Aeristitia for sentencing." His tone roughened. "Sometime during the night, we were sequestered, and Mairi's village was attacked. She was killed and Bran, well, you already know his story."

Chloe's thoughts reeled. "Bran is one of you?" Of course he was. How could he not be?

"Yes. He is Nephilim, born of an angelic father and a human mother."

Her mental picture of a boy with ruddy cheeks vanished. In its place, she remembered the man with a cane. He resembled Nathaniel and Saul enough to be blood related. Now she realized he probably was the nephew in question, which explained why neither man included him in their earlier argument. They were, or at least Nathaniel was, protecting him from Saul's plans.

Desperate for a moment to process the information, she asked, "What happened next?"

"We were found guilty, transported to Dis, and given to Delphi. My brother became a soul harvester and I became the Weaver. I've spent the latter part of my eternity weaving soul cloth from harvested souls while he spent his hunting down marked souls and executing them. As you know, I've completed my share of collections as well."

Her spine tingled at the mention of collected souls. "A marked soul is damned, then?"

"Yes. Murderers, pedophiles, rapists...they're marked for punishment and their souls are harvested for our use."

"All those dreams I had...you weren't after me." The realization took her by surprise. "You were doing your job and I got caught in the crosshairs somehow."

"If I had known I was hurting you, I would have approached you sooner." He met her gaze. "Whatever this bond is we have, it enabled you to experience me harvesting damned souls."

"Then I'm not crazy." Relief wended its way through her until she sagged from the respite. For a while there, she'd wondered. "Everything I thought happened, everything I dreamed, was real." She scarcely believed it. "Wait—the dreams started after my accident. My doctor said I almost died. Do you think my brush with death caused our connection somehow?"

"I know it did." His ominous tone made her shiver. "What do you remember?"

"Not much," she admitted. Snow and fear, but the rest blurred in her memory. "Why?"

His eyes closed. "I was there."

Shock made her knees buckle. "Did you cause it?"

"No." His tone went sharp. "I witnessed it. Your soul called to mine. I knew I shouldn't have stayed, but I couldn't leave without seeing you for myself." His exasperation was clear. "No one came to claim you. You wouldn't have survived the journey to Heaven. Your soul would have been lost and I couldn't let that happen, so I helped." He held out his hands. "You were beautiful, your soul the loveliest sight I'd seen in such a long time."

"You saved me." Certainty filled her as wisps of memories

floated to the surface. The perspective was wrong; it wasn't hers, but his. Through him, she relived him bent over her body with a needle and thread, heard her ask him to stay. "That's what Saul meant when he said you bound me to you. How is such a thing even possible?"

"Part of your soul had left your body, but it was still tethered. I cut a piece from my own and sewed it to you. Forced your soul back into your body long enough for paramedics to arrive, long enough for them to save your life."

Her hand went to her scar and tracked the puckered edge. "Didn't it hurt?"

His bitter laughter jarred her. "Like you wouldn't believe."

"Why would you endure such pain for someone you didn't even know?"

"I can't say." She watched as he scratched his head and wondered if he noticed how often he indulged the nervous habit. "I asked myself the same thing, so many times. Did I risk it because your soul was that unique? Or because I worried Bran would suffer the same fate if something ever happened to me? Was it because I found the consequences unfair? Or because of some other reason I can't fathom?"

"If you didn't know we were connected, then why did you come back?"

He stared across the street and her heart plummeted into her toes.

"When I bound you to me," he said, "I contaminated you. I left a stain on you and the master seraph, Delphi, noticed. He marked you because of it."

"He…marked me? Like damned souls marked me?" Her legs gave out and she sank to the floor. "It wasn't a coincidence you found me. You came to collect." She swallowed a knot of sick fear. "You came to kill me."

His answer came without hesitation. "Yes, I did."

"Can't you tell this Delphi person it was an accident?" Her heart pumped wildly. "Wouldn't he understand he made a mistake and I'm not like that? I'm not any of those things you mentioned."

"No, you're not," he agreed. "You're also not supposed to be alive. You should have died in that accident. There's a balance, and I shifted it when I saved you."

"You mean like the butterfly effect?" A flap of gossamer wings and everything changed.

"Something similar, yes. To make an exception is to invite chaos. Children won't be born that should be or lives will end before their time, all to accommodate a life that should have ended."

Chloe could have been a paper doll as easily as his news tore her in two. Part of her had wanted to run screaming when she realized her lover would become her executioner. The other part had shut the panicked portion up in a box and locked out the pathetic whimpers for a second chance she'd already been given.

With numbness came clarity, and with clarity came something too desperate to be acceptance. She was grasping at straws to save herself and she knew it.

"You waited, though. To collect me." She considered their visitors. "That's why Saul and Bran came." She frowned. "What were you waiting for?"

"For love to find you," he said simply. "When a person who is loved dies, their soul emits a beacon of light, bright enough to draw Heaven's attention. It's how my angelic kin know where and when they are needed." He paused. "When you died, you weren't tethered. There was no beacon, no guiding light. There was nothing."

"So when you saved me, it was to give me time to find someone to love?" Her pride stung at the thought of being laid so utterly bare before him. "I guess I wasn't fast enough for you. After you realized I had been marked, you came to see for yourself what was taking me so long."

His response was lost in her frustrated growl of fury. She was such a fool to have ever trusted him.

"When Saul showed up, you two fought over what exactly?" She stood and dared him to contradict her. "Who gets to finish me off now that I'm in love with someone?"

Bright blue eyes snared hers and the anguish in them made her chest ache. His lips parted, sounding out the words even as he thought them. "You're in love."

Heat flared in her cheeks. "I think I'm finished with this conversation."

She covered her face with her hands and turned toward the window. It didn't help. His gaze seared her back and made her spine itch. The denial she wanted to fling at him dried on her tongue and hung suspended in her thoughts.

Had she really said she was in love? Her heart beat an emphatic *yes*.

No, no, no. She couldn't love him. Not when things would end this way. It wasn't fair.

Nathaniel grasped her shoulders, turned her, caught her chin, and forced her to look up at him. His hard eyes said he wasn't going anywhere until he got what he came for, and she suspected that was her answer. "You said you were in love." He waited.

She cleared her throat and glared at him. "And you said you were here to kill me."

His dark expression heated. "I want you to say the words."

"I want to live to be a hundred." She locked her knees so they wouldn't shake. Or worse, take a step into him and tell him exactly what he wanted to hear.

Their bond crackled with his desperation. His hands curled at his sides and she knew if she took that step, her resistance would be over. She would be his willing lamb to lead into any slaughter.

What flowed between them, soul to soul, was pure communion without the filters of their mouths or mistakes to muck things up. Only their bond kept her brave enough to face him. It rushed warmth and comfort in contrast to his inscrutable expression.

Nathaniel crowded her space, his tone cool and distant. "You couldn't have stopped me if I wanted to kill you. I was alive when this world was spoken into existence. Claiming one soul requires no effort on my part."

If he wanted to scare her, he was doing a bang-up job. "Then why wait? Why not get it over with instead of fighting with Saul like a couple of five-year-olds calling first dibs?"

His familiar presence enveloped her. "I don't want you to die. That's why. But you will, and knowing I can't save you is killing me."

Desperation thickened the air and her tongue. Words passed beneath their skin now. Sound fast became obsolete. Answers, she needed answers. "You protected me from Saul."

"I did." He nodded as he lifted a strand of her hair and rubbed the curl between his broad fingers. "I always will."

The temperature in Chloe's apartment skyrocketed. "Not

because you wanted a chance to finish the job but because…?"

His head lowered as he buried his face in her hair and his lips found the shell of her ear. "I did it because I love you. More than anyone or anything I've ever known."

She exhaled shakily as his lips slid down the column of her throat. His prickly cheek scrubbed across hers; then his teeth closed over the skin at the base of her neck.

"When I came here, I didn't think I cared if you meant them. I only wanted to hear you say them once." He pressed a kiss to her cheek; then his hand rested on the leather holster at his hip. "I was wrong. I do care. I learned a long time ago that words are worthless if you don't mean them."

"This is crazy," she said. They would have no life together, no future if Delphi had his way.

The snap at his side popped open.

"We only have a few hours left." And everything in her wanted them spent with him.

The eerie scissors took their place in his hand and looked as if they were meant to be there. "I'll be outside if you need me," he said. The blades opened, sank into the air, and sliced a glittering gold seam.

Peering closer, Chloe realized Nathaniel had cut some sort of portal. So that's how he moved from place to place so fast. Her breath caught as he stepped forward and his foot vanished. He glanced back one last time, and her need for him unhinged her inhibitions.

She took the steps, grabbed his arm, and pulled until both of his feet were planted on the floor. The air sizzled as the fissure closed behind him.

Chloe stepped closer and cupped his face in her hands.

"You broke my heart." She smoothed her thumbs over his cheeks. "Don't lie to me again. Whatever happens, we stand together. Deal?"

He gave an almost imperceptible nod.

"Good." She pulled his head down. "I love you, Nathaniel. Whatever you are, however this ends, you deserve to know you are the only man I have ever and will ever love."

Chapter 28

A SHIVER COASTED through Nathaniel as Chloe's words stroked his senses and their lips parted on a bittersweet kiss. He held her close, inhaling her familiar scent and savoring this moment before reality came crashing down around them and the inevitable slashed through their bond with a copper blade.

"I guess running away isn't an option?" Chloe said as her head came to rest against his chest. "Wherever we went, Saul would find us, wouldn't he?"

His arms encircled her. "He's not the one we have to worry about." The tense muscles in her lower back loosened as he kneaded with his thumbs. "If something goes wrong, if Saul can't convince Delphi to give him more time, then he will be the least of our worries."

"I thought you wanted Delphi to come for me."

"For us, yes." He pressed his lips to her apple-scented hair. "But I'd rather he not be in a murderous rage at the time."

Her head snapped up and busted his bottom lip. "What do you mean *us*?"

Blood filled his mouth with a copper tang. "When I saved you, I broke Delphi's law. I interfered with the death of a mortal. The punishment for that is banishment to the soul pits."

"Then he doesn't know what you've done," she said slowly. "If he did, you wouldn't be free now." She glanced away. "He wouldn't have to know at all if you let Saul finish the job."

"Let him finish the job?" His jaw popped. "Chloe, he would kill you." And Nathaniel knew his brother well enough to know that Saul would make him watch. And watching Saul kill Chloe would destroy Nathaniel more than eternity in the soul pits. "I knew the consequences of my actions. I broke the rules twice. Once when I lied for my brother, because I loved him and wanted him to have his chance at happiness with Mairi, and then a second time when I spared you from death, because I…I had to. I love you. If it could save you, I would break them again."

Her voice wavered. "If I'm going to die anyway, can't you…"

"No." He caught her chin, forcing her head back until her startled gaze snapped to his. "If you die now, with the mark still on you, you'll be sentenced to the soul pits as well. I must speak with Delphi. If I explain what happened, he can pardon your soul. It's my fault you're still alive, that your soul is marked. What I did to save you caused this. His brother, Gavriel, could escort you to Aeristitia, where you belong. You'll have the peace and comfort there you deserve."

Her face scrunched in a not-quite-hopeful expression. "Why do I sense a 'but' here?"

"I can't take you to Dis, where Delphi lives. Mortals can't withstand its temperatures for more than several minutes at most, and we would risk him stripping you of your soul without hearing me out. And I can't leave you here alone and unprotected. Saul has searched for a way to save Mairi for a long time. Now that he's seen you, he thinks reviving her is possible. He doesn't understand that I stitched our souls together while you were alive, before your soul left your body. He sees only the end result and thinks that justifies whatever means necessary to possess the shears and retrieve her soul." Nathaniel touched cold metal at his hip, and it soothed him. "He'll stop at nothing to learn the trick, and once he has, you'll be of no value to him." The thought of Mairi made him tighten his grip on the shears. "He thinks we have a score to settle."

Chloe stared where his hand gripped his shears. "He wants your scissors?"

"The *shears* are a powerful tool. They end lives, sever souls from their bodies. They aid me in the making of soul cloth, in my duties as Weaver. They are integral to my position, to my survival. Besides their more grisly duties"—which she had intimate knowledge of—"they can also create portals to anywhere from across the room to across the world. The others can only access this plane and Hell, but Saul wants into Heaven. Mairi's soul is in Aeristitia, and the only way for him to reach it is to travel there and tether it himself. The shears are the only way he can reach her."

"So our plan is to go to the cabin and wait for Saul to show up." Her throat worked over a lump. "Then what happens?"

"I left word with Bran to ask Delphi to meet us there." All Nathaniel could do now was pray the master seraph wanted the missing soul enough to leave Hell for it. "Then I make my case, and Delphi judges us all."

"Earlier, when Saul tried to…I heard him inside my head."

Chloe frowned. "I get that I hear you because we're…" She swallowed. "How is it possible Saul can do the same thing?"

"Harvesters share a mental bond with their marks. When Saul comes near you, he senses the uncollected mark and a connection sparks. The bond forces harvesters to skim surface thoughts and memories." His tone was soft. "It's part of our punishment, reliving the horror of those acts."

Anger on his behalf sizzled through their bond. He gave her a smile that comforted.

"Okay." She exhaled. "So how do I keep your brother out of my head?"

"I'm not sure," he admitted. "The bond was never meant to work both ways. That you can hear my thoughts and respond to them is…I've never experienced that before. For me, the bond is a steady murmur of thoughts, memories. Once I've seen that first flash of insight, I'm usually gone. With you, it's different. The longer we're together, the easier it is for me to tune you out."

"Hmm." She began pacing. "So it should work the same for me."

"I don't see why it wouldn't." He rubbed his jaw. "I'll admit, what happened in that alley has never happened before. I didn't hear Saul. I heard Saul *through* you. I couldn't make sense of what I saw or heard, but I couldn't tune him out, either. You, though, came in crystal clear."

"Great." Chloe's sharp exhale blew the hair from her eyes, which brought his attention to the dark smudges beneath them. "Yet another thing that's off about me."

He swiped a thumb over the soft skin. "I'm sorry I got you into this."

She lowered his hand and pressed a kiss into each palm.

"You did what you thought was right." Her smile was overly bright. "I got a second chance, and I got to fall in love with you. It's hard to feel too bad about that."

"Chloe…"

"No more apologies." Clamping a hand over his mouth, she said, "Let's do something. Go somewhere. I don't want to sit here and wait." She glanced around her apartment as if seeing it from a different perspective and her hand slipped. "There's so much I always thought I'd get around to. Places I wanted to see, things I wanted to do, but I never wanted to leave home." She laughed. "I've barely left Main Street."

"There's nothing wrong with that." Once he'd had a home and been content in it as well. The boundaries of her world were laid out in terms of Piedmont's city limits, as his had been restricted to Aeristitia's corridors. As he smoothed his thumb across her knuckles, he decided she was right. They should collect happiness while they could. "So where are we going?"

"I hadn't thought that far ahead." She chewed on her bottom lip. "I mean, I've never been anywhere." She looked to him. "If you had one night, one destination, where would you go?"

He kept her waiting while he considered her request. Her choice of coffee table books were all heavy travel tomes, featuring clear skies mirrored in crystalline waters. The sheets on her bed were a whimsical shade of blue and dolphins blinked up from the pattern of her pillowcases. He remembered the dainty seashells embossed on her plates and cups and the choice was easy.

"I'll take you to Whitehaven Beach, off the coast of Australia." His speculative smile earned him a nervous glance. "If we leave soon, we'll have time to watch the sunrise." The last they might ever see.

Locking down that line of reasoning, Nathaniel refused to let desperation color their final moments together. He would save Chloe. He had to. This stolen time would be his parting gift to her, a precious memory for them both to cherish, a retreat for his mind while his body burned in the pits.

Indecision warred in her expression. Traveling so far out of her comfort zone required trust he no longer deserved. He couldn't blame her if she said no and chose to stay home in familiar surroundings, though destiny would find them either way.

"If we go"—she made a face—"and I don't like it…"

"I can have you home in seconds, *meira*."

Her cheeks flushed a vibrant pink and drew his fingers to stroke the high color.

"You've called me that before," she said. "What does it mean?"

"*Meira* is a Hebrew word. It means 'to illuminate.' " His touch followed a line down to her collar where he picked at the tiny buttons fastened at her throat. "You are my light, the closest I will ever come to Heaven again."

Her flush lit up her face. "Thank you." She leaned in, wrapped her arms around him, and sighed. "Neve should be finished closing the store by now. I'd like a minute alone with her if you don't mind." She picked at his shirt pocket. "I guess saying good-bye isn't an option."

"It's safer for her if you don't." During his time with Chloe, Nathaniel genuinely began to like Neve. He knew Chloe was even closer. The last thing he wanted was for Neve to be harmed. She loved Chloe enough that if she thought her friend was in danger, she'd never back down. That stubborn streak he had counted on to tether Chloe's soul just might get Neve killed if she confronted the wrong person to keep Chloe safe.

"I know," she said. "I worry about her. How she'll take it when I disappear."

She took a reluctant step toward the door. "I'll be right back."

He punched numbers on his phone with one hand, then freed the shears from his hip with the other. Next, he pulled a whetstone from his pocket and hit the Send button. "I'll wait here."

Chloe left Neve with a smile and a promise they would talk in the morning about how her first night at the fair went. Who she met and which books she shared. It was a lie, but the truth was much too dangerous to share.

When Chloe reached the top of the stairs, Nathaniel stood and his possessive gaze touched on her, making the tightness in her chest relax and her next breath easier.

"It was harder than I thought it would be saying good-bye without telling her anything, leaving her to wonder. Neve is…" She was the best friend Chloe had ever had. "I'm going to miss her."

"I'm sorry things between you ended this way." A kitchen towel hung from his fingers. His shears and a stone sat beside a bottle of water on her coffee table. "Neve is a good woman."

Bile rose in her throat. He'd sharpened the vicious things.

A smooth sidestep to the right, and he blocked her line of sight. Grateful for help breaking her thrall, she glanced up with a smile, then stopped dead in her tracks.

Nathaniel's eyes narrowed on a point beyond her shoulder. His arm shot out, fingers curling toward her. His mouth opened on words she couldn't hear because her ears burst with a sudden *crack* of sound. Images assailed her, made her head swim.

Saul. His presence permeated her senses like before and her skin crawled from the fervid desires channeled between them. Their connection engulfed her. His thoughts forced their way inside her head, twisted and unnatural.

"You're looking well, pet." Saul stared at her too long for her comfort. "I need a moment alone with my brother. Why don't you pour us some drinks and let the men speak privately?"

"If you want a drink"—Chloe straightened her shoulders—"the kitchen's that way."

"Huh." Saul appraised her. "Did you grow a spine since the last time we met?"

"Chloe." Warning thickened Nathaniel's voice. "Come here."

"I'm tired of running." Months of nightmares and self-doubt had exhausted her.

Nathaniel walked slowly to her side and put his arm around her shoulders. "Our agreement was to meet tomorrow, Saul."

"Yes, well." Saul sat on the arm of the couch, so close she could reach out and touch him, which would *never* happen. "A funny thing happened to me on the way to meet Delphi. Reuel brought Trates and Arestes topside for a visit. They said Delphi had given them instructions on where to escort me, but I'm thinking his idea of a waiting room would look a lot like a soul pit to me." He chuckled and it was an ugly sound. "That Delphi, he does love playing judge, jury, and executioner. Even without the trial."

"You fled punishment." Nathaniel's anger spiked. "Now you've led him here, to her."

His hand clamped on to Chloe's arm, and she watched his gaze touching on points around the room as if he expected more company at any moment.

Focusing on Nathaniel's touch, Chloe narrowed her connection to Saul until his thoughts went silent. All that was left was the familiar sensation of her mind brushing Nathaniel's.

"Can you hear me?" She projected the question at Nathaniel but kept an eye on Saul to test Nathaniel's theory. *"Saul?"*

He didn't as much as blink.

She tried again. *"Nathaniel?"*

"I'm here." Nathaniel's thumb smoothed over her skin. *"I can't hear Saul. Did you block him?"*

"I think so." Saul's presence made pressure build behind her temples, but she locked her jaw and locked him out of her head. *"Is it a good thing if Delphi comes? I mean, if he's here, then things might go according to plan."*

"They might." Nathaniel sounded uncertain. *"Let's hope he arrives sooner rather than later."*

"We don't have long," Saul said. "I'm here to negotiate, not argue." A shark could have given a more convincing smile. "You have something I need, and in return, I'll give you something you want."

Nathaniel barked out a laugh. "You have nothing I want."

"See, that's where you're wrong. Delphi will come for your woman, and he won't rest until her soul is harvested. You know that. She will die, and this time, there's nothing you can do to save her. But"—he leaned forward—"share your knowledge with me, and I will help you bring her back. Second chances are difficult, but thirds are a near-impossible feat…without practice. Such mastery requires time you don't have and experience I have in excess and will share."

"Your word carries less weight than air." Nathaniel's breath warmed Chloe's neck as he said, "I have no way of knowing you can do what you claim, nor would I want any part in it."

"What you've accomplished with Chloe on your first try is admirable. Luck has always favored you. But I must ask you, can you do it again?" His tone gentled. "We're brothers, Nathaniel. It's our duty to aid each other, and I can think of no greater gift than sparing our lovers from fates neither deserves."

"You can't save Mairi," Nathaniel said. "With no host, no form, she's too far gone."

Chloe suppressed a shiver. If Saul attempted to revive them, Chloe imagined the results would be horrific. What he wanted to do…wasn't natural. Whatever his practice had accomplished so far, the results must not be sound. Otherwise, he would hardly be here now, asking for help Nathaniel couldn't give.

"Hosts can be acquired and forms relearned," Saul said. "Her salvation would be complicated," he admitted. "That's why I need you. I can't resurrect what I can't reach, and Aeristitia is off-limits for me." Saul glanced at Nathaniel's hip and frowned. "You do have your shears here, don't you?"

"And if I do?"

Saul smiled, once again at ease. "Then we come to some sort of mutually beneficial agreement."

"We can't trust Saul." Chloe leaned against Nathaniel. *"He's up to something."*

"I know." Nathaniel rubbed her shoulder. *"The question is what?"*

"There's one way to find out." Chloe fisted Nathaniel's shirt, revulsion churning in her stomach as she allowed her connection to Saul to widen. His excitement caused her heart to race in response, nauseating her further.

"Let her die, brother. Unlike you, I'll show mercy and bring your lover back—the exact same way I did all the others." Chloe felt Saul's amusement thrum in every thought. *"I'm sure you'd grow to love her new appetites... eventually."*

She pressed her thumbnail into Nathaniel's back and directed her thoughts toward him. *"He's thinking that if you let me die, he'd bring me back—with new appetites. What is that supposed to mean?"*

"I'm not sure. It sounds as if he's attempted to bond souls to new hosts. Whatever his method, it must not work or he wouldn't be so interested in you." Nathaniel's hold on her loosened, which was a good thing considering she had lost feeling in her arm. *"I'll keep him talking. See if you can pick up more information we can use to barter with Delphi."*

"I'll try." Hiding her face behind Nathaniel's arm, she squeezed her eyes shut tight and pushed at the weak barrier Saul had placed between them.

Images burst into her mind, blinding everything else from her vision.

A charred mountain range inside a massive cavern filled with red haze. The only light came from pits belching flames. A long stone wall ran over the baked clay ground.

"I think we both know time is running out," Nathaniel said. "Lay out your terms or leave."

"Very well," Saul said, turning serious. "In exchange for my favor to your woman, I expect an equal favor in return." He paused. "You are to go to Aeristitia, find Gavriel's journal, and use it to locate Mairi. Then bring her back to me."

"No." Nathaniel's answer was firm.

"Have you even considered *your* punishment?" Saul asked. "After all, you picked a big rule to break. How about this? I'll extend my offer, two souls for the price of one. If you're banished to a pit, I'll bring you back first. You'll be together." He smiled as he mentally tacked on, *"Scavenging the Hell plane in misery for all eternity."*

Chloe kept her expression neutral as the reality of his offer flickered through her mind with perfect mental snapshots of other souls he had re-created this way. How wrong they were. They were nothing but mindless killing machines left to prey upon each other. Nathaniel was right. Whatever Saul had done clearly wasn't working as he intended it to. Yet he hadn't given up experimenting.

Nathaniel's voice hardened. "I have no way of knowing if you could bring back one soul, let alone two."

Saul clicked his tongue. "Even now, when I am the only person who can save your mortal's life and benefit us both in the process, you refuse to share your power with me." He withdrew the copper dagger from his hip and pointed it at Nathaniel. "Do you think Delphi will listen to you? He won't. So what if you have the shears. He gave them to you because he thought he could trust you. Congratulations. You've just proven he can't. Delphi only cares about one thing, and that's making an example out of those who break his law."

"I'll take my chances," Nathaniel said. "And pray he listens."

"You surrender too easily." Saul laughed. "Help me, and she can live. You can be together."

His promise was too good to be true, and Chloe knew it. She dug into Saul's head and his thoughts proved him a liar. More images flickered past. More rambling made her head ache. Still she looked into him, sifting through his thoughts, and his knowledge poured into her.

Steep cliffs. Howling winds. Heat. So much unbearable heat. And shadows. Movement from below. A secret army fortified in the heartland of Hell. They would overthrow Dis. Make this plane a safe haven for his abominations.

Chloe felt Nathaniel's regret seeping into her and heard his voice in her head. *"I'm sorry,* meira. *He can't be trusted. Even if he could bring us back, we wouldn't be who we are now. We would still have lost each other."*

She slipped her hand into his in a silent show of support. They still had one chance left. Delphi might still be persuaded to help them. All she needed was proof: a location, a snippet of thought damning enough to win Delphi to her and Nathaniel's side. Her total focus became unearthing any information that could save them, and she fed those images to Nathaniel. He could make sense of the landmarks she had never seen and the images depicting acts she had never imagined.

"I can't risk it," Nathaniel said. "We will face Delphi's sentencing."

With a snarl, Saul launched himself at Nathaniel, blade in hand. "You'll face mine first."

Nathaniel shoved Chloe backward and she fell, grabbing at the coffee table to keep from busting her head against the corner. Cold metal met her palm and she closed her fingers around the shears.

A flash of light exploded and *something*—a man unlike any she had ever seen before—stepped from empty air. His ink-black hair hung past his shoulders, vanishing against the darkness of his tailored clothing. His fathomless eyes surveyed the room as his three sets of wings, shimmering with ebony feathers, nestled against his back.

Feathers. Wings. *An angel.*

His cold gaze settled on Chloe, seemed to peer beneath her skin to the soul Nathaniel had spared. He ruffled his feathers and the scent of sulfur tickled her nose, teased her stolen memories, and sparked recognition.

No. This wasn't an angel. Nothing born of the Heaven Nathaniel had described to her could exude menace the way this man did. This was Delphi. The governor of Hell was standing in her living room.

Delphi scowled between Saul and Nathaniel. "What is the meaning of this?"

Each man froze. Saul's desperate charge halted. Nathaniel plucked the blade from his hand, then relaxed his defensive pose.

"This is why I had no need to hear you speak on your behalf, Saul. I knew whatever words you said in your defense would be false." Delphi's icy tone made Chloe shiver. "Over the past two weeks, you have claimed to have no knowledge of the lost soul's location. Yet you stand here next to it." His gaze settled on Chloe. "In her very presence, as I should have known you would be. You are ever leading your brother into temptation, and this occasion is no different. Your actions have proven the truth I knew your words would deny, and you will be punished accordingly."

"No, you misunderstand." Saul placed a hand over his black heart. "My son's health has improved. He was able to recall an important detail I worried, in your anger, you would refuse to hear." He gestured toward Nathaniel. "After I had gone home for the night, I was under the impression another harvester would carry out my assignment. Nathaniel took this soul's collection on top of the one he'd already volunteered to harvest. He failed in his duty, not me." Saul straightened his clothing. "I came here to confront him and he attacked me." He locked eyes with Chloe and he poured himself into her mind. *"Tell me what you know of how he bound you together, and I will save you both."*

"You're lying. I'm in your head, Saul." She stared at him. *"I know. I won't bargain with you."*

"Then you condemn yourself and your lover to death." His eyes narrowed. *"Enjoy your eternity."*

Chloe turned to Delphi. "Saul came here to bargain with Nathaniel. He wants access to Aeris—to Heaven." Delphi transferred his frown onto her. "He wants a soul being kept there. He thinks he can bring her back. Mairi, her name is Mairi." She was rambling but she couldn't stop. "He offered to resurrect me if Nathaniel brought her to him. He said—"

"Is that the best you can come up with? I'm happy for Mairi, glad she's where she belongs." Saul chuckled. "Besides, resurrection is forbidden. I wouldn't even know where to start." He shook his head. "You can't even think up a decent lie to save yourself."

"Enough." Delphi lifted his hand. "This ends here. Now."

Time ground to a standstill.

Sweat rolled down Chloe's spine. Would he rip out her

soul from across the room? Nathaniel stepped between them and the forgotten shears seemed to vibrate beneath her palm. She slid her fingers into their smooth grip. Pain scalded her hand as the shears reached inside her, found her commonality with Nathaniel, and gave their grudging acceptance of her mastery.

If Delphi didn't believe them, then maybe she could show him the creatures, earn some points tallied in their favor. Fear made her hand tremble, but if she was going to Hell and lose Nathaniel, then she would take Saul and his abominations with her.

She loved Nathaniel, so much, and if her death was the only way to save him...so be it.

"If you won't listen," she said to Delphi, "then I'll have to show you."

Before Nathaniel could act or Saul react, before Delphi's lifted hand revealed her fate, she stabbed the air and sliced a portal. She couldn't look back. If she saw Nathaniel, saw the horror of his realization written on his face, she might not have the strength to leave him.

Focused on the heat, on the fire pits from Saul's memory, she went to her knees and allowed herself to fall through the glimmering portal as she'd seen Nathaniel do. Cool air evaporated from her lungs as darkness enveloped her. Sulfur plugged her nose and made her eyes burn, but that wasn't the worst of it.

The skin covering her palms and knees hissed and crackled. The ground burned so hot, she jumped to her feet and cried out as she blistered. The stench of flesh roasting on her bones made her gorge rise.

White light brought her head around in time to see Saul tumble through the portal after her.

"Clever girl." His teeth flashed in the darkness. "I underestimated you."

Vicious snarls rang out from below at the sound of his voice. She had the sick feeling wherever they were was very, very high and whatever made those sounds was very, very hungry.

He lunged forward and Chloe dove aside as the portal's light flickered. She skidded across the scorched ground as a scream rose in her throat, met with the heated air, and dissolved.

Saul lunged a second time and she rolled away, blinking back tears as her forearms burned. The pain blinded her senses until a split-second's relief cooled her flesh as her body whistled through air and she fell. Their portal closed and took the faint light with it.

Impact stole her breath when she hit the ground. She gasped as Saul straddled her waist. Wind stirred by his wings blew sweltering sand into her eyes as his rough hands cupped her jaw.

"I never considered the side effects your bond with Nathaniel would have." He studied the shears in her hand. "Whatever he did to bind your souls has enabled you to use his shears. They must recognize that part of him in you, which means they can feed off your soul as well." His eyes glittered. "That means with your soul in my possession, the shears will obey me. I won't need my brother's cooperation." He cast Chloe a pitying look. "I'm afraid I won't be needing your body, either."

Chloe clawed at his hands and writhed, but his weight pinned her to the ground.

Another burst of light shined overhead. Chloe sensed

Nathaniel's arrival but couldn't see him. He must have followed their trail, his portal opening where hers had.

Delphi…he must have chosen their side. How else could Nathaniel be here without his shears? Hope gave her an adrenaline boost. Gathering her strength to forge a mental connection, Chloe warned him, *"Watch your step. There's something down here."*

Saul stiffened over her. "I'm sorry it came to this." She gagged as he pressed a savage kiss to her swollen mouth. Her lips burst from the force and blood ran down her chin. "But Nathaniel would have made the same choices I did to save you."

The pressure on her jaw increased until her head snapped sideways on a sharp *pop* and everything faded.

"Nathaniel…"

"No. Don't waste your energy." His voice broke. *"Hang on, Chloe."*

"I love you." The words were too weak to travel through their bond. *"Always."*

"Chloe? Stay with me. I'm on my way…"

"Too late." The last dregs of consciousness faded and blackness enveloped Chloe. She jolted one last time as an inhuman roar filled the cavern. Nathaniel. Her beautiful angel. Not even he could save her this time.

Chapter 29

MINDLESS WITH FEAR, a feral roar ripped from Nathaniel's throat as he caught a familiar shimmer from the corner of his eye. It couldn't be. If that light was Chloe's soul, then...He ran full out toward the cliff's edge and leaped into the yawning void.

A freight train of upward motion slammed into his gut, knocking him backward. Nathaniel grunted as he landed in a sprawl. His head was still spinning when Saul pinned him down one-handed. Saul's fingers crushed his throat as he slammed Nathaniel's skull against the ground. Through the bloodred haze covering Nathaniel's vision, he spotted the brilliant light bathing Saul's fist.

Saul had wound a soul around his wrist and hand, using it as a glove. Its vibrant sunset colors lit the darkness around them. He clutched the shears through the insulating barrier.

"You." Nathaniel summoned the depths of his strength. He surged up, caught Saul around the throat, and crushed his windpipe. When that wasn't enough, he shook his brother until Saul's eyes refused to focus. "What have you done?"

"Given you…," Saul panted, "a taste of my personal Hell."

"Chloe." Nathaniel tested the bond with Chloe he knew was gone. Hoping he was wrong. No response, though he winced against the flare of light as the soul responded.

For a second, his grip around Saul's throat went slack, allowing Saul to wheeze out a laugh. "Tell me, brother, are you thinking of precious little Bran now?" He panted. "Or have you finally gotten a taste of what this cursed eternity has been to me?"

Oh yes, Nathaniel knew now what his brother had endured. An instant flickered past where Nathaniel wondered if this was the moment that would break him. Would he turn from all hope of salvation as his brother had done? Or would he embrace the justice he had been created to deliver? The sharpness of Saul's teeth set Nathaniel's on edge. Justice. Yes. It was all that was left to him now.

"You killed her." His voice broke. He didn't care, not about his brother, not about his punishment, not about Delphi, not about anything. Nothing mattered without Chloe.

Saul lifted his glowing hand. He gave it a shake as if her soul were a bangle to be settled on his wrist. The shears caught the shine of her soul and glinted dully.

Nathaniel's spine bowed as his lips parted and his agony was given voice. She was lost. And Saul…he would pay. Some vital hope fragmented, shattered his mind while muscle took over.

His fingers tightened around Saul's throat until his knuckles popped. Lifting him by the neck, Nathaniel slammed him onto the blistering ground. Rolling to his knees, he palmed Saul's face and crushed down until his fingernails filled with skin and sand, smashing Saul's skull against the jagged rocks until he heard a crack and warmth coated his fingers.

It wasn't enough. Nothing would ever be enough again.

Grabbing Saul's hand, Nathaniel unwound the severed spirit until he held the root of Chloe's soul in his hand. Then he reclaimed his shears and faced his brother. Nathaniel's chest ached with the guilt of how badly he had failed Chloe.

His gaze snagged on the soul bag at his brother's hip, and he knew what he would do.

Snapping the ties with a firm yank, he freed the bag and ripped the mouth open wide. With his empty hand, he tossed it to the ground beside them.

Stale air swirled as the vicious portal opened, searching for anything not grounded in flesh to consume. Nathaniel's hold on Chloe tightened as he ripped open the front of Saul's shirt and snatched the pendant from around his brother's neck. He was about to give the portal a snack.

Saul's eyes widened. He scratched and clawed at Nathaniel as his skin dissolved. His mouth became a whirl of black glitter shaped on a soundless scream. He became as insubstantial as the air the bag inhaled in greedy gulps.

He writhed as suction from the portal found purchase and breathed him in.

Saul would burn for eternity. If Nathaniel joined him in the end, so be it.

There was no life for him after Chloe. Her death had hollowed him out, left him as soulless as the husks of mortals whose souls he had harvested. What did it matter how Delphi punished him? Nothing was worse than knowing he had failed Chloe.

Back on his feet, Nathaniel made for the cliff's edge,

where he'd first seen the glimmer of light. Shining in his hand, Chloe's soul illuminated a shallow ledge and he jumped down to the rocky outcropping.

At his feet, a bloody jumble of charred and broken limbs jutted from the rocky ground. As he lifted Chloe's remains into his arms, her soul withdrew as if confused by his discovery.

Tears burned Nathaniel's eyes, but the heat evaporated them before they could fall. Each stroke of his thumb down Chloe's cheek drove home the fact that he would never again hear her laughter or feel her touch, never see her smile or taste the full curve of her lips.

Nothing Delphi did to him now could be called anything short of mercy.

The axis of his world had tilted when he met Chloe, bent toward her as a flower in search of sun. Without her, his existence slipped back into darkness. Death, his centuries-old companion, made a welcoming bed and asked Nathaniel to lie in it.

Nathaniel jerked as hard fingers squeezed his shoulder.

Delphi sounded pleased. "Balance has been restored."

Willing to plead with Delphi, Nathaniel caught that cool hand in his. "Please, spare her. She is an innocent in all of this. I beg of you, summon Gavriel. Let her soul return home."

"My brother can no more enter Hell than I can Heaven." He pulled away. "This mortal's soul is blighted. It cannot journey to Aeristitia."

Silken warmth surrounded Nathaniel as Chloe's aura engulfed him, covered his face and neck with ghostly kisses of assurance before she abandoned him and strained toward Delphi.

"What is it, child?" He allowed her light to fill his hand. A strangled snarl rose in Nathaniel's throat, earning him a sharp glance from Delphi. "Silence, Weaver. Let her soul impart its message."

Delphi plucked the root of Chloe's soul from Nathaniel's hand as if picking a flower.

It guided him toward the ledge, then shrank against him, muting her light.

"I see." His lips set in a grim line.

On numb legs, Nathaniel lumbered to Delphi's side with Chloe's body in his arms.

In the valley below, thousands of opalescent creatures growled and snapped at one another. Nude and filthy, their human shapes belied their animalistic manners. Wild red eyes, sharp with hunger, lit the pitch-darkness surrounding them. Still more scrabbled across the ground as they exited what looked to be a doorway carved from obsidian stone.

"There must be thousands of them." Delphi peered into the darkness. "Saul must have worked centuries to create this number." He frowned when he noticed the arch and the milling bodies beyond it. "More hide inside that cavern." His expression turned pensive. "Resurrection is a divine talent, which means Aeristitia has a traitor in her midst." Glancing toward Nathaniel, he said, "And for no one to have reported the absences in their soul pits, he must have had allies among the harvesters as well."

"I couldn't tell you if he did." And he no longer cared.

"We must leave this place." Delphi gave the creatures one last glance. "Now, before they catch wind of us. They're vampiric, sustaining themselves on the souls of the living or eating the flesh of their own." He further shielded Chloe with his hand. "She's fresh. They'll scent her first." He grasped Nathaniel's shoulder and black mists swirled around their ankles and swallowed them down a different kind of portal.

When he could see again, they stood between pillars of white marble with scowling seraphs to either side.

Delphi motioned Arestes forward. "I need you to take care of this." He gestured toward Chloe's body.

The seraph inclined his head with a somber expression. "I will ensure her remains are properly tended." He opened his arms, expecting Nathaniel to pass her over.

Though Nathaniel was aware he held only a shell and that he should give her into another's care willingly, he couldn't let Chloe go. His fingers tangled in her hair as he cradled her broken body to his chest.

Across the way, Chloe's essence flickered in Delphi's hand. Urgent in its attempt to draw his attention, it was as if she wanted to reassure him she was still her, still with him, just different.

Another time he would have laughed as a woman born of flesh comforted a man born of the spirit, assuring him the soul lived on even after the body died. With less resistance, he surrendered her body to Arestes. Her soul had no use for its broken casing now.

Delphi stroked the fluttering spirit with featherlight strokes. "My thanks to you, little one." His attention shifted from her to Nathaniel. "You defied me, tampered with the fate of a mortal, which is expressly forbidden. I should have reclaimed your shears and left you stranded beyond the wall to wander through Hell until those creatures devoured you."

The fistful of light Delphi held struggled against him. He frowned at it. "Quiet down or you'll wear yourself out." Then he addressed Nathaniel. "Despite your *second* lapse in judgment, I find myself in the unusual situation of being indebted to your mortal and having a fair idea of what she'll ask for as her due."

Nathaniel's focus riveted on Delphi's hand out of fear his fingers would open.

Perhaps sensing how little of Nathaniel's attention he held, Delphi passed over Chloe's soul gingerly. "She has saved you, Weaver. Remember that, and honor her for it."

Chloe's love had shattered him, healed him, remade him into a better man than he had been the day he met her. She thought he had saved her life, but she was wrong. She had saved his.

Accepting her soul with sweat-slick palms, Nathaniel tried not to tighten his grip, but the urge to hold on as tight as he could to his beautiful Chloe was too much and he failed. Mistlike warmth crept through his fingers to twine around his torso. Exerting the minutest pressure, Chloe gave the best hug she was capable of giving. It was the best he'd ever gotten.

"Do you still have Saul's pendant?" Delphi asked gruffly.

Surprised to find the chain still dangled from his limp fingers, Nathaniel handed it to him.

Delphi tied a knot in the broken length. "Come." He beckoned Chloe and she went.

At first, the links passed through the column of light, but as he held the links outstretched, the wavering mass beneath took shape. Became more human in appearance and gradually filled out in detail. Subtle changes shifted across her skin as if the soul had already forgotten Chloe's form and labored to reinvent her appearance.

With a final surge of incandescence, the remaining light absorbed into the new skin it had created and a perfect replica of the Chloe he had known suspended in the air before him.

Life surged through her, making her gasp for air her newly formed lungs forgot to supply. Her large brown eyes whirled over to Nathaniel, and she reached for him. The movement broke the invisible cord holding her aloft and she fell.

He lurched, slid on his knees, then caught her in his arms. Once down, he lacked the strength to rise. All he knew was the sweet apple scent of her hair and the smooth softness of her skin. His arms shook with gratitude as they enfolded her.

Confusion swirled through Chloe as her wispy limbs solidified. Moments earlier, she'd been a swirl of dancing colors, desperate to impart a message her limited form struggled to convey. Now she was sort of wrapped in skin. Aware it wasn't hers, though it looked familiar.

Forgetting all the new sensations bombarding her, she focused on one thing, the most important thing—Nathaniel. In the struggle to see him better, she'd fallen; no longer insubstantial, her body had weight and it obeyed the laws of gravity even in this strange place.

Before she gasped from her surprised free fall, Nathaniel caught her in his arms and crushed her to him. She couldn't breathe to complain and didn't want to. His arms were a heaven she had feared never reaching again.

Coarse patches of dried brown gunk on his shirt rubbed against her tender skin. This odd rebirth had left her nude and her skin baby soft. Then she noticed Delphi and realized she had an audience.

"Can I borrow your shirt?" Her voice rang strange through untried ears.

Nathaniel stared down at her, unblinking. His hands trembled where they held her. His expression was one of shock, as if he couldn't believe what he saw was real.

Her lips met his throat and he shivered. "The shirt?" She stroked his cheeks, his jaw, forcing him to feel her hands on him and acknowledge her.

His glazed eyes snapped into abrupt focus, and he pulled the shirt over his head and down over hers in one smooth motion. Seams ran down her sides because the shirt was inside out, but she didn't mind. It fitted her current self-image to perfection.

Across the way, Delphi cleared his throat.

Chloe scrambled to her feet, but Nathaniel plucked her from the ground. Once he stood, he placed her bare feet on his shoes so her delicate soles wouldn't burn. Then he wrapped a firm arm around her, forcing her to lean back into him. "I don't understand," she said to Delphi.

"You have nothing to fear from me." His harsh features softened. "I owe you a debt of gratitude, and I always pay my debts."

"I did you a favor," she said, wondering at how quickly everything had happened.

"And I have done a favor for you." His gaze touched on the pendant hanging around her neck. Then he glanced at Nathaniel. "Two, if one counted such things among friends."

Her cheeks burned. "I didn't mean to be rude."

"I'm sure." The slow curve of his lips transformed his face into something as fearsome as it was beautiful. "You sacrificed yourself to show me Saul's army with no reason to think your actions would lead to any outcome other than your death, and his."

Silence seemed like the best policy at the moment. If he wanted to give her credit for more than wanting to save her and Nathaniel's hides, then she wouldn't stop him.

"Now here is where I find my problem." Delphi brushed a length of midnight hair over his shoulder. "Nathaniel altered your base composition when he shared his soul with you. The human, Chloe McCrea, was marked for death, and she has died. That debt has been settled."

"I was human when I died."

"No, you weren't. If you had been, I couldn't make the offer I'm about to extend." He crossed his arms. "Your soul is an odd mix of human and angel because Nathaniel is part of you, even though as the Soul Weaver he cannot claim to be either of those things himself. I didn't realize what he'd done until I held your soul myself. Since you were still alive when he bound you two together, instead of a resurrection, he essentially created a new type of Nephilim."

"Delphi," Nathaniel argued, "her parents were human. She was—"

"What she was born as is not what she died as," he said, silencing Nathaniel with a raised hand. "In special cases, as with your nephew, I've been given leave to appoint emissaries of those Nephilim who choose to serve Heaven's cause."

Behind her back, Chloe pinched Nathaniel. *"Let the man speak."*

His answering growl rattled her teeth since her body was pressed so fully against his, but he conceded the point and let Delphi continue uninterrupted.

"You were able to use your bond with Saul to gather information, and you gave your life to share that information with me. I won't forget your sacrifice." Delphi kept his gaze locked with hers. "Nathaniel has given you an inadvertent gift. I believe in time, such a skill could be honed. Your new talent perfected."

He smoothed a hand across his jaw. "In their current state, I'm unsure of how or if Saul's army of immortals can be destroyed. It would be foolish to think they will simply disband because their leader was lost." His expression darkened. "Saul had divine assistance, which means he may not be incapacitated but recovering even now." He looked to her. "And there are others among us who helped hide his secret. They must be found and punished."

His momentary pause let his words sink in. "I could use someone with your abilities to help me divine friend from foe. You could save many human lives, as well as those of our kin, by unearthing the traitors among us."

Chloe's sudden increase in value became clearer. If she could tap into Nathaniel's and Saul's minds, she could do the same with any other harvester. But that meant… "I would have to remain marked for the bond to work on others, wouldn't I?"

Nathaniel's voice sliced through their conversation. "Chloe would be at too great a risk. If she connects to a harvester, her soul would be vulnerable, even as a Nephilim. To say nothing of her mind, the psychological effects of what she would witness."

"The choice is not yours to make, Weaver." Delphi dismissed his concerns without preamble. "She would remain marked, but I offer her the chance to wear a second mark as well." His bared teeth gleamed. "Mine."

Cold fury surged through her bond with Nathaniel.

"What about a second mark?" Digging in her heels, she shoved Nathaniel back before he plowed into Delphi but only by the skin of her teeth. "Let's all calm down, okay?"

Agonized blue eyes blinked clear of their rage. "I apologize, *meira*." He added, "Delphi."

Things were heading south fast with Nathaniel so strung out, and Delphi wasn't helping matters. Didn't he know not to wave a red flag at a bull unless he wanted to be shish kebabed?

She wasn't fool enough to think she could rein in Nathaniel for a second longer than he allowed her to, and if he decided she was in danger, nothing would stop him from protecting her. Even at the cost of their fragile negotiations.

Delphi appeared undaunted. "You've seen my brand before, I'm sure. It's the silver mark embedded in the skin of Nathaniel's shoulder. When he exchanged his wings in order to wield the shears, he became my emissary. The mark is my proof of ownership, as well as a protection."

"If I agree"—Chloe forced her fingers through Nathaniel's fisted ones—"then what do we get out of the deal?"

"In exchange, I offer you full ownership of the pendant you now wear and the ability to move between planes. You may live where you will as long as you heed my summons and you may wear humanity when it suits your purposes," Delphi said. "As Nathaniel is mine, so now will you be."

Her head spun at the thought. His offer meant her continued existence, but it was a high price to pay. And Nathaniel…Delphi hadn't mentioned his fate.

As if sensing the direction of her thoughts, Delphi countered his proposal. "I also offer you the guardian of your choice since your new situation will come with its share of danger."

Nathaniel tensed behind her. Chloe thought he held his breath.

Her words tripped out in an eager rush. "I choose Nathaniel."

Delphi paused long enough to make her sweat.

"Although he has shown questionable judgment in these past weeks, I will need his shears and talent in the coming days." Delphi's gaze met Nathaniel's. "You are to be this soul's guardian. If any harm comes to her, the blame will be yours, as well as the punishment."

Nathaniel pressed a hand to his heart and gave a solemn nod, the best he could do with her plastered to his front.

Delphi continued. "After careful reflection, I've also decided you are no longer fit to harvest souls. I must ask you to surrender your soul bag." Nathaniel tossed it over almost before Delphi finished his request. "The others will fill your pit for you, and you will only access it while in Dis, during your weaving time."

When Delphi glanced back at Chloe, the almost-smile teasing his lips let her know everything would be okay. They were back on his team and he was oddly pleased by his newest addition. "Your request is granted."

"Thank you." She elbowed Nathaniel's gut.

"Thank you for saving her," he grunted, "and for sparing me."

Delphi gave them a nod. "Give me your pendants."

Chloe dropped hers into his hand. The sensation of her skin dissipating bottomed out her stomach. The rainbow-glitter outline it left behind was similar to Nathaniel's composition. His contribution to her makeup was a golden patch curling over her heart.

Nathaniel handed over his pendant and assumed his other form as well.

Within Delphi's closed fist, light spilled through the cracks of his fingers. When he opened his hand, a pair of silver bands sat on his palm. He placed each one on the ring fingers of Chloe's and Nathaniel's left hands.

More than a little freaked out by the way her flesh regenerated beneath the metal and spread outward, Chloe eagerly sought something to keep her attention focused elsewhere and found it in Nathaniel.

Biting her bottom lip, she had to admit he looked kind of sexy when he was all gold dusty.

Delphi took her hand in his and twisted the ring. The engraved inset spun while the band remained in place. "Turn it counterclockwise and your spiritual form will be revealed. Clockwise, and you resume your former, human appearance."

As she stared down at what amounted to a magical spinner ring, she never would have guessed she would end up as a glowing glitter being with a built-in dimmer dial.

Her life, her death, all of it kept getting more and more curious.

Delphi released Chloe's hand, then ensured Nathaniel understood the trick before he stepped back. "Now, have we reached an agreement?"

Decision time had arrived. *What to do, what to do.* Nathaniel's concerns were valid. Delphi's proposition was a dangerous one. If the harvesters realized she was spying on them, they would never welcome her mental invasion. Yet, if she mastered her fear and took this massive step forward, she could save them. The magnitude of the situation was incomprehensible, but the alternative was no life, no Nathaniel, and banishment all around.

The power to ensure their future *together* was in her hands. All she needed was the courage to claim it. This might be a foreign existence, and her new position might frighten her, but she had Nathaniel, and it would be enough.

She gave him one last chance. *"Is this what we want?"*

"An eternity spent by your side?" He smiled his bone-melting smile. *"I can think of nothing I want more."*

Now she turned to an expectant Delphi and kept the tremble from her voice. "We accept your offer."

"I somehow thought you might," he said, helping her turn so her chest met Nathaniel's. "This will sting."

He reached beneath her borrowed shirt and cupped her shoulder blade. Heat built between them as he seared his brand into her delicate flesh. When she hissed, he blew cooling breath across her skin to lessen the sting, earning a vicious scowl from Nathaniel.

"There," Delphi said. "The brand will heal in a moment. In the meantime..." He placated a still slightly feral Nathaniel by lowering her shirt with a brush of his cool fingers across her hip. Then he stepped back. She turned again, wishing she could stand on her own but figuring Nathaniel wouldn't let her even if she could. "Nathaniel will educate you on the new laws of your existence and how to control your spiritual form. As to your mental preparation, I will need time to decide how best to proceed without alerting anyone to your purpose." His lips twitched. "I'm certain you two will find something to occupy your time until then."

Nathaniel's fingers kneaded her hip, a promise of what he already had in mind.

Turning on his heel, Delphi said, "I would ask one last thing of you both, and that is for you to keep in mind that my forgiveness is not inexhaustible."

She took the warning for what it was. "I understand."

"I hope for your sakes that you do." He shoved his hands into his pants pockets and strolled through the high archway. A single feather floated from his wings on the stale air. A few steps later, a second downy fluff drifted in the same direction as the first.

Chloe wondered at the loss, then tilted her head back. "Is he supposed to shed like that—oomph."

Nathaniel crushed his lips to hers and their matching smiles bumped their teeth together. "Let's get out of here."

She hadn't heard a better offer all day.

Chapter 30

MORNING SETTLED AROUND Chloe's shoulders with tangible weight. As she lay in bed, glancing around her room, she felt apart from this place...the only home she had ever known.

A sigh from Nathaniel blew warm air across her nape. His arm tightened around her, tucked her closer against his body. "How are you feeling?" His voice was husky and made her skin pebble.

"Good. Alive." Chloe studied her hand, saw the gooseflesh rising and the ring that could make that same flesh vanish with a twist. "Strange."

"I can imagine." His lips pressed against her neck. "Any regrets?"

"No." She twisted in his arms until they faced each other. "Not one. You?"

"Where you're concerned?" He leaned in, and she met his lips halfway. "Never."

"I'm sorry about your brother," she offered.

His expression tightened. "Saul chose his own path."

"Still…" She traced the hard line of his jaw. "I'm sorry you were the one who—"

"It's done." He captured her hand and kissed her finger. "It had to be done."

Nathaniel would need time to grieve, to cope with what he'd done and mourn the man Saul had once been. Chloe respected that and wouldn't push. She did have to ask, "What happens now?"

He shifted so his hips fit against hers, rocked against her. "What would you like to happen?"

She slapped his shoulder. "Didn't that happen enough last night?"

He didn't hesitate. "It's never enough."

"I'm serious." She pinched him to get his attention. "This is the first day of our new lives, and I've been thinking…about what Delphi said." She forced out the words. "If I do this job for him, I'm going to make enemies. I can't—I won't—lead them back here. This store meant everything to my parents, to my grandparents. I can't risk it becoming a battlefield or Neve becoming a target. When I think about the times your brother came here—saw her—I just…"

"Shhh." Nathaniel drew her against his chest. "It's not your fault. If anything, I should have protected you both better."

"It's not that. I don't blame you for what happened." Impossible when he had risked everything for her. "But this is my home. I've always lived here. I don't know if I can live anywhere else." Chloe withdrew from the comfort of his arms and rolled onto her back. She stared up at the ceiling and tried to gather her nerve. "I was thinking—that is, if you wanted—you and I might find a place. We could start over, together."

"Chloe." He palmed her cheek and turned her head toward him. "You and I are forever. If you want to make a clean break with your old life, I will support your decision." He went quiet, but their bond hummed with words unspoken.

"What are you thinking?" She'd rather hear his thoughts out loud.

"Other harvesters don't have shears, but they do have special knives for slicing rifts. No matter where we go, they will be attracted to you because of the mark on your soul, and they will sense me because they are my kin." Determination hardened his gaze. "Saul had help. If he knew who you were, where you lived, and what our connection meant, he might have told others. It might be safer for Neve if we stick closer to your home. We could watch over her until this matter is settled."

Hope blossomed in her chest. "Do you think we can?"

"It's your decision." The twist of his lips would have told her the turn his thoughts had taken even if his thoughts, their connection, hadn't darkened with his mood. "If you want to stay, we can. If you wish to go, then we will."

"But the others can find us." Her soul was a beacon that called to them. "And they'll always be a rift away from us, no matter where we go because of the knives you mentioned."

"I should have thought to ask Delphi to provide you with one." Nathaniel frowned. "I left Saul's in Hell."

Chloe struggled to sit upright. "I thought Delphi brought you to me."

"He would have, probably." Nathaniel sounded unconvinced. "I didn't give him the chance. I used the knife I took from Saul and sliced my own rift."

"He's not a nice man, is he?" Delphi wore the same lethal

attractiveness as Nathaniel, but his was razor sharp, his expression cruel.

"He is what he has to be." Nathaniel set his jaw. "He seems to like you."

She reached behind her, rubbed the symbol beneath her skin. "I'm not sure if that's a good thing or not."

Because it wouldn't do him any good to lie to her, Nathaniel said, "I'm not either."

Her stomach quivered. "I didn't think to ask, but I'm guessing the whole not-exactly-living thing means my pills are useless."

She fisted the sheets. This was a whole new world and a whole new set of anxieties for her to master. Going without would be hard. She wasn't a cold-turkey kind of girl.

"As long as you're wearing skin," he said, "human medicine will work for you."

"Wearing my human suit." She flexed her fingers, watched the metal of her ring glint. "I don't feel like I'm not human."

"Your soul *is* human." He turned to her, looking troubled. "I never was and never will be."

"It's too late to warn me off now." Chloe stood and stretched. "I kind of like being a glowing glitter being with a built-in dimmer dial. Besides, I'm curious. I mean, when our bodies become insubstantial, can we still touch each other? Can we still…?"

Nathaniel's eyes took on a predatory gleam as he rose and stalked her across the room. "I don't know. Maybe we should find out."

"Oh." She tried to sound disinterested. "So you've never…?"

"There are no female harvesters, and I don't know any

Nephilim who can shift forms." He tugged her against him. "Well, none that can shift between the spiritual and the physical shapes at least."

"Shape-shifters?" Chloe patted his chest. "You know what? I don't want to know. Not yet. Let's save this conversation for our rainy day fund, okay?"

"All right." He tilted her chin up. His thumb slid across her bottom lip and she became very aware that he was still naked, still aroused. "Do you need more time to make your decision?"

"I'm, um…" Chloe took a step back to clear her head. "No. This is my home. Everything else has changed. I'd like this one thing to stay the same, at least for now, until I get my legs under me. Then, who knows?"

With her new life expectancy, she was feeling more optimistic about beating her fears and embracing her new existence with hope.

Chloe headed for her dresser and fished out her usual work clothes. "Are you coming down with me? Neve will be here soon to open the store. The last time I saw her, she was convinced you were to blame for the bruises Saul gave me."

Nathaniel's expression darkened.

She held up a hand to ward off his anger at the memory. "Try not to take it personally. She came from a bad situation. Her kids…She just doesn't want to see me end up where she did. Give her time to see she's wrong. I don't think anything either of us says now will smooth things over."

"I can respect that." He picked up the bloody remnants of his outfit from the previous day. "I think I'll head home and grab a shower and a change of clothes; then I'll meet you back here." He scratched his scalp. "Bran's not up to it, but maybe Reuel can help me move a few necessities."

"Reuel?" Chloe hadn't heard that name until now.

Nathaniel watched, maybe for her reaction. "He's a harvester."

Chloe shuttered her expression.

Bring a harvester here? She wanted to say *I don't think so*, but the way he said it, the pulse of warmth through their bond, told her Reuel was more than just a harvester; the two men were friends. Good friends. That meant Chloe would have to befriend him, or at least try. They were all on the same team, so it made sense to learn the players. Really, that was part of her job description, wasn't it?

"The other harvesters are my friends, my family. Several Nephilim are too." He cupped her shoulders. "Will that be a problem? If you'd rather we live someplace else…"

"No." Shoring up her resolve, Chloe patted his hands. "I have to learn how to interact with them if I'm going to do the job Delphi's given me. Besides, I'd rather meet them on my own terms, and it's not like they couldn't find us wherever we went. No. It's better this way. I'll just have to put on my big girl panties and deal."

"Before you put those panties on…" He scooped her up in his arms and tossed her back onto the bed.

A delighted squeal escaped Chloe as her back sank into the mattress. She twisted and crawled, but she didn't make it far. Nathaniel wrapped his hand around her ankle and tugged her beneath him. She was tempted to twist the ring and make him work for it, but when his body covered hers, she found she didn't mind being caught at all.

Chloe paused with one hand on the doorknob and took a

slow breath. Neve cast a shadowy outline across the closed blinds from where she stood on the porch. A smile crept up on Chloe. Not long ago, Neve had shown up just like this on her doorstep. Life had been so different then.

"Hello? Chloe?" A concerned voice dragged Chloe from her musings.

"I'm here." Chloe flipped the blinds open, turned the sign facing out, and opened the door.

"Morning." Neve held a plate filled with goodies shielded by tinfoil in one hand and carried a box tucked under her other arm. Plants peeked over the box's edges. "Look what I've got."

Chloe peeled back the foil. "Are those scones?" The plate tipped when Neve tried to sidle past her into the store. "I'll take these off your hands."

"I bet you will," Neve said on a snort.

"Hey, I'm helping." Chloe bit into her breakfast with a blissful sigh. "Cranberry and orange?"

"You guessed it." Neve set the box on the counter by the register. "I was wired when I got home last night."

"Last night?" She let her second scone go cold in her hand. She hadn't thought to ask Nathaniel how the eating thing worked.

"I was at the fair last night. The literacy booth?" Neve plucked the scone from her fingers and bit down. "Is that ringing any bells?"

Chloe winced. "I knew that." Yesterday had been an eternity ago. "How did it go?"

"I think it went well. I lost my helpers about halfway through. It got hot and they were tired of working when they could see every other kid in town enjoying the fair. I ended up calling the sitter and paying her to chaperone the kids around and then take them home. Oh. And the plants were left over from another booth. The person just packed up and left them there." She patted the box. "I couldn't leave the poor things to wither and die."

"The store could use some greenery." Chloe's mother had kept ferns, but they had been the fabric kind. Chloe had tossed them out once the sun started bleaching them and never thought to replace them.

"Well I'm glad you approve." Neve began unboxing the plants. "They'll be much happier here in the store than they would be where I'm staying. I don't get this much light."

Rubbing a leaf between her fingers, Chloe realized she hadn't thought to ask where Neve was staying and Neve hadn't offered her the information. "Are you happy there?"

Neve kept right on arranging the plants. "Home is where you make it."

Chloe was beginning to realize the truth of that statement.

"There's something I need to tell you." Time to woman up and tell Neve the truth.

"Why the serious face?" Neve braced her elbows on the box. "Is it Nathaniel? Did he come back here after I left?"

"He did." Chloe spoke over Neve's objection. "We needed to talk."

Her gaze zeroed in on Chloe's throat, where the bruises had been. Neve frowned. There were no bruises there now. "And?"

Chloe said on a rush, "Nathaniel is moving in with me."

Neve's eyes rounded. "What?"

"I wanted you to know because you're my friend and because I didn't want you to be concerned if you caught him moving around the store before or after hours." Chloe reached for her friend, patted her hand. "I love him, Neve. I want him here with me."

"But will he stay?" she blurted. Her eyes shut. "I'm sorry, I didn't mean that the way it sounded. Or maybe I did. I still could have phrased it better. Does he realize you're…?" She rubbed her hands down her face. "Besides the fact I saw the bruises. Chloe, please, don't—"

"I have never laid a hand on Chloe in anger, and I never will." Nathaniel's voice drifted down the stairs. He took them two at a time until he reached Chloe's side. "What happened to her is unforgivable, but the person responsible has been punished."

Neve's brow wrinkled.

"What he means is"—Chloe shot him a look—"his brother, Saul, was a very violent man. He followed Nathaniel here, twice, and the second time things got out of hand."

Eyes narrowed, Neve glanced between them. "You said he *was* a violent man."

"He's out of Nathaniel's life." Saul would never harm any of them again.

"I don't know, Chloe. This is a huge step, and it's all happening so fast." Neve cast Nathaniel a measuring glance. "If you love her, you can wait a while, right?"

"Neve." Chloe firmed her voice. "I appreciate that you're looking out for me, but I'm a grown woman. I can make my own decisions. I'm not asking you for permission here. I'm telling you he's going to be a part of my life, one I hope you, as my friend, can learn to accept."

"I won't hurt her or take advantage of her." Nathaniel

put an arm around Chloe's shoulders. "I promise you that."

"You've made a lot of promises today, Nathaniel," Neve said. "Make sure that you keep them." She turned on her heel and headed for the storeroom.

Chloe pressed her face into Nathaniel's side. "I think that went well."

He rubbed her back. "I don't know which was worse, facing Delphi or facing Neve."

"Delphi," they said in unison.

"Okay. I have to get to work." Chloe withdrew and gave Nathaniel a nudge toward the door. "Don't you have a porch to stain? If we're staying here, you're finishing the job."

Nathaniel grunted something about maybe moving after all was a good idea.

"Aww." She closed the gap between them and patted his cheek. "I'll make it worth your while." She wiggled her ring finger. "Aren't you even the least bit curious about souls mating?" The quickening of his breath made her grin. "Why, I bet if you stained the porch fast enough, we'd have time to conduct an experiment before sundown."

Tonight her harvester training would begin. She'd caught that errant thought of his earlier. Nathaniel wouldn't rest until she could protect herself from anyone looking to collect on her mark.

He kissed the tender inside of her wrist. "You drive a hard bargain."

She braced her hands on his chest and shoved him toward the door before the heat in his eyes melted her will to resist. "You love me for it."

"I do," he agreed, his expression solemn. "I always will."

Chapter 31

NATHANIEL CLIMBED THE stairs leading to the apartment and found Chloe standing before their bedroom window, people-watching. It seemed she did that more often these days. He gazed at her while she stared through the glass, still more comfortable inside than out.

Today she wore strappy sandals and an airy dress that kissed the backs of her knees. The light pink accentuated her pale skin, made her appear softer, more fragile than he knew she was.

Her soft sigh sliced through his sense of well-being and made a frown tug at his lips.

Chloe's education in harvesting was taxing. The things she saw weren't meant for mortal comprehension. Learning the basics of soul harvesting, witnessing the act firsthand through Nathaniel's memories and his perspective, were brutal lessons. He'd tempered those harsher duties by teaching her to carve rifts from this room to a different beach every night. She seemed content, but times like these...he wondered if she was.

Fear she might be unhappy made contingency plans roll like dice through his mind.

"Hey." Her small smile reflected in the glass and eased the tense ball in his gut. "I wondered when you'd be getting home. We just closed shop. How's Bran?"

"He's good." Nathaniel eased a step closer.

With a small nod, Chloe stepped to the right and took her smile with her. She braced on a bookshelf so new it hadn't been given a final sanding. It was one of many he'd built for her throughout the apartment.

Wanting to hear her voice again, he said, "I think he'll be walking without a cane soon."

"I agree." Her fingers worked the delicate buckles at her ankles; then her shoes hit the floor with a thud. "He's stubborn, like his uncle." Turning her back to him, she asked, "Can you help me with this zipper?"

"I think I can manage it." Catching the metal tab, he lowered it slowly, allowing the pad of his thumb to trace the curve of her spine. Sliding his hands inside, he pushed the fabric from her shoulders. It pooled around her ankles, revealing a lacy bra and matching coral panties. Cream-colored ribbons created a decorative seam his fingers itched to unlace.

When she turned, light spilled over her flawless body and his breath caught in his throat. She was a miracle to him, a gift he would cherish through all his living days.

While she plucked pins from her hair, his greedy gaze drank in the sight of her. The freckles once sprinkled across her nose had vanished. The small beauty mark on her side was likewise gone. Even the scar over her heart, the one that had intertwined their fates, was nothing but a smooth expanse of skin now.

He reached for her just as she bent to pick up her things and touched nothing but air.

"I think I'm going to take a shower." She headed for their bedroom with the dress draped over her shoulder and the shoes hanging from her fingertips.

Nathaniel's chest constricted with every step she took away from him. He turned his back before she closed a door between them. Tightening his fists, he vowed he would make her happy in her new life. Damn the consequences, he would find a way even if it—

"Are you going to make me wash my own back?" Chloe's bare feet meant he hadn't heard her approach. She traced a finger down the crisp line of his shirt, tapping the buttons as she went, until her finger rested at his belt buckle.

He couldn't answer, not while she wouldn't look him in the eye. Hooking a finger in his belt loop, she turned and led him trailing after those cream ribbons.

Inside the bathroom, steam fogged the mirror and water thundered into the shower basin. She unhooked her bra and discarded it with her panties before she stepped under the spray. Uncertainty made him pause with his fingers on his belt until she popped her head around the door.

"Hurry up," she said, "or we'll run out of hot water."

His clothes were tugged over his head, shoved down, and kicked aside. She held out a wet hand and he took it, allowing her to lead him inside the stall.

A bar of soap sat in the palm of her other hand. Lather bubbled between her fingers and covered her washcloth. "Turn around."

His taut muscles relaxed under her gentle hands as she washed the worst of his anxiety away.

The past several months had taken a heavy toll on them, the past few weeks even more so. Even during the past week, Chloe's brush with death kept him awake at night. He would lie in bed, listen to her even breathing, and pay back the sleepless nights he'd given her an hour at a time.

As her scrubbing lulled him into a boneless state, his shoulders slumped. When his heavy eyelids closed, he decided he could curl around Chloe, sleep for eternity, and be content.

Until her washcloth dipped between his legs and she cupped him through the fabric. Then his eyes shot open and all thought of sleep vanished. "I think that area is clean enough."

"I'm not so sure," she murmured.

A light squeeze of her hand and he suddenly shared her doubts. He groaned and leaned into her touch. If she wanted him cleaner, so be it. She could rub him raw if she wanted. Anything to keep her hands on him and to see the sadness wiped from her face.

"Did I hurt you?" Her grip loosened.

Clamping down on her wrist, he kept her hand right where it was. "No, it feels good." So good he spread his legs wider and gave her room to play.

"There's something I want to try." Pink blossomed in her cheeks. *"I can't say it."*

"Then show me." He tucked a lock of wet hair behind her ear. *"We'll do anything you like."*

When she sank to her knees, his almost buckled. Though she had shown interest in exploring his body, he'd been too greedy to give up his discovery of hers.

Her gaze flicked upward. *"I've never done this before."*

He had figured as much, but still his strength left him at her words. *"You don't have to do it now."* He would be happy to taste her, pleasure her. But it was nothing compared to her coming apart around him.

She closed her hand over his erection and pumped her fist with shallow strokes designed to drive him wild. *"I know, but I want to."*

Her dark eyes, so earnest, drew him in and made his spine tingle with desire.

"Ready?" Her voice was husky with intent.

Lines puckered her forehead, and he could tell she was puzzling out how to proceed.

Stroking her cheek with the back of his hand, he said, "If it makes you uncomfortable, you can stop at any time." His finger parted her lips. "I won't come."

And one day, he would stop making her almost-impossible-to-keep promises.

He watched, enraptured by the barest hint of her tongue as it flicked out and licked the side of his shaft. He gasped and braced his hands against the tile when her expression shifted from inexperienced hesitation to one of unexpected delight.

His forehead met tile, but it did nothing to cool the suffocating heat rising around them. Her timid exploration was killing him and he could think of no better way to go.

When she licked a slow circle around the crest of his erection, his fingers dug into grout. As her lips parted, and she took him in a few precious inches, he locked his hips so he wouldn't thrust.

He wanted her first time experimenting this way to be on her own terms. She should learn what she enjoyed. Find her boundaries, while he made mental notes of what made her eyes close and cheeks flush with shared pleasure. After all, there would be plenty of time for reciprocation later.

The warm pressure of her lips around him, the long and torturous slides of her hand up his shaft, clenched every muscle as he struggled to hold back his orgasm. "*Meira*, you have to stop now."

Her unfocused eyes met his, then widened as understanding hit her.

Not waiting until she stood, he lifted her. When her legs locked around his waist, he pressed her against the wall. Her breasts thrust out on a gasp as the warm flesh of her back met frigid tile. Her nipples pearled under his gaze. Dropping his head, he sucked one of the hard buds into his mouth and scraped his teeth over the sensitized nub.

With his hips pinning Chloe in place, she couldn't move. His hand found her sex and she writhed and scraped her fingernails down his shoulders. His thumb stroked her clit as he sank two fingers deep inside her. She gave a hoarse cry as she tightened around him. "Please." Her strangled plea at his ear broke through his focused haze.

Fisting his cock, he rubbed the smooth head against her soft core, then pushed inside. They both moaned at the sensation of finally being completed. Two souls, two lovers, sharing a need for each other he would ensure lasted forever.

His grip dug into her hips as he lifted her slowly and lowered her even slower over his erection. Delicious friction made his muscles tremble. Then Chloe closed her teeth over the skin at his shoulder and the frayed thread of his control snapped.

"More." Her nails stabbed him, demanding more, and he gave it to her.

Deep thrusts slid her body up the slick wall. The tighter she clutched him, the harder he pushed, until she screamed his name.

"Love you. So much." A heartbeat later, he hurtled over the edge into orgasm. His strength drained until he dropped to his knees. Kneeling in the basin, with their bodies and minds connected, he promised her, *"I will do whatever it takes to make you happy."*

Her puzzled smile gave him hope. "I am happy."

"When I came home, you seemed distant." His gaze wouldn't budge from her mouth, refusing to learn what her eyes might reveal. "I thought now that you've had time to think, you might regret choosing this life, might regret choosing me."

Chloe cupped his face, tilting his chin up as she smoothed her thumbs across his cheeks. "I am a little overwhelmed. This all happened so *fast.*" Sudden warmth ignited in his chest. "Do you feel that?" Love rushed through their bond until his head swam with the images she projected. "That's me, loving you with everything I've got. I told you, we're forever."

His throat tightened. "Forever."

She kissed the corner of his mouth. "Silly man." Her tone coaxed his eyes to hers, which shone with amusement. Her lips brushed his as she spoke. "How long did you think love lasted?"

About the Author

Born in the Deep South, Hailey is a lifelong resident of Alabama. Her husband works for the local sheriff's department, and her daughter is counting down the days until she's old enough to audition for *American Idol*. Their dachshund, Poochie, helps Hailey write by snoozing on his dog bed in her office.

Her desire to explore without leaving the comforts of home fueled her love of reading and writing. Whenever the itch for adventure strikes, Hailey can be found with her nose glued to her Kindle's screen or squinting at her monitor as she writes her next happily-ever-after.

Twitter: http://twitter.com/#!/HaileyEdwards (Hailey Edwards)

Facebook: http://www.facebook.com/authorhaileyedwards

Website: www.haileyedwards.net/

CPSIA information can be obtained at www.ICGtesting.com
Printed in the USA
LVOW061931011212

309677LV00001B/124/P